Longbow

The Saga of Roland Inness
Book 1

Wayne Grant

FIRST EDITION

ISBN-10: 1502490560

ISBN-13: 978-1502490568

Longbow is a work of fiction. While some of the characters in this story are actual historical figures, their actions are wholly the product of the author's imagination.

Cover Art by Brian Garabrant

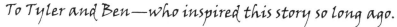
To Tyler and Ben—who inspired this story so long ago.

To Seaborn,
For your ride
home from Camp
Greenbrier.

MMXV
Joe

Jacob O Bank
Bank

Longbow

Prologue

It is the Year of Our Lord 1189 and England is in the thirty-fifth year of the reign of Henry II, the first and greatest of the Angevin kings. It has been over one hundred years since William the Conqueror imposed Norman rule over the fractious peoples of the island kingdom. That rule has brought peace, but at a price. For the conquered Saxons, Danes, and Celts of the land, the Norman yoke lies heavy.

In the larger world it is a time of change and uncertainty. Europe is stirring to the calls from Pope Gregory for a new crusade. The great Kurdish general, Saladin, had captured the holy city of Jerusalem from the Christians and the Church wanted it back. It was a fit time for heroes and legends to arise. This is the story of one such.

Chapter 1

The Shot

Roland Inness stood perfectly still in the shadows of the deep glade. He had seen a hint of movement out of the corner of his eye and knew not if it augured danger or opportunity. All around him the wood was silent but for the far away screech of a crow announcing dawn in the mist-covered valley below. In these foothills dirty grey snow still clung to the low places, long past the time for the spring thaw.

The boy was taller than most of his age and sturdily built—though painfully thin. His dark hair hung loose, almost to his shoulders, and brushed against cheeks that had grown hollow during the long winter of famine. He had arisen long before dawn, when the stars still hung bright in the sky and had followed paths he knew well far down the mountain's flank in search of game. He was much nearer the lowlands than his father would have allowed. But this dawn, he hunted alone.

The valley below and these foothills were the property of the Earl of Derby. Far beyond where his eye could see was rich farmland where green shoots were just beginning to show through the dark soil. In the high hills and moors where he and his Danish kin had been driven by the Normans generations ago, the soil was rocky and poor and food scarce in the best of times. And these were not the best of times. The autumn harvest had been a disaster and the winter had been long and snow bound. Old men said it was the cruellest in memory. Long before spring, food had grown scarce and starvation stalked the farmsteads on the high flanks of the Pennines. The winter had taken his mother, weakened by hunger and wracked with fever.

The early snows had driven deer to seek shelter and forage at lower elevations and the late spring had kept them there. In another month, they would be moving up the valleys and into the highlands where it would be safe to hunt them without fear of offending the Earl. He thought of his younger brother and a sister, just now able to walk. They had cried in the night, their bellies empty. They could not wait another month. Poaching on the Earl's land was a flogging offense, but the boy knew the thing he held lightly in his left hand made the stakes deadlier. It was a longbow. If he were caught with this weapon by the Normans he would not be flogged. He would be hung.

The bow was slightly longer than the boy was tall and rough in appearance. For all its lack of beauty, it was the most lethal weapon in all the world. It could propel a shaft with a bodkin arrowhead two hundred yards and pierce chain mail—or even plate armour at closer range. The Danes had brought the weapon with them in their Viking longboats and had carved out a kingdom with it in a new land. The longbow was feared, outlawed and suppressed by the Normans, for it was the only weapon that could defeat their armoured knights—yet in a hundred years of their rule, the bow had not completely disappeared. The art of constructing it was still known to some among the Danes and Rolf Inness, the boy's father, had patiently taught his oldest son the craft.

In his tenth year, he had begun. First, in winter, Roland had cut a stave from the strong and supple English yew, making certain that he had both centre and sapwood. Hidden in the rafters of the family's rude hut, the wood was left to cure for almost two years. At the winter solstice just passed, his father had judged the stave ready for fashioning. For days he had carefully drawn his blade over the wood, following the grain as he had been taught. Once the dimensions were proper, he had worked a piece of antler over the entire length to smooth and toughen the surface. It was not the beauty in the wood he sought, but its strength. Finally, he had attached pieces of carved bone to each end that were notched to secure the fine flax bowstring. When he was finished it was truly no thing of beauty, but his father had been pleased and that was well enough.

Once again, he sensed movement at the far borders of his vision and could not resist a slight turn of his head to bring it into view. It was a roebuck, still lean from the long winter, but enough meat for a fortnight! The knot of hunger in his own stomach urged him on. His Lordship would not go hungry for the want of this deer. Danes and Saxons may starve, but the Normans never went hungry—ever. He slowly raised the bow at his side and nocked the arrow, his eyes steady on the prey. It would be a long shot, but he had made longer.

Roland strained against the stiff draw of the bow until the fletching of the arrow touched his cheek. He breathed evenly, as he had been taught, focused on the vulnerable point behind the deer's shoulder and loosed the shaft. The arrow leapt true and the buck was instantly down and thrashing in the brush at the other side of the clearing. Roland unsheathed his rude knife and leapt across the open space to where the deer struggled. Quickly, he slit the animal's throat and let out a long breath. As the buck grew still at his feet, he slung it over a low branch to bleed out and let himself feel the excitement of the kill for a moment. This meat would be smoked in the cave above his family's hut, and they would survive another hard season in the midlands of England.

He pulled his prize to the ground and as he started to position the antlers across his shoulders to drag it the long way back home, he stopped and grew still. Something was not right in the forest. A lifetime in these woods had given him a keen sense for when something was amiss and he felt it now. Below him the cries of the crow had grown more insistent and then another sound came from down the mountain, the distinct yelp of a hunting hound on a scent!

He glanced down at the buck and noticed for the first time the sweat glistening on its flanks. This animal had been in flight and had only paused in this glade for a moment, near the end of a long chase. He heard another yelp from below, closer now. Hounds were in hot pursuit, and not far behind would be the Lord's gamekeepers and men-at-arms.

Roland's joy at the kill was instantly gone. His heart was hammering in his chest as he fought to stop the rising panic that seized him. Now the sound of the hounds was distinct as they responded to the freshness of the scent left by the roebuck in its passage. In moments, they would burst from the woods below along the old game trail. The dogs might be distracted by the downed buck while he fled, but the men who followed—they would immediately understand what had happened here and put the dogs on the trail of a new quarry.

Roland hesitated but a moment to wrench his arrow from the dead deer. *No point in leaving evidence—or a perfectly good shaft!* He sheathed his knife, flung his bow over his shoulder, then turned and ran like the devil was on his heels across the clearing and up into the denser underbrush. The hounds would surely be put on his scent in a matter of minutes and would run him down in short order unless he could somehow elude them. *He had to think!* As soon as he was out of sight of the clearing he stopped and gathered himself. At that moment, a savage wailing arose as the dogs burst upon the fallen deer. *No time!*

On the verge of despair, the boy suddenly had a vision of a place not far off that might be his salvation. With renewed energy, he turned onto a half-obscured game trail and ran along the flank of the mountain. As he ran, the wild baying started to recede. Then, he heard a new sound—the faint but distinct sounds of men shouting. The Lord's men had found the deer. How soon would they put the hounds on his trail? He stopped for a moment to listen, straining to hear what was happening back in the glade. The sounds had died to almost nothing, but then there was a high-pitched yelp—the yelp of a hound that had found a scent.

"Blast!" he cursed. They were on to him.

He bolted down the trail, redoubling his speed as he headed for the place he hoped would save him. Roland had spent his entire young life in the high hills of the Pennines, chasing deer or just running for the joy of it. Now he ran with no joy—only desperation. *There it was!* A small but energetic stream emerged from the mist and ferns above him, cut across the game trail and leaped over a boulder field that tumbled out of sight down the mountain. He plunged in up to his knees and started to pick his way down the streambed. The water was numbingly cold and soon he could barely feel his legs. A hundred yards down the mountain he stepped out onto a muddy bank where he, quite deliberately, left the imprint of his leather shoe. From there, he entered the boulder field that disappeared in the mists below. After working his way for several yards downward, he carefully retraced his steps.

The hounds were well-trained hunters. They would know in but a few moments that he had not crossed the stream on the old game trail above him, and would begin to search the stream banks to pick up his scent. He could but hope that the Lord's men would think he had taken the easier path downstream, and would urge the hounds in that direction first. It would not take the dogs long to detect where he had left the stream. Everything rested on the hunters believing the hounds were on the right track, and that he had fled downhill across the boulders.

Roland picked his way back across jumbled rocks to the muddy bank and carefully stepped backward into his own footprint as he reentered the stream. Now it would simply be a race.

To his left and slightly downhill he could hear the excited howling of the pack as it discovered the old game trail and turned in his direction. The streambed was steep and slick with moss and slime. The tumbling water clutched at his leggings, but he no longer noticed the icy cold of the stream as he scrambled madly upward. The baying of the pack was growing louder now and he could faintly make out the sound of rough voices not far behind. His lungs were burning as he lunged upwards through the torrent and despite the icy spray, his mouth was as dry as sand. Then, soaked and numb, he found himself once more where the game trail crossed the stream. A hound yelped just out of sight in the dense woods to his left. The boy rose to his feet and plunged further up the streambed—into the ferns and mist above.

He had barely clambered fifteen yards uphill when he heard the dogs below him splash through the stream. Roland moved with care now, for the men could not be far behind, and he must not be heard. Even though he was concealed in the brush and ferns that crowded in on the stream, he needed to put more distance between himself and the hounds, lest they catch his scent directly. He moved with desperate care higher up the mountain.

As he climbed, he realized that the hounds had gone silent—casting for his missing scent further along the game trail. Then the baying began again as they retraced their path to the stream. Here the sounds mingled with the shouts of the men who followed.

Roland could not make out what the men were shouting amid the frantic wailing of the dogs and his own ragged breathing. He lay very still and listened intently, as the sounds below started to grow fainter—receding downhill. *They had taken his feint!* The boy said a swift prayer and moved once more uphill.

Far down the hill, the dogs sent up an excited howling as they sniffed out his exit from the stream and the men shouted at the discovery of his footprint. For the next hour the sounds rose and fell, as the trail was lost amid the jumble of stone. By this time, Roland Inness was far away and over the crest of the nearest ridge. In the boulder field, a tall, spare young man with the face of a hawk turned and looked grimly up the mountain.

"He's foxed us," he said, to no one in particular.

"Beg pardon, my Lord?" said the nearest of the men-at-arms.

Sir William de Ferrers turned and spat on the ground near one of the hounds. "He knew we'd think down…and he's gone up, I'll wager."

"Up the mountain, my Lord?"

"Up and over, you idiot! And long gone. We shan't catch him this day—but he can't stay hidden forever. I will find this fellow who would take our game and outrun our dogs. There can't be many of that ilk." Sir William signalled the men to assemble. He looked up the mountain once more, as though trying to pierce the wall of trees and rock to discover his quarry. Then he turned and sent the nearest hound whimpering with a well-aimed kick.

"Collect the kill and get these stupid mongrels out of my sight" he growled. The dogs cringed and the men scampered to obey.

Chapter 2

The Devil's Day

Lord Robert de Ferres, the 3rd Earl of Derby listened intently to the young man in front of him. William, his only son, was not long past boyhood, but he was already a veteran of the constant struggle to maintain control over their domains. Ruling the wild lands—and occasionally wild inhabitants—of their vast holdings in the midlands of England required constant vigilance.

His report had, thus far, been only mildly troublesome. Some peasant had been stupid enough to fell a stag being pursued by the future 4th Earl of Derby. It *was* a bit surprising that this unknown poacher had managed to elude his son, whom the Lord knew to be a relentless and skilful hunter. He was about to receive a second surprise.

"Guards, leave us. I wish to speak to my father alone," commanded the young man. The two men-at-arms who had flanked him while he recounted the day's events turned wordlessly and left the Earl's chamber.

"My lord, you will understand that I did not wish to alarm your men," Sir William began, "but you must know that this poacher— whoever he is—used a Viking bow to make his kill."

The Earl stiffened for a moment then rose and walked to the edge of the hearth where a glowing log cast enough warmth to take the chill out of the room. He stretched his gnarled hands, scarred in many battles, toward the welcome heat.

"A longbow? What is your evidence of this?" he asked quietly.

"The arrow was gone of course, but the wound was unmistakable. The poacher slit the animal's throat and would be roasting a haunch as we speak if we had not been hot after the beast. This one is experienced in the forest and steps lightly, but I could still trace his path back to where he stood to make his kill."

"And?"

"I stepped off the distance – it was near two hundred paces from where the stag was struck."

The Earl's head sank to his chest as the painful logic of his son's conclusion sank home. Nothing but a longbow could kill at that distance.

"Aye, William," he sighed. "I see your reasoning…but the men do not know?"

"No, Sire. They are but little keener than my horse at noticing such things."

The Earl considered his son with his usual mix of emotions. His heir had been smart enough to divine the meaning of the day's events and to keep this worrisome news to himself—and for this the older man was thankful—yet here too was the part of his son he abhorred.

His firstborn had all the qualities of a formidable leader, but for this one flaw of openly disdaining those beneath him, both noble and peasant. From earliest childhood, he had shown himself to be intelligent and brave. He was the swiftest runner and most cunning gamesman among the boys his age, but his father's pride in his son's victories had often turned to ashes as the boy taunted those he had vanquished. The Earl could care less if the boy were arrogant. *God's breath, but he had arrogance aplenty himself!*

In truth, a humble man could not rule this land, but a man too prideful makes enemies unnecessarily. And even the great Earl of Derby could ill afford too many enemies. Neither his pleading nor punishment had driven the arrogance from the lad. It was an unfortunate flaw in one who would someday be master of Derbyshire.

9

"William, this poacher must be found and this bow seized *discreetly*. For that reason I give you the task, but have a caution. The last time we encountered such a bow was when you were a babe. We had to fight for our lives to quell the uprising that this infernal device made possible. I lost over half my men-at-arms trying to put down a bunch of peasants who still haven't forgotten that their sires were Vikings."

The older man shuddered slightly as he recalled the events of twenty years ago, when the peasants of Danish stock had risen all over the north and had almost swept the Norman lords from these lands. It had been the longbow that had made the fight a close-run affair. In his own lands of Derbyshire, it had been unsafe for any knight or noble to venture far from the castle walls—even in daylight. Many a good knight had gone down with a goose quill shaft through his chest, even with armour on. It had gotten so bad that he and his men had actually been besieged for a fortnight in Peveril Castle until reinforcements had arrived.

They had finally crushed the revolt through sheer military might and a heavy dose of terror, but it had been a humiliating event for a warrior of Robert De Ferrers' fame. King Henry had dispatched troops to relieve his garrison—and literally save his life. And the King never forgot the debt that the Earl of Derby owed him. He kept a short leash on the nobleman for years thereafter. Robert De Ferrers still chafed when reminded of the King's succour.

In the end, he had his men round up suspected ringleaders among the Danes in the dead of night and put them to the sword when they would not betray their comrades. One band had held out for weeks on the high flanks of Kinder Scout mountain, but had finally been driven out by brutal cold and starvation—into the arms of the de Ferres men patrolling the high country. Another band had to be rooted out of the great cavern close by Castleton—known to the locals as the "Devil's Arse"—with fire and sword. It had been a brutal time and one the Earl did not want to see again.

In the years that followed, an uneasy peace had settled over his lands, but he had few illusions. They had finally recovered two of the Viking longbows and survivors among the rebels had admitted that they had never had more than twenty of the weapons. With only twenty longbows, these ignorant peasants had almost upset his world. He must not let it happen again!

"William, you know where to look. Only the Danes know the secrets of constructing a longbow, but *have a care!* They have grown quiet these score of years since their last rising. Do *not* incite them!"

"My lord, you may rest easy. I will find this man and his bow. These scum shall not rise against us again." There was grim determination in the young noble's voice, as well as something more. His father recognized it for what it was—pleasure.

***

The sun was near mid sky when Rolf Inness stepped through the low door of the hut his family called home. He was a big man with a thick tangle of beard that fell over his chest and long hair braided in back. He moved nimbly for a large man, but with a noticeable limp. The weather was still chilly in the early spring and his old injury was flaring up. The wound from a deflected broadsword stroke had never healed properly, but it had not completely crippled him either. At least he was still moving around, while the man who had laid on the stroke had died in the next instant.

As he gazed across the small stony patch of cleared land bounded by forest on all sides, he tensed. Something was coming— and quickly—through the woods. Whatever it was made no sound, but a hare broke cover from a bramble near the wood line and that was all the sign he needed that something approached.

Then he saw his oldest son burst from the tree line at a full run. Rolf Inness moved as quickly as his damaged leg would allow to meet the boy, who was staggering across the turned up clods of the field. Roland's breath came in gasps and his worn clothing had been made even more ragged from his headlong flight over the ridge.

"What's happened boy?"

"Father…I felled a roebuck over the ridge," he gasped fighting for air. "…Lord's men were on its trail…Didn't know…didn't know!"

"Did they see you, lad?" His father grabbed him by his

11

shoulders holding him at arm's length.

"Are you pursued?" The man looked past his son to the wood line, half expecting a squad of the Lord's men to burst out at any moment.

"No, father. I checked the backtrail. No one follows," said the boy, gaining his breath. "They found the buck and put the dogs on my trail, but they never saw me. If they had my trail, I would know it." Rolf Inness knew his son's skills in the forest surpassed his own. If the boy had been followed, he would know. The man relaxed his grip on the boy.

"Aye, lad. They'd be close at hand if they'd tracked your sign, so we're safe for now." As he spoke, he continued to scan the tree line. If the Earl's men were determined they would be back, and would likely find the trail that led to this small field. He glanced down at the bow, which the boy still held tightly in his left hand.

"Roland, how far was the shot that brought down the roebuck?"

The boy managed a weak grin. "Near two hundred paces, downhill, father. I took him in the shoulder just as you taught me." He paused and added, "I fetched the arrow before I fled."

The man's gaze grew tense once more. He pulled the young boy to his chest and hugged him tightly.

"Roland, my boy, it was a fine shot, but would to God you had missed!"

"Father...?" Roland looked up puzzled.

"Lad, if any in that hunting party have their wits about them and any skill in reading sign, they will know the distance of the kill. Only one thing can kill at such a range. They will know it was a longbow and will comb the countryside for the man who wielded it—and they will certainly start with your backtrail."

The grim truth of his father's words struck him. He had been told tales since he was a small boy of the great peasant uprising led by the Danes with their longbows so long ago. He knew the Norman lords feared the weapon and the people who knew the secret of its construction.

"Father, what are we to do?" the boy asked urgently.

Rolf Inness paused deep in thought.

"It may be that none will recognize how the buck was felled.

But we cannot stake everything on that hope. If they know it was a longbow they will not rest until they track its owner down."

He paused again and looked at his oldest son. There was pain in his eyes.

"God help you boy…but you must flee. They will come and they will know a man as creaky as I could not have eluded them in that forest. You will be suspected, simply because you are capable of the deed—and Normans need naught but suspicion to hang you or worse."

Roland looked at his father in dumb amazement.

Flee? Surely there was some other way!

"Father, we can hide the bow where they will never find it! Perhaps they will not have noticed the distance. Don't make me go!" he pleaded. The thought of becoming an outcast, even from the brutal life he lived in these hills, panicked the boy.

"Boy, we can hope, but we must prepare," Rolf Inness said grimly. "You must hide yourself in the forest for as long as they search and that may be for a very long time. I've taught you well. You will live if they do not discover you. I'll send your brother and sister over the ridge to Odo's with warning, for all the Danes will be suspect. He will look to their safety until this is done. I'll pack what food we can spare, but before the sun is another hour higher in the sky, you must be gone. Go up the side of Kinder Scout—hide there and watch. If they do not come within a day, it may be safe to return. If they do come, they will know about the bow and the lot will be cast. If they know I had a son, we will tell them you died of the fever in the winter." The man gave a bitter laugh. "They will have no way of knowing any different, since they take little notice of who lives and who dies among us. So watch and pray, son."

As his father finished the boy could see bright tears beginning to brim in the older man's eyes. Roland had never seen his father cry. He was stunned. Life had been hard throughout his childhood, but it was all he knew. He was not ready to be outlawed and outcast, to rely only on his own devices.

"Father…we were starving."

"I know, son, I know," he whispered in the boy's ear, as he gently pulled him close. "You're my good lad and will always be, but now…now you must be gone." His voice grew commanding.

"Look at me, Roland!" He forced the boy to look him in the eyes. He could barely stand to watch the strong face that he had always known lose its battle with grief.

"Stay alive! Do you hear me? Stay alive and God will provide—somehow." Rolf Inness turned and ducked low into the hut. A few moments later he returned with a small sack of food that he thrust into the boy's hands. A boy of perhaps ten years and a girl child with her mother's golden curls followed behind him. The younger fought back tears, frightened by the fear she saw in the faces around her. His brother had a grim look about him Roland knew well. He was a boy always ready for a scrap.

Roland hung his head as he took the sack then picked up the longbow that he had dropped in the dust and flung it away in disgust. All of his pride in fashioning it and the hours of practice to master it had brought him here. He wished his father had never shown him the secret! He turned toward the forest, which loomed to the rear of their hut, and the rising flanks of Kinder Scout. He had spent much of his short life there, but now it appeared to be an alien place full of peril. He felt his father's hand on his shoulder.

"Roland, you'll be needing this," his father said, holding out the bow he had retrieved from the dirt. The boy recoiled, but the man spoke urgently. "Don't be a fool. Ye have a good heart, boy, but it'll have to harden if you're to live. So take the bow, keep it hidden…use it well." The man quietly unstrung the bow and carefully wrapped it in a length of rough cloth.

"I will, father," the boy said grimly, as he took the bundle. His own eyes had begun to sting with tears.

"Now go!" the man said, pushing him gently toward the dark woods. "…and God go with you!"

Roland sprang forward like an arrow released. He could not look back. He sought the shadows of the ancient trees and began to climb rapidly. The boy knew where he was heading—a rock outcropping halfway up the slope where he could observe the farm below from concealment. He had often done just that as a child, in those rare times when he hadn't been labouring beside his father in the fields below or seeking out game for the cook pot.

The boy moved quickly over familiar ground and soon reached the rocks where he lay down flat near the lip, gazing on the farm below. Roland had spent fourteen years here—he had never known another home. It was true that his family didn't own this land—no Danes owned the land they worked—but it was still home. As far back as he could remember, he and his father had tilled the rocky soil of this place and hunted the game in the forest. His brother Oren, four years his junior, had helped them scratch out a subsistence—when he didn't get in the way. The girl, Lorea, though barely beyond infancy, busied her small hands in the endless toil of the farm.

It was a hard life, but he knew none better. Until the winter famine, food had been reasonably plentiful and Mara, his mother, had the skill to make it last. She was buried in a small plot beneath an ancient oak that rose from the edge of the wood. He looked longingly at the little hut. It may be built of wattle and daub and have dirt for a floor, but he had been happy there.

He watched as his brother gathered Lorea in his arms and disappeared down the single path that wended its way along the ridge connecting the tiny farms dotting this high country. They would stay hidden until the danger had passed. Oren had stopped briefly to look up in his direction and wave before moving off down the path to spread the warning to their far flung neighbours. Seeing his brother's wave brought a painful lump to the back of his throat.

Hours crept by as the sun bent lower in the sky and Roland waited. He watched his father attend to the routine chores of the farm until last light, but rarely ceased to scan the tree line surrounding their little clearing. A hawk startled him in the dusk as it burst from an unseen perch in the wood opposite and snatched an unfortunate mouse from the field, but nothing else stirred. Night came on, but not sleep as he waited through the long hours to see what fate the morrow would bring him.

Dawn broke and the sun burned away the mists in the small hollow below and the boy hoped, for the first time, that fate had spared him. Then his breath caught in his throat. From the exact spot where he had emerged from the woods but half a day past, a man appeared—then quickly two more. *Soldiers!* They moved with an arrogant lack of caution across the field toward the hut. He noticed a fourth man trailing more cautiously behind, as though expecting to be skewered by a shaft from an unseen longbow at any moment. He couldn't be sure at this distance, but the man resembled the Earl's son, William, whom he had observed on many occasions during market days at Castleton.

It mattered little to Roland that a nobleman led the squad. He knew that his fate was sealed. They must know about the bow and he could never return. Still, he watched with desperate urgency as his father approached the advancing soldiers. The lead man struck the peasant to the ground without preamble, and the two that followed dragged the man to his feet. They held him as the young leader approached.

Roland desperately wanted to hear what was being said, but he was far out of earshot. He could see that the Earl's son was questioning his father, who kept shaking his head. Rolf Inness was clearly telling them nothing of value. For his stubbornness he was beaten with remorseless skill by the soldiers. As the blows rained down the boy's mind turned from shock to building rage. Slowly he rose to his feet, his hands clenching at his sides. For a moment he couldn't move, couldn't breathe.

Even at this distance, the boy could see that Sir William was losing patience with his father's stubborn silence. In a horrible instant he knew what would happen next. He tried to cry out, but his mouth seemed not to work. He watched in horror as the nobleman turned to the one soldier not holding the prisoner and nodded. Without hesitation, the man unsheathed his sword and thrust it to the hilt into the defenceless man's back. Rolf Inness slumped to the ground and did not move.

The boy's stomach lurched and his heart seemed to stop beating for a long moment as he tried to take in what he was seeing. He stayed frozen to the spot as the soldiers moved quickly, under the young Lord's orders, to torch their hut. Finding nothing left to destroy, they moved off down the same trail that his brother and sister had taken the day before.

Roland hardly noticed the rising flames from the hut as his eyes remained fixed on the motionless figure in the field. No man, not even one as strong as his father, could survive such a blow. Rolf Inness was dead, murdered with only his son for a witness. He had brought this fate down on the man he loved most in the world and had stood there and done…nothing.

The boy stumbled from the rock, sank to his knees and retched into the bushes. For a long moment he stayed rooted to the spot in silent anguish, then rose to his feet. Movement seemed to break his horrified trance. He retrieved his bow and, cursing to himself, he ran—down the mountain to the edge of the wood and on into the clearing where the tilled earth began. No one was there to challenge him as he ran, stumbling toward the man who lay face down in the sod.

Gently he turned his father over and cradled his head in his lap. The dirt where Rolf Innes had fallen was stained dark by his blood. Roland wanted to weep, needed to, but the shock was still upon him and he simply rocked back and forth in the soft dirt, a low moan growing in the back of his throat.

"Father…Father…I've killed you. He wanted to scream, but his voice was like a whisper. Then slowly his rage returned. It overwhelmed his shock and grief as he thought of how these Normans had slaughtered the man he held in his arms—the man who had given him life. He looked down into the face of his father, then gently laid him in the soil he had tended for so many years. His heart ached to think of the children returning to find him like this, but there was no time to tarry. He glanced around and needed little of his tracking skills to see where the killers had gone. They had taken the same trail Oren and Lorea had taken the day before. No doubt they had other Danes to question before this day was done.

He unwrapped his bow and strung it. Turning a last time he looked long upon the man lying in the dirt—knew he would never see that face again. He made the only farewell that came to him.

"They will pay…Father. I'm so sorry." Then he was gone. His mind curled around one clear thought.

If these men were seeking a longbow, he would give them one!

He knew this path well and every blind turn in it. With but a moment to secure his quiver of arrows, he was off. The boy followed a game trail that paralleled the old path for almost a mile, then headed up and over a rise. The path below wound around the ridge to avoid the elevation. He ran with the grace and speed of a forest animal, which in truth is what he was, what his father had

17

taught him to be. He paused for a moment as he climbed the ridge to listen and could hear the faint clank and murmur of men on the trail well below.

His prey had been easily overtaken, but he must choose his ground carefully. He had only his bow for a weapon and must not let them close on him or he would be finished. Perhaps joining his father in death might be a fitting end to this day, but he knew he would not take that course. It shamed him that he wanted to live and was afraid to die. It shamed him, but it was the truth. He shook his head as he ran as though to banish all such thoughts for another time. For now there was a hunt to finish and a reckoning to be had. He hoped that God would forgive him—but these men must die!

As he ran, he pictured the spot he sought—a steep rise that overlooked the trail on the other side of the ridge. He was breathing heavily, not from the exertion of overtaking the soldiers, but with the anticipation of what he was about to do. The familiar spot appeared just below him on the slope, and he quickly found a position behind a fallen tree. He removed four goose quill shafts from his quiver, fitted one to the bowstring and thrust the others into the dirt beside him. The boy's mind raced and his heart hammered as he waited for the Normans to appear on the path below.

He heard them long before they came into view. They were talking and laughing, as men often will after a battle—but this had been no battle.

"*Murderers*," the boy thought, grimly.

They came into view, walking quickly, but with no evident fear of attack. The three men-at-arms were in the lead, with Sir William de Ferrers following. At this distance, there could be no doubt as to the identity of the leader. Roland paused for a moment. This was no roebuck he was stalking--it was a man. The church said that vengeance was the provenance of God.

"*This is not church,*" he muttered to himself.

The boy drew the longbow smoothly, sighted and released in a fluid motion. An instant later, the arrow seemed to simply appear in the leading man's chest. He was dead before he hit the ground. The others froze in shock at the sight, which sealed the fate of the second soldier. Roland released another shaft. It buried itself in the man's neck and he toppled on top of the first, clutching at his throat as a froth of blood foamed from his mouth. The boy forced himself to remain calm as he nocked his third arrow. This one was for the man who had ordered his father's death! He took careful aim at the tall young man down on the path, who was now looking frantically into the forest for his attacker. He let the shaft fly.

Somehow, William de Ferrers sensed he was the next target of the hidden bowman. Instinctively, he grabbed the man beside him and jerked him forward. An instant later, a longbow shaft buried itself into the hapless soldier. From some hidden place above the trail he heard a guttural cry of frustration and a man, nay a boy dropped onto the trail and raised his bow. Without further hesitation, the nobleman leapt off the path and into the woods, which sloped away beneath him. He felt a tug at his sleeve and a quick sting as a deadly shaft ripped through the fabric and disappeared ahead of him. He ran like death itself pursued him—as indeed it did, for Roland Inness was now pounding down the trail to where his target had disappeared into the dense thickets. The boy was propelled by rage and had the advantage of knowing these slopes by heart, but his quarry had never lost a footrace as a boy and was now driven by wild panic.

He dogged his prey for almost an hour, and would have taken him but for ill luck. De Ferres reached the valley floor barely ahead of his pursuer and used the open ground to gain speed and put distance between them. As Roland burst from the woods he saw the man for a moment before he disappeared over a low rise.

He drew an arrow from his quiver. When he gained the rise ahead of him he would have a clear shot. He leapt forward then froze. A troop of the Earl's men had emerged from the wood to his right, on what business he knew not. They had not seen their master's son disappear over the hill, but they would clearly see the boy if he continued his pursuit. Roland cursed under his breath as he realized his prey would escape. He edged back into the tree line and was never seen by the passing soldiers.

In an agony of frustration, he slumped down on a rock and tried to organize his thoughts, but could not. For hours, he had operated on fear and rage. Now grief began to overwhelm him. He tried to push it away but failed. He rolled off the rock and curled on his side, shuddering, and wept like a baby. He wept for his father, his family and himself. He felt like he would never stop the tears and didn't try.

Then, from frighteningly near, a gruff voice spoke to him.

"Are you dying boy?"

Chapter 3

The Monk

William de Ferrers, heir to his father's great estates in Derbyshire, York and Nottinghamshire—and the future 4th Earl of Derby—stumbled out of the forest gasping for breath. He cast a quick look over his shoulder, half expecting to see a phantom with a drawn longbow at his heels. He hesitated but a moment then resumed his flight, knowing that at any moment he might feel the jolt of a shaft in his back. He made for a nearby rise and felt immense relief as he crested the top and descended into the protected ground on the other side.

The young man had never experienced this kind of blind panic before. As befits a future Earl, he had been trained in the skills of combat and had been an apt pupil, besting those older and more experienced through his skill and ferocity. But those contests had been controlled. Blades were dull, disabling strokes avoided. Most importantly, none of his opponents would ever take the risk of actually injuring the son of their liege lord. It was an advantage that the boy had never truly understood as he often mocked those he bested.

In the past hour, William de Ferres had come to realize that this scum of a peasant boy cared not a whit that he was the son of

21

the Earl. As his breathing slowed and the panic began to retreat, he looked down to see a dark stain on his britches. He had pissed himself!

A blazing anger replaced the fear. The audacity of this boy! To assault the person of a nobleman was an unspeakable crime. He must be found and brought to justice—*then flayed alive!* He would make of this boy an example that would strike fear throughout Derbyshire. The young man abruptly halted his eager thoughts of revenge, as another fear overtook him.

No, there must be no public hearing or execution for this man. He must die swiftly and secretly—and his story with him. No one must ever know that William de Ferres had run like a frightened child from a peasant. *No one.*

***

Roland leapt to his feet as soon as the strange voice had spoken and had an arrow nocked when an unexpected blow behind his knees sent him sprawling. He tried to spring back up to meet his attacker but was pinned to the ground by the end of a rough hickory staff. Its owner loomed over him with a slightly puzzled look on his face. Gazing down at him was a rather round, but powerfully built man of middle years clothed in rough brown robes. Roland recognized the robes as that of a monk, but could not identify his order. Framing the man's somewhat round and red face was a fringe of brown hair. Set in that face was a lopsided grin and a pair of piercing brown eyes that seemed to look right through his own.

"Why are ye weeping like a bairn, lad? Are ye hurt?" the man asked, keeping the staff firmly planted in the boy's chest. Clearly this man, this monk, meant him no harm, for surely he could have knocked him senseless when he had the advantage.

"I'm not hurt," Roland managed to reply as he quickly wiped his eyes dry.

"So answer my question then!" insisted the monk as he nudged the boy gently with the blunt end of the staff that still pinned him to the ground.

Roland was a Christian, or at least his mother had hoped he would be. There were no churches up in the highlands of the Pennines and few clergy deigned to make the difficult hike up to

22

the Danish farmsteads. Many of his neighbours still favoured the old, fierce Norse gods, Odin and Thor, but his mother, Mara had believed in the one Christian god. His father, Rolf, had little use for gods of any sort, but had not chosen to quarrel with his wife over the matter. Roland hesitated. He wanted nothing more than to be left alone, yet something about this odd monk's gruff concern opened a rush of emotion inside him.

"I've done the devil's work this day!" the boy blurted. He paused, then continued, defiantly, "And would do it again."

The monk looked appraisingly at the boy, unfazed at his outburst. He raised his staff and held it lightly in both hands as the boy scrambled up to a sitting position.

"Aye, son, the Devil is often about in these parts, but come now, tell Father Augustine your story. Confession is ever good for the soul, and perhaps I can help in some small way." The monk's voice was rough, but kindly.

For reasons he could not fathom, Roland trusted this man. He took a deep breath and began to tell the story that had started with a dead stag and ended with his father and three soldiers dead, his family in hiding and him a fugitive from the Earl. The monk eased himself to the ground and listened intently, his face becoming grimmer as the story unfolded.

When Roland had finished, he gave a great sigh. Speaking of these things had lightened his burden only a bit, but any relief from his guilt and grief was welcome. The monk sat silently for a few moments.

"So ye killed three men with that?" He pointed to the bow at the boy's side.

"Aye, but I missed the one that most needed killing!" Roland said, with bitterness in his voice.

Father Augustine reached for the bow, but Roland snatched it away and held it close by his side, a look of challenge in his eyes. The man stepped back and nodded.

"Ye're wise not to let a stranger, even one such as I, lay hands on your weapon lad. It's a Viking bow, is it not?'

"Aye, Father…I made it myself," the boy said, with a mixture of guilt and pride.

The boy's words brought a look of surprise, even shock to the

23

monk's face.

"You know the craft?"

"Aye, I learned from my father—who taught me well."

Father Augustine nodded, absorbing this new information. He started to speak, then paused and shrugged his shoulders.

"Lad, God works in strange ways that we mortals cannot comprehend. You must seek his forgiveness for striking down those men. I'm certain he will be merciful—under the circumstances." The monk made the sign of the Cross in the air and bestowed his blessing.

The boy straightened himself and replied, "For those I've killed, God may do as he must, but I'll seek no leave of *God* to finish what I have started. The Earl's son will die, and for that, I care not whether I am forgiven."

The monk sighed as he saw the hate burning in the young man's eyes.

"It is always thus, my son, though it is my prayer that a day will come when some justice will abide in the land and all can foreswear vengeance."

The boy shook his head slowly.

"Pray on Father, but for that day to come, all Normans must die."

"All, my son? Not all Normans are cruel, nor are all Danes virtuous. And Saxons…well who can say? You are a Dane I reckon?"

"Aye, Father."

"Well young Dane, I have learned from painful experience that little separates the races of men. All are sinners, even Saxons like me. I expect you will find this as well, if you live long enough." The monk saw the scornful look on the boy's face as he spoke.

"What's your name, lad?"

"Roland Inness, Father," the boy answered.

"Inness? The monk repeated, "…Inness? He seemed lost in thought for a moment. "And what'd yer father's name be?"

"Rolf Inness, sir," Roland replied.

The monk leapt to his feet and slapped his meaty thigh.

"God works in strange ways, indeed. I should have seen it! By damn—*pardon my language Lord*—but ye're the spitting image of your sire! *Rolf Inness, by God.* He was but a few years older than you when we rose against the Normans." Father Augustine seemed transfixed by memories as he continued. "We almost beat them, lad. It was a *close* thing, and it was the bows that your father and the other Danes crafted that made it so. Aye, it's a hell of a weapon. Your father was a dead shot with it and damn brave to boot." He paused, seeing both astonishment and pain on the boy's face.

"I never knew Rolf escaped, son. Those few of us not hunted down by De Ferres and the King's men scattered in every direction. Some further into the hills and some, like me, over the sea. I can but thank the Lord that he survived these many years and grieve along with you at his loss. I will pray for his soul, lad, though I doubt that will be needed."

Roland tried to take in all of this information. He knew his father had somehow been a part of a long-ago rebellion against the lords—that he had been wounded and had somehow managed to survive the brutal repression that had followed the breaking of the revolt. His father talked hardly at all about those days. This strange monk had already given him more to chew on than his father ever had!

"Father, you are a churchman. How did you come to fight with the rebels?" the boy asked. It was passing strange that a man of God should speak with such relish of long-ago battles.

"Ah, Roland, I was not always a man of the church," he grinned. "Nay, I had little use for all the unseen things of the world as a young man nor did I have the temper to find grace…but somewhere along my way, grace found me!" He paused to look about him at the forest and the nearby clearing. Worry shone in his eyes. "This is neither the time nor place to tell my story. I will say only that these past years I have sought to do more good with the scripture than I have done with the sword."

The monk rested a hand on the boy's shoulder.

"Roland, ye've acted as a man would this day, though ye still be a boy. It's a rough way to grow. Someday I may have the chance to tell ye more of your father, but now the hornet's nest has been stirred and ye'll not be safe in these parts. I will find your brother and sister. God will provide for them—with a little help from Mother Church," he said, kindly.

Roland steadied himself against the monk's firm grip on his shoulder. He could barely speak for the ache in his throat as he thought of the young ones.

"I'm deep in your debt, Father," he managed to croak. "I could not bear to think what would become of them without my father to protect them."

"Fear not for them now lad, but for yourself. I can see ye mean to have your vengeance, but you'll have none if ye be dead. Sir William can wait a bit on his doom. His men will be on your heels soon. Ye must move quickly away from these lands and stay to cover. The forest folk will be wary but not all would be your enemy—especially to one who knows the secret of the longbow!" The man finished with a gleam in his eye.

"And if you get in a tight spot, you might use my name. There are many in the forest who regard it well."

Roland nodded. "I'll tell them Father Augustine sent me this way!" he said.

"Oh, heaven forbid boy. They'd not know that name and would as like skewer you as help you. The outcasts who live in the forest know their humble friar by another name. Tell 'em, ye're vouched for by *Tuck*."

Chapter 4

Flight

"I said no!" The Earl of Derby shouted. He had held his temper in check for weeks as he urged his son to drop his fruitless search for an invisible bowman. His patience was now at an end. The quarry—whoever he may be—was either safely gone to ground or long gone. The endless searches and interrogations ordered by his son were creating a growing ill will among the peasantry. He had even begun to hear furtive rumblings of complaint from his own men-at-arms. Now this hothead wanted to close the borders of Derbyshire and detain all travellers for questioning! This was too much.

"But my lord, we cannot just let this villain escape…he murdered three of our men! The peasants will think us weak!" he fairly choked out the words.

"*Weak*? *Weak*? More likely, they already think us daft! Aye, it's a dangerous thing to let this go unpunished, boy," he said with barely controlled fury in, "but you have only yourself to blame! I bade you use restraint in this matter and before the sun had set you had killed one of my peasants!"

"But my lord, as I told you, the path led directly to this man's farm."

"So this made him guilty?" interrupted the father "Considering

27

all who knew him vouched for the fact that this man was a cripple, I rather doubt he was your bowman! And since he was long dead when you got my three soldiers skewered by the real culprit, his innocence looks a bit more compelling!" By now Robert de Ferrers had worked himself into a full rage. The younger man shrank back a bit. His father was reaching his elder years, but at times like this, one was reminded that Lord Robert had a well-deserved reputation for ferocity. The man had not held this fractious region of the midlands for thirty years by being weak. Few would wish, even now, to tangle with the Earl of Derby in a fury.

"Get you out of my sight 'til I give you leave to return. Do not let me hear that you are ordering my men about on this phantom hunt, or that you be unsettling the peace of my peasants!" Concluding his audience, the Earl motioned his son away with an irritated wave. The younger man retreated from the Lord's chambers and hurried to his own, seething as he went.

"I'll not use your precious soldiers, old man, but I shall have this blasted bowman—like it or no!"

His valet was fussing over the garments he had laid out for his master's evening attire when William de Ferrers entered his bedchambers.

"Randolph! Leave that. Fetch me Ivo—and be quick about it!" The valet stopped in his tracks, a stricken look on his face.

"My lord? You want me to fetch... Ivo...here to your own chambers?" He said the name with a tremor in his voice.

"Can you not understand a simple instruction, you dolt?" shouted Sir William.

"Aye, my lord." Randolph scurried from the room in close to a panic, and was back in less than half an hour's passing. He stepped into the room and cringed off to the side of the doorway.

"My lord, I...I've b-b-brung him," he said.

Through the door walked a man short of stature but broad and powerfully built. He wore the garb of a woodsman, but with small additions that marked him as a man whose station had risen above that of the common peasant. The belt that girt his waist was of fine black leather with a few small jewels inset. From the belt hung a lethal looking dagger with a single ruby set in the hilt. The man's face would not have been remarkable except for a prominent scar, which ran from his left ear across his cheek to the corner of his mouth. He was burned brown from exposure to the sun, but this scar shown white, like the belly of a dead fish on the riverbank.

Ivo Brun was the best game tracker in Derbyshire, but this was not his claim to fame. Brun was a killer—and one renowned for his ability to find and dispatch even the most carefully concealed or protected victim. The mere mention of the man's name was often sufficient to settle many petty squabbles among the lesser nobility, for it was within this class that the man found both his employers and his prey. Only the nobles had the resources to pay his price. It was said that he had his own peculiar code of honour. He would kill no woman, priest or small child—unless they got in his way—nor would he claim payment without proof that he had succeeded in his task. None could remember an instance when Ivo Brun had not collected his payment. He stood placidly before William de Ferrers. His face an indifferent mask.

"Yer Lordship sent for me?" His voice lacked just enough of the usual deference to border on an insult, but not enough to call him on it. In truth, William de Ferrers was a bit frightened of this man and did not choose to take issue with his tone, no matter how irritating. This was the second time in less than a month he had encountered a man he knew to be capable of taking his life. He now prepared to set the one against the other.

"Yes, Ivo, I have a job for you...."

***

Roland awoke with a start in pitch-blackness. It took him a moment to realize where he was. He peered out from the rough shelter he had made from spruce bows in the deep thicket to see that the first signs of dawn were in the eastern sky. He moved slowly, for a fortnight scraping out an existence in the forest pursued by dogs and soldiers had left him gaunt and worn. His flight had taken him far from the high forests of Kinder Scout. He had no wish to bring any further trouble down on the Danes and had resisted the urge to return to familiar ground. He travelled mostly at night, staying to game trails in the forest that had, by chance alone, led him northward toward Yorkshire. He had stayed alive by hunting and occasionally filching scraps of food from peasant farms near the forest's edge. He hated the theft, but had no choice, for the constant patrolling of the Earl's men had driven much of the game from these lands. He was at least thankful that spring had finally broken the grip of winter. He no longer shivered himself to sleep each night.

Shaking off the weariness that seemed to creep deeper into his bones with each day on the run, he took up his longbow and slung his quiver over his shoulder. *Only three arrows left.* Replacing them would be impossible until he found a secure refuge. It had been two days since he had eaten. With game scarce and neither fruit nor nut available so early in the spring, starvation had returned as a real possibility. The gnawing pain in his stomach had actually dulled with time, but he knew he must eat or die. He decided to head back to a clearing where he had found his last meal, a few tasteless roots he had grubbed from the ground. They would at least fill his stomach.

The place was not far and he approached it cautiously. The Earl's men were not skilled in the forest, but they were relentless. The boy knew he should not return to a place he had disturbed, but saw little choice. A tiny movement ahead caught his eye and he froze, scanning the opening into the clearing. Now nothing moved—*but something had!* He stayed still and strained to see. Even in his weariness, his hunter's eye did not fail him. Hardly visible in the dawn light, frozen as still as the boy, was a rabbit crouching by a tall clump of grass. The boy's stomach spasmed and his mouth watered. *Meat!*

Barely breathing he withdrew an arrow from his quiver, making no sudden moves. He knew the rabbit watched him and might bolt at any moment. He forced himself to go slowly. At last his bow reached the shooting position and he released. Too late, the rabbit saw the motion and leapt forward. He was struck before his leap was complete. The boy could hardly suppress a whoop. He had had no meat for over a week. This would give him strength! He stumbled into the clearing to retrieve his prize and found that the rabbit had managed to crawl off into a tangle of brambles to die. The trail was clear, though thorns pulled at his ragged clothes as he moved to fetch his meal.

"There he is!"

Longbow

Roland whirled to see half a dozen men-at-arms entering the clearing not twenty yards away. With no further thought for the rabbit he bolted through the clutching brambles and into a thicket. *How could he have been so careless!*

The boy heard three arrows pass through the foliage on either side of him as he forced his way through the dense underbrush. He heard the men moving along a game trail that circled the thicket. They would reach the other side long before he did! He angled to his left and frantically sought a path to freedom. He could feel his panic rising as the saplings clutched and held him back.

"Psst!"

The boy almost jumped out of his skin. Squatting stolidly amid the underbrush just a few feet away was a large and dangerous looking man. He was bearded and his hair was long and caked with red clay. Small bones and other amulets were woven into its braided strands. His clothes were made entirely of deerskin like some ancient Pict and a wicked looking axe lay across his thighs. He was chewing on a root.

Unhurriedly, the man arose and motioned for Roland to follow. The boy did not want to, for this man looked as though he were from another age—and a very savage age indeed. Shouts from the far side of the thicket ended any debate. The wildman was slipping away through the tightly spaced saplings and Roland fell in behind him. He could barely keep up with the loping stride of the man, but was relieved that the sound of the soldiers was starting to fade in the distance.

Somehow his guide had found the smallest of trails which led down into a ravine so overgrown with brambles and covered by dead fall that it formed something of a tunnel. The sounds behind were very faint now, but he could make out an occasional curse as the soldier fought through the tangle of thorns seeking him. More quickly than seemed possible, they were beyond the reach of the Earl's men. As the way became easier, Roland quickened his stride and caught up to the man.

"Who are you?" he asked between gasps of breath.

The man hardly slacked his pace to answer.

"Best ye dunna know. Not good for ye—or meself. Tuck told us to watch fer ye… and *here* ye be!"

Tuck!

He had been too frightened to take the friar's advice. As he had moved from one hiding place to another, he had seen evidence of forest folk, but had steered clear. He was far from home now and knew not if the name Tuck carried any weight in these parts. Apparently it did—at least among such rough folk as this!

"Is he near?"

"Nay, 'e spoke of you over a week ago."

"He is your priest?"

"Aye, mine and more like me who live away from the rest. Some would be hanged if they showed themselves. Others don't like the crowds. Tuck's our shepherd. We are his flock."

For a moment Roland wondered if the man was one of those who would be hung if caught. The thought was not so frightening as it once would have been. He himself would swing if de Ferrers ever laid hands on him. Suddenly a thought struck the boy.

"Did he speak to you of my family?"

"Oh, aye, 'e has 'em safe away. Out of Derbyshire I'd guess—but 'e didn't say."

Roland stopped and sagged against sapling, his knees suddenly weak. He had spent these past days fearing for his own life and scrounging for sustenance. He had tried to keep thoughts of Oren and Lorea away, but they would not stay away. He had brought their world down around them with one bow shot and now they were both orphans and fugitives.

But thank God—and Tuck, they lived and were safe.

"Come now, lad. Buck up. We've give 'em the slip, but they could get lucky and strike our trail. Must be off."

Roland nodded and straightened himself. Silently they travelled trails seldom used even by forest creatures until at mid-morning they arrived at a small cleft that cut into a low, rocky hill. The entrance was overgrown with a wild variety of vines and briars, making it almost impossible to see. His guide carefully separated a mass of vines and stepped forward, holding it for the boy. Now the way was so narrow that two men could not pass at once. Only a short way on, the man stopped again and pointed to the side of the deep ravine with a grin. There, tumbled boulders had formed a small alcove that looked dry and secure.

32

Longbow

"A home fit for a hermit," the boy thought.

For three days he sheltered with the wild man of the forest. Food here was scarce as well, but at least he felt safe for the first time since his flight. He considered staying longer, but the man had seemed to read his thoughts and made it clear that the he was welcome only for Tuck's sake. He could rest here for perhaps another few days and move on. Then his companion returned from foraging with strange news.

"The soldiers are gone—back to the castle. I saw no sign of search parties today." Roland's face lit up, but the man raised his hand.

"There's more. The folk at the forest edge speak of a man alone, askin' questions, looking for a boy such as you—a dangerous man. I watched and I saw this man, near the clearing where we met, and…" the man stopped with curious look on his face.

"And…?" the boy prompted.

"And 'e knew I was there."

The hermit paused as the import of his words sank in.

"If a man knows I'm about—when I choose to be concealed— 'e's dangerous indeed," the man said. "I've heard tales of only one man in the Midlands who could do it—Ivo Brun." The boy flinched at the mention of that dreaded name. Though he had never seen the man, he was well known by reputation. It had been Brun who had helped the Normans hunt down the Danes when the rebellion had been crushed.

"'E will find this place, and soon," the hermit continued. "We must go separately, and with haste."

The man had hardly more possessions than the boy and they wasted little time on leave taking.

"God bless you sir and have a care!" The boy could not conceal the sadness in his voice. His companion had been strange indeed, but after weeks of no human contact he had been a blessing. It was painful to part.

"Aye, lad and same to ye. If I live to see Tuck, I'll tell him of this. You be gone now and go swift and tread light. It's a bad man that seeks you!" Without another word the man stepped through the vines at the entrance to the cleft and was already out of sight when

Roland followed.

He knew now that he could not survive long in Derbyshire. He was grateful the soldiers had been called off, but they were village dwellers for the greater part and had been more a nuisance than a danger. But this man who stalked him now, Ivo Brun, was a tracker of renown and a killer of even greater fame. There was no doubt William de Ferrers would not rest until Roland was dead.

"You'll die by my hand before I die by yours", the boy muttered quietly. A month on the run had done nothing to cool the boy's hatred of the man who had ordered his father's death.

The boy looked down at himself. His somewhat gangly but wiry body was noticeably gaunt from the privations of winter and weeks on the run. Settling accounts with William de Ferrers must wait. For now he had to get beyond his enemy's reach. He set off at a steady trot towards the east as the sun was beginning to decline in the west.

A full moon rose over the horizon which gave just enough light to speed him on his way. All through the long night he travelled, stepping lightly and masking his trail where he could. He stopped now and again to be still and listen. Nothing stirred on his backtrail that he could detect, but every instinct told him the pursuit would be there.

Just before dawn, he reached the edge of the forest and looked about. Beyond a stubbled field that had not yet been turned, lay a road—the King's Highway. He knew it ran from Sheffield up to York. Roland had come this way once before in his search for game and had seen the road. From the forest's edge he had noted that it was a busy thoroughfare, filled with knights, peddlers, monks and gentry.

His father had told him that the road to York, like most of the serviceable roads in England, had been built to last by the Romans eight hundred years before. The boy's experience with the world beyond his farm, the forests and heights of Kinder Scout and Castleton was very limited, but he recognized this highway as both a risk and an opportunity. When he had come here before, he had not been prepared to take the risk. Now, he had little choice.

There could be no way to track him on this heavily travelled path, and strangers were expected to be about on the King's

Highway. Perhaps he would not attract any special attention. He was going to have to take his chances in the open and hope for an opportunity to make a place for himself, either with the travellers on this road or with whatever lay at its end.

Which way to go? The question took little consideration. To the south lay Sheffield and the lands of the Earl of Derby. That way lay grave risk of capture and an unpleasant death. So it would be northward toward York, a great city that his father had spoken of, but of which he knew little. For the next few minutes, Roland picked the brambles from his hair and did his best to make himself presentable. With a final deep breath he stepped out of the woodline and walked rapidly toward the road. At this early hour, no one was in sight—and for this, he was thankful. He would rather no one saw him emerge from the forest. In a few moments he reached the edge of the road and swung to his left—to the north and Yorkshire. He was a traveller like everyone else.

He fought the urge to look over his shoulder. He could feel the presence of William De Ferres and his hound Ivo Brun behind him. He had no doubt he would return this way one day to collect his blood debt, but for now he must put distance between him and all he had ever known. He trudged toward York and the unknown.

Chapter 5

The Road to York

On closer inspection, the King's Highway was not as grand a thoroughfare as it appeared from a distance. While the old Romans who had built this road were master engineers, eight hundred years of use and abuse had taken a toll. The road ran straight and level as one of his bow shots, but every few yards there was a missing stone or a crumbled edge to the roadway. Roland had to tread carefully to keep from breaking an ankle in the gaping holes. Still, this was the finest road that he had ever traversed and a sight better than the rutted country lanes that led down from Kinder Scout to Castleton.

As the dawn arrived, he hardly noticed the beauty of the day. It was late April and a chill lingered in the air, though the days were gradually warming. Many of the trees that lined the fields on either side of the highway were going from bud to leaf with the changing season. As the sun emerged, the sky was rapidly turning from grey and gold to blue.

He hadn't eaten since fleeing the hermit's cave and his hunger was a constant companion. It was a companion in a foul mood. He *had* to get something to fill his belly, but there appeared to be nothing left to scrounge in the fields nearby. Then he smelled something!

Longbow

Faintly at first, and then stronger, came the smell of a wood fire and of meat roasting! Roland's mouth immediately began to water and his stomach groaned as though it had a mind and voice of its own. Off to his right, in a little finger of wood that cut across the fields and swept up near the road, he saw a thin stream of smoke rising in the still morning air. He paused for a moment and surveyed the road ahead and behind. No one was moving yet in the first hour past dawn. Furtively, he slipped off the crest of the highway and into the brush that grew alongside.

Employing all of his stalking skills, he crawled and crept for what seemed an eternity in the direction of the cook fire. At last, he was able to survey a tiny clearing. At its centre was a small fire and—as his nose had already informed him—there was a hank of meat roasting on a spit. On one side of the clearing, a great dapple grey destrier was hobbled and hitched to a tree limb. Roland had never seen a horse this magnificent and it marked its owner as a knight of some consequence—no doubt a Norman.

Beside the huge horse was a reasonably handsome black mule. A pack of considerable size rested against a large oak and a largish lump wrapped in a blanket rested against the pack. Another blanket lay in a heap next to the tree. Clearly, this was a traveling knight with a companion, perhaps a squire. Roland presumed it was the squire who was already up and about somewhere attending to his duties—perhaps seeking water or more fire wood.

Once again the irresistible smell of roasting meat met his nostrils and he felt himself drool involuntarily like a cur. Then, as if in sympathy with his mouth, his stomach began to rumble.

"Grrrrrhhh…." Roland clutched at his gut. *Gad, it was loud!* The stillness of the surrounding woods made the sound seem unnaturally clear, but then it settled and the boy brought his gaze back to the clearing.

I am no thief, he thought, but scruples would not fill his stomach—nor would caution. A quick dash across the clearing and a likewise quick escape into the nearby thickets and they would never catch him—or their breakfast. He slowly rose to a crouch. From the corner of his eye he saw a blur of movement, then an explosion of stars and darkness.

Roland knew not how long he had lain senseless as his eyes

flickered open. He started to move, but was made instantly aware of an uncomfortably sharp object pressed none too gently into his chest.

"If ye move, I'll run ye clear through," a voice above him said.

The boy opened his eyes and followed the long gleaming blade of a broadsword up to its owner. Behind the sword loomed a boy, but little older in appearance than himself. Boy he might be, but there was a look of grim malice in his eyes. Roland's mind searched frantically for some means of escape, but none seemed possible. He fought back panic and tried to conjure up words to say that would not be his last. Then, oblivious to all else, his stomach again began to whine and complain, loud enough for any to hear.

His captor stepped back a pace, but kept the sword pointed at Roland's throat. He shook his head.

"Well thief, I could hear that from as far away as York! By the sounds of it, ye've eaten a live dog." His captor said with scorn as he nudged the sword tip into Roland's gut.

"Beg your pardon sir, but if I had a dog...I would surely have eaten him—live or dead—long before this." Roland blurted.

"Ahhh," said the boy, arching an eyebrow, "for a starvin' thief, you're a bit of the jester now. But by the look of things, you're a poor thief and your jests are none the better. Eating dog is not funny."

For a moment the grim look on the squire's face eased into a smirk. "'Course I can't say as I've ever met a *starvin'* Englishman before—tis a fat country it is. Nor have I found the English to be all that amusing."

Roland looked at his captor. He was about an inch shorter, but much broader and more muscular than Roland. He had a shock of sandy coloured hair, flecked with rust, and his face was fair-skinned, with a patch over the nose of randomly sprinkled freckles. His English was understandable, but spoken oddly. Roland was used to the accents and dialects of English used by his fellow Danish farmers and the distinctive Derbyshire accent of the other locals around Castleton and Sheffield, but this was different.

"Are you not English then?" Roland asked as pleasantly as any one would with a blade at his throat.

The boy took a quick look at the slumbering knight by the big oak. He appeared to still be sound asleep. He turned back to the boy on the ground.

"Don't be insulting me, ye sneak thief," he hissed. "Can ye not see I'm of a much nobler and deadlier race? *English?*" The boy spat on the ground.

"So are ye a...a...*Scot?*" Roland cringed slightly when he said the word. Mothers in the Midlands and north would frighten misbehaving children by invoking the threat of the ferocious clansmen, who would pour out of the highlands when least expected and leave nothing but smoking ruins behind. He had never encountered one, but Scots were no imaginary bogeymen.

"A *Scot?*" The boy was now clearly irritated. "Would I not be wearing one of those...those...*wee little dresses* they fancy, if I was a benighted Scotsman?" The boy took a moment to swivel his hips to make his point. In other circumstances the boy would have laughed, but the arm that held the sword to his chest had not moved.

"You are under the blade of true son of Erin—ye dog-eating Englishman!" the boy announced with a flourish, emphasizing his point by nudging Roland uncomfortably with his blade.

It took a moment for this information to register with Roland. *Erin? Erin?...Erin!* Oh God, this squire was an Irishman! He hadn't heard much of the Irish, but what he had heard was not good...not good at all. They were supposed to be more truculent than the Scots, and twice as crazy!

Roland gauged his words even more carefully.

"I meant no offense, Sir—for surely I've often heard that the Irish are a ... brave and true folk—not at all like the plunderin' Scots." Roland said this in his most diplomatic voice, glancing down at the sword point that still hovered uncomfortably close to his chin.

The boy snorted.

"We Irish are not so stupid that an Englishman can cozen us with flattery. Now what am I to do with you? Run you through? "

"Did I hear someone mention eating dogs?" The voice came from a little distance off and Roland allowed a quick glance to locate its owner. A large man dressed only in a long jerkin was standing by the large oak happily taking his morning piss. He finished up and with bare feet picked his way carefully through the forest debris toward the two boys. The man scratched his backside and yawned as he surveyed the scene. He was a very large man indeed, with hairy legs like moss covered saplings and a neck like a bull. He had a ruddy complexion and a face somewhat overwhelmed by a large crooked nose. What there was of his hair was closely cropped and receded to about mid scalp, revealing a number of scars which must have once been near lethal wounds. Not a handsome man, even a fearful looking one, except that his eyes were cheerful.

Roland's captor was quick to answer. "I was about to skewer this here fellow for creeping up on us, my lord," he said, pointing to Roland, "but he claimed to be a dog-eating, Englishman. So I thought you might be wantin' to meet such a rare bird before I spilled his giblets."

The large knight waved his hand as though dismissing such a thought. He looked at the boy on the ground.

"So ye say ye like the taste of *dog* do ye? Before the boy could reply the man continued. "I've eaten dog meself on campaign a time or two, I have, and—if you're proper hungry—it's quite tasty. Why, in Burgundy four winters ago, those Frenchy dogs soon wised up and wouldn't come near our English camp for fear of the cook pot. Had to eat our own shoe leather in the end, by God." He patted his stomach a moment and gazed off into memory. "A nice dog would have come in handy that winter," he sighed wistfully and turned back to the boy who his squire still held at sword point.

"So what'd be yer name, lad?"

"Roland Inness, my Lord" he replied.

"*Roland?*" The man looked at him quizzically. "That doesn't sound right English to me. In fact, it sounds *Norse!*"

Roland spoke carefully, but with a touch of defiance. "It is a Norse name, my Lord...and a proud one! My great grandsire was a Viking and my sire says I'm named for him. He came in the longboats with the other Danes and torched half this island, I'm told."

Though the Scots and Irish had a fearsome reputation, they themselves had long feared the marauding bands of wild Norsemen who could slip quietly up an estuary and assault a village, monastery or castle with little warning. It had only been with the conquest of the Normans, themselves descendants of Norsemen, that the threat of Viking invasions had ended.

The knight squatted on his haunches and motioned the boy on the ground to sit. Roland slowly rose keeping a weather eye on the Irish boy who still held the broadsword in a threatening position.

"So how did a proud spawn of Vikings come to be slithering on his belly trying to steal food this fine day?" he asked. "…And what's that ye've wrapped in those rags?"

Roland froze for a moment. The longbow on his back was the one thing that could tie him to the dead men back on Kinder Scout. Mere possession of such a weapon by a peasant was a crime in itself. He had to think quickly.

"This?" He jerked his head over his shoulder at the object slung on his back. "Nothing but a rod I use to fashion shelter from the rain, My Lord…or to crack a head, if I need to defend myself. I do not deny I was about to steal your breakfast and I am sorry of it, but I've been three days with nothing."

"No dogs in these parts?" the knight asked with a grin.

"None I could catch, my Lord."

"Well then, mutton will have to do. Get up boy and come warm yourself by the fire."

The big man arose, scratched at an itch under his arm and lumbered back toward where the meat was sizzling over the coals. The Irish boy drew the sword back, planted its point on the ground and leaned forward over the tall hilt.

"Go eat thief, but I'll be watchin'" He eyed Roland for a moment longer then motioned toward the fire. No further invitation was needed as he scrambled to his feet and moved into the clearing.

"So, young Inness," said the knight as he sliced a slab of meat off the skewer and tossed it to the boy, "as we have your name, you shall have ours. I am Roger de Laval, Master of Shipbrook and Defender of the Welsh Marches and the nasty piece of business there with the sword is one Declan O'Duinne, my trusty squire."

"Pleased to make your acquaintance, my lord" said Roland as he launched into the hank of mutton, the warm juices running down his chin. The man across from the fire was a Norman knight and he had many reasons to hate him, but was thankful for his charity at the moment.

"*Live and let live for now,*" he thought to himself and concentrated on the meat.

***

Three leagues away, a short stocky man with a pale scar on his face moved steadily through the morning mist with his eyes intent on the faint trail ahead--a trail that would have a rich reward at the end. Thus far his hunt had gone as expected. The Earl's men who had stumbled across a fugitive near here days ago had been lucky fools at best, but they had given him a place to begin his search. The forest folk hadn't been very inclined to be helpful, but he had his ways of extracting the information he wanted. He now knew that a stranger had been about in this part of the forest, and that his quarry was closer to a boy than a man. The description of the stranger he had persuaded the locals to provide was flimsy, but useful, nevertheless, for it roughly matched what little information Sir William had been able to impart. He thought for a moment about his brief meeting with the nobleman.

The Earl's whelp had been too terrified to get a good look at the bowman. Ivo Brun had a good sense for people and for terror. He had quickly pegged the young man as cunning, dangerous—and a coward. *But he pays well.*

Of particular value was information he had squeezed from several frightened peasants that the boy carried a long, thin object wrapped in rough cloth on his back. This could only be the weapon that troubled the mind of the young Lord William.

He had cast in a widening circle from the clearing where the soldiers had seen the boy, searching for some sign amid their clumsy trampling, when he had sensed that he was being watched. He only hesitated a moment before continuing his search but that had been enough. The watcher was gone. *Well enough—he would follow this new track!*

It had not proven easy, for his quarry had been careful. The trail he followed had been made by a big man, so this could not be the one he sought, but perhaps this big man had knowledge of the boy. In time he came to the rocky cleft covered with vines. Brun did not enter for he could clearly see that two trails had left the deep ravine—and within the past hour. He recognized the first—the big man—and paid it little attention. Ivo Brun cared not for whoever might have aided the boy. That was not his concern.

The other trail was made by a lighter foot and would be his bowman. That trail headed east. He turned his back to the setting sun and followed the trail toward the approaching night. This boy knew the forest well and left but a faint record of his passing, but for Brun it was enough. His pursuit was slow but steady until darkness finally stopped him. He had tracked men in the dark before, but those had been men who were fleeing in a panic and had no skill in the woods. They left a trail as clear as a Roman road. He could not track a boy this skilled at covering his tracks by moonlight. He found a nook beneath a deadfall, curled into a ball and went quickly to sleep.

At dawn he picked up the trail and by mid-morning, he had arrived at the edge of the forest. An open field lay before him and beyond that, the King's Highway. The boy had passed this way near dawn when the dewy grass made his faint tracks more visible. The traffic on the road was fairly heavy by now, but the man paid little attention. He knew the trail would be lost on the highway, so he had to gamble on which way the boy had gone. This young fellow had been smart enough to elude everyone but him for the past fortnight, so he would be unlikely to make a foolish mistake at this point. He would not turn south toward Sheffield, where he would soon be back in the domain of the Earl of Derby. *No, he would have gone north.* Satisfied with his judgment, Ivo Brun turned left on the King's highway and joined the line of travellers journeying north—to York.

Chapter 6

Stalked

Roland's belly was full for the first time in weeks and after several days of no sleep the boy had to fight the urge to curl up beside the fire and drift off. The squire, O'Duinne, had moved off to continue preparations for the day's travel, but continually cast glances towards him. The boy had to concede that he would have done the same if the situations had been reversed.

Sir Roger De Laval had quickly finished a huge helping of the mutton and was now pulling on a pair of breeches over patched linen drawers. He tucked in his long shirt and reached for a tunic in the bag by his side.

"So where are you bound, lad?" he called out.

Roland saw no point in concealing his destination from the man who had just shared his food.

"York, my lord."

" Aye, we as well. Come here and help me with these boots."

Roland scrambled over to where the knight was now sitting, casting a quick glance at the squire who was, at that moment, packing the black mule. After a good deal of shoving and pulling, the boots slid on the big man's feet and he stood. The boy noted that the faded black tunic Sir Roger now wore displayed what must be the de Laval coat of arms—a rampant white stag. It was a proud symbol for this knight of fierce countenance, but genial manner.

By now the mule had been packed and the huge warhorse saddled. Roland helped the squire scatter the remaining coals of the fire and smother them with earth. It was time to depart. The boy was anxious to be off. He knew he could not be tracked along the worn path of the Roman road, but he still felt the need to put distance between him and the man he knew would be pursuing him.

No invitation had been issued, but Roland sensed that Sir Roger might not object to his company on the journey north. The boy was tempted, but hesitated. Traveling with a well-armed knight would offer him far more protection than he could muster on his own, but de Laval was a Norman. There could be no doubt of that—both the fashion of his name and the quality of his mount marked him as one of that warlike race. *"Murderers,"* he muttered to himself and felt the heat rise in his cheeks as he thought of the vengeance he owed the Normans. Vengeance might have to wait, but until then he wished to have no truck with them. Then, the words of Tuck came back to him. *"Can't have your revenge if you're dead."*

He would bank his hatred for now. Like much else in his life, settling accounts with Normans would have to wait for a better day. Given the chance, this day he would travel with the enemy to York. At last the party was prepared. Sir Roger mounted the huge charger that had been waiting patiently, munching grass near the fringe of the road, and clucked softly to the horse. The animal almost seemed to shrug, and then swung his head toward the roadway.

Sir Roger half turned in his saddle and shouted back.

"Walk with us a ways young Inness. It will give Declan someone to jabber to besides me self."

And so began the day's journey. The two boys trailed behind the knight, with the squire leading the black mule. The day had warmed considerably, and soon other travellers roused from their encampments and appeared along the road. As they walked, Roland came to understand what had motivated Sir Roger's invitation. With no prompting, Declan O'Duinne began to expound at length on their fellow travellers and the state of the world in general. He nudged Roland and nodded toward a monk sitting by the roadside extracting a stone from his sandal.

"For the love of God, now there's the only skinny priest I've seen since misfortune brought me to England!" he exclaimed in a hushed voice. "Irish monks, now they're all bony as storks, but the English clergy are as plump as your spring robins. Never miss a meal, I'd wager...or a flagon of ale!" he snorted. The squire seemed to have completely forgotten his earlier hostility towards his new companion.

"Look!" he again nudged Roland and pointed out a man pulling a small cart behind him. "A peddler! Now there's a proper trade for a poor lad like me self!" He lowered his voice a bit so Sir Roger could not overhear. "I'll never rub two coppers together as squire to a knight who loses money every year on his lands." He whispered to Roland.

Roland interrupted this speech—which would probably have lasted till mid day—to ask a question.

"Sir Roger is poor then?" The idea seemed far-fetched to the boy. All noblemen and gentry were rich.

"Well, he'll not have to beg in the streets of York, I suppose, but it's a fact that he has no money for his squire. What little he does have can mostly be traced to the Lady de Laval, who has a head for commerce." He grinned and shook his head. "Sir Roger is a soldier and is a bit lost managing an estate. He prospers when the King needs warriors and is...*adrift*...when there is peace. And with Henry on the throne there has been a lot of peace these past years."

The boy paused and his voice took on a more serious timbre, "My master fought beside Henry in France and Wales and in my own Ireland. That's how I came to be a squire to an English knight and a story that cries out to be made into an epic poem!" With that, the boy launched into his life story.

"The O' Duinne's of Ulster are descended from a cousin of King Donnchad Donn mac Flainn, a ruler of great wisdom and courage..."

Roland's mind and gaze began to wander, as his companion detailed the history of the O'Duinne Clan. After weeks as a fugitive in the forest, he felt horribly exposed walking leisurely among the crowd on the highway. He observed each traveller that approached for the presence of a threat and tried to attract no notice, as he frequently glanced over his shoulder at the road south. The boy had no illusions that he had reached safety. The fervour with which he had been hunted by the Earl of Derby's men made it clear that his killing of three soldiers would not be soon forgotten—or ever forgiven. For a moment, in his mind's eye, he could see the face of William de Ferrers in that instant when he had loosed an arrow towards the man's heart. Only some instinctive urge to self-preservation had saved the young heir to the Earldom of Derby that day—that and the swiftness of his flight from Roland's pursuit.

Roland knew without doubt who was behind the frantic search that had dogged him for so many days. He also knew that it would not end soon. He was relieved that the soldiers had been withdrawn from the search, but troubled by the new threat from the lone stalker who had so frightened the wild man of the forest. William de Ferrers truly must want him dead in the worst way. Roland thought for a moment about his dead father and clutched the end of the longbow concealed on his back.

"The feeling is mutual, my lord," he whispered grimly to himself, turning his attention back as Declan O'Duinne continued the epic story of his rise to squire.

"So Sir Roger, seeing the fighting spirit and unwavering courage that tis the very nature of the O'Duinne Clan, stayed his blow and spared me dear father's life that day. My sire, seeing this man was a true knight indeed, bade me serve him as squire from that day forward—and so I have these past three years."

Taken with his own thoughts, Roland had obviously missed a good portion of Declan's saga. He had no notion of how or why Sir Roger and the head of Clan O'Duinne had come to blows—or to what purpose, but the end result made him pause.

"Sir Roger…he spared you father's life?" he asked quietly.

"Aye, Master Inness, and none could have gainsaid him had he taken it! The fightin' in Ireland these past years has been more than can be borne. Clans and subkings fight the English and each other like savages…like *animals*. It is the curse of the Irish that we cannot live in peace with ourselves, much less with the English who seek to lord it over us. To see an act of honour in such a place is a rare thing. Sir Roger is a fine soldier—and a fierce one at that—but he's a finer man and, while we have our differences, I've been proud to serve him, even if he be a cursed Englishman!" This last Declan said with a smile.

"Honour in a Norman is something I've never seen," Roland replied, "...nor mercy. Your Sir Roger is a rare bird indeed, Master O'Duinne."

Declan O'Duinne took a long look at the boy walking beside him, and grinned.

"On that we can agree then. Ye may call me Declan."

Roland grinned back.

"Pleased to make your acquaintance."

***

Two leagues behind, Ivo Brun trudged steadily northward. As he walked, he paid special attention to the edges of the forest where travellers often stopped to rest during the heat of the day, to take their meals, or to encamp for the night. He did not want to pass his prey unawares. As the morning progressed, more and more travellers joined the pilgrims and peddlers on the highway. Brun, from time to time, circled off the roadway to get a better view of the travellers ahead. Somewhere up there was a boy with a longbow who was worth a great deal of gold to him—dead or alive. *Dead was always simpler,* he thought to himself. He picked up his pace and began to pass those ahead of him, as he sought to close the gap on his quarry.

***

As the day progressed Roland learned more about his traveling companions, simply by listening to Declan O'Duinne's never ending narration. It seemed the squire and his knight were en route to inspect a small land holding two leagues beyond York that had been a part of Lady de Laval's dowry when she had wed Sir Roger. This seemed to be a regular annual duty the Lady De Laval had decreed. The Irish boy had begun to describe the route to their destination when he stopped and seemed to suddenly remember his manners.

"So Roland, where do ye hail from and what's your business in York," he asked politely. Roland froze for an instant before answering. There seemed no malice in the squire's manner, but he must take care. He had much to hide.

"I travel from Derbyshire to a bit beyond York," he said. "I have an uncle there who has offered me work tending his swine. His only son died of the fever in the winter." It was a bald-faced lie, but the only tale that had come to him.

The Irish boy looked aghast.

"*Hog farm*! Why ye'll be smelling like a filthy swine and up to yer waist in pig shit, Roland…and those boar hogs!" Declan shuddered. "They can fair rip a man's leg off with those tusks." The boy put his fingers to his mouth to portray the killer tusks of the boar hog and snorted furiously. Roland was forced to laugh. He couldn't remember when he had last laughed. It felt good.

"But Declan, you yourself were complaining about making no money as a squire. My uncle is really quite prosperous supplying pork to Yorkshire. Why don't you stay and join me. Uncle could always use another swineherd." Roland made this offer, knowing what the response would be.

Declan seemed injured at the suggestion. "We O'Duinne's are of warrior stock and cannot be chasing piggies around all day! A squire's pay may be poor, but it's a proud callin'. Besides, if I were no squire, I'd be a peddler, where ye can make some real coin—and not smell like a pig sty!"

As they walked, Roland thought about what his next move might be. There was no uncle waiting beyond York with a pig farm to give him sanctuary. He was on his own, with nothing but his wits between him and disaster.

"Roland, me lad, you must give up the soft, but smelly life of shovelling pig crap for your supper," Declan continued in a lower voice so that Sir Roger could not overhear. "Look at me! I plan to see a good deal of the world and have a few adventures along the way. If I'm lucky—and all Irishmen are lucky—I may one day be a knight meself and own land granted by a grateful king for me valour!"

"*Or*, you may be shovelling horse crap for your supper and get a broadsword through your gizzard for your trouble," replied Roland. Declan gave a short laugh, but seemed to find this last jab a bit close to the mark.

For a while, the boys walked along in silence. Declan

O'Duinne's words had given his mind something to chew upon. Only a month before, his whole world had been on Kinder Scout. Farming and hunting were all he knew and all he had expected in this life. And now that life was gone. In its place were two imperatives—survival and vengeance. How to make a life from those?

Declan had become a squire and believed that he could someday become a knight in his own right. *Was this possible?* He knew nothing of the rules for such things other than a king made knights and a king could do anything he wished. *Kings...* Roland knew little of them. Henry was King and had been since before his birth. He was reputed to be a great warrior and a just man with truculent princes for children, but Roland knew little else. He had once heard that the King liked to hunt in Nottinghamshire to the east and wondered if he used a longbow like the one on his back. The whole world of kings and knights and adventures seemed distant and unknowable to him. His only previous encounter with a knight had been with William de Ferrers, who was now his mortal enemy. Roland's thoughts were jolted to a halt, as he tripped in a deep hole in the roadway and fell on his face.

Declan laughed and pointed and Sir Roger also seemed amused.

"I guess you Viking Englishmen are more used to a longboat than walking on solid ground!" he roared and seemed greatly amused at his jest.

Declan pulled Roland to his feet and the boys resumed their position to the rear of Sir Roger. *"Never been in a longboat,"* Roland grumbled, to no one in particular.

"Ah, that'd be just as well, since we won't be needin' one on this trip," Declan declared cheerfully. "We'll be fordin' the River Wharfe near noontide and see the walls of York by dusk. If we step lively, we should be safely through Micklegate Bar before dark I'd wager. There is an inn favoured by Sir Roger, just over the River Ouse bridge, and it has a tolerable stable for his squire to find lodging." He paused for a moment and then asked, "Will ye be travellin' on to your uncle's? It'll be well past dark before ye could get much north of the city."

Roland thought quickly.

50

"I'd hoped to arrive at Uncle's today," he lied, "but doubt I could find the place in the dark. So I'll needs find some shelter in the city and finish my journey on the morrow."

Declan smiled broadly. "Ah, look no farther, Roland me lad! The stable at the Black Ox won't be as fine an accommodation as yer uncle's...*pig estate*...but it's reasonably snug." He slapped Roland on the shoulder, then added by way of explanation, "The horses and mules rarely appreciate me stories—so I'd favour the company!" Roland simply nodded, grateful that he would not be thrown on his own devices in York. He had never seen a true city.

With that issue resolved, the boys settled into a steady pace as the warmth of the day grew. As predicted, they reached the ford at the River Wharfe a little past noon. It had been a cold spring with a slow thaw and the waters of the ford were cold, but only waist deep. Sir Roger's horse stopped just short of the opposite bank and proceeded to drink his fill, as the knight watched the two boys lead the pack mule past him and on to dry land.

On the opposite bank a knot of travellers had just plunged in to make the same crossing, but one held back surveying the view ahead. The man's tunic was filthy from a combination of sweat and the dust of the highway. He had kept a killing pace all that morning and had passed dozens of travellers heading north. He paid little heed to the sweat and dirt that grimed his face and clothes. All of his concentration was on the line of travellers crossing the river. There on the opposite bank stood a boy with an object slung over his back—something long and thin and concealed in rags. *A longbow!* It had to be.

Here was Ivo Brun's target in the flesh. The boy was a bit above medium height and somewhat gangly—like a colt. His hair was dark and his clothes ragged, as they would be after weeks in the forest. This precisely fit the description he had squeezed from the forest folk. Brun's hand moved absently to the hilt of his dagger.

"There's a lovely boy," the man muttered, keeping his eye on the figure on the opposite bank. "Ivo will wait till none are about to slit your gullet and earn me pay."

He eased slowly into the river and began to cross. He was in no hurry now. It would be child's play to follow and kill the boy at the right time.

A hundred yards ahead, the two boys, refreshed from their dip in the river, were in high spirits. Declan O'Duinne felt moved to song and took up some indecipherable Irish ballad in his native Gaelic. The boy had an unschooled, but surprisingly pleasing, tenor voice. It seemed a number of their fellow travellers agreed and urged him to continue. Declan tried to draw Roland into his minstrel show, but the boy firmly refused. Roland knew that he could no more carry a tune than carry Sir Roger's horse. In this pleasant fashion, the afternoon passed until a commotion was heard near dusk from farther up the line of travellers. Sir Roger spurred his horse forward and soon returned.

"York lies but a half league ahead. We shall be there before full dark. By the saints, I could use a pitcher of ale!" The large knight wheeled his huge charger back around and urged the horse into a faster walk. Roland and Declan had to lengthen their stride to keep up. Roland could have burst from excitement. He had never seen a proper city before. Castleton was hardly more than a collection of huts at the base of Peveril Castle and Sheffield, which he had only seen a half dozen times, was little more than a village—but York! This was purported to be a mighty city with high stone walls encircling the entire place and two castles guarding those walls.

A mile further on, they topped a rise behind Sir Roger and there lay York before them. Its wall seemed huge and endless and Roland could see two separate fortifications on small hills within the city, each topped with a banner fluttering in the light breeze. In every direction from the walls, flat, neat fields in their early spring green sparkled in the gold of the setting sun. It was a sight to remember.

At this point, the line of travellers approaching the city had turned into a throng—nay, a mob—as other roads converged on the southward entrance to the place. Every style of dress and station was visible in the vast assemblage lumbering toward the southern gates. Beyond the walls, Roland could make out a few roof tops and what seemed to be infinite columns of smoke rising from cooking fires and chimneys and forming a white and grey cloud over the place. This was a city indeed!

Longbow

Ahead, the mob disappeared through the huge arched gate that Declan had called the Micklegate Bar. Finally, Sir Roger's party began to pass through as well. On either side of the gate stood two men-at-arms, who were surveying the travellers with alternating looks of suspicion and boredom. To all who entered, the massive ramparts surrounding York were an awesome display of Norman power—and were meant as such. When they had conquered this island but a few generations back they did it with heavy armoured cavalry and secure fortresses erected at carefully selected locations throughout the land. From these secure bases they had been able to continue to extend and tighten their grip on a conquered but restless mass of Saxons, Danes and Welsh. Not one Norman fortress had fallen to rebels in all the years since the conquest.

Roland thought back to the rare tales his father had told him of the rising of the Danes against the Normans before his birth. For the first time, he understood the courage behind that rebellion. That men, armed with stolen swords, staves and, of course, the longbow, could have challenged the power of those who had built these walls was beyond his comprehension. He wondered if he had the courage to face that kind of power and knew, in a moment of realization, that someday he would know the answer to that question.

As they entered the city, Roland's head swivelled from right to left as he took in the colourful chaos that was York. Street vendors hawked their wares from every doorway and alleyway. Strangely exotic women smiled and giggled at the boys as they passed and spoke boldly to Sir Roger, who merely smiled and waved.

"Sir Roger is the most loyal husband in Christendom" whispered Declan to Roland, careful that his master did not overhear. *"The Lady de Laval can be as prickly as a gum ball on occasion, but His Lordship is besotted with her."*

Roland wasn't sure why Declan was passing him this information, but he nodded anyway and continued to take in the incredible sights and sounds. In short order, they were passing over a stone bridge which spanned the River Ouse. The river was broader than any Roland had yet seen and ran straight through the city. On the northern side of the bridge lay a pleasant looking inn with a sign sporting a likeness of a black ox. This must be their destination. Sir Roger dismounted and handed the reins of his horse to Declan, who, in turn, handed the rope attached to the black mule to Roland.

"Follow me," he said, and led the great grey horse into a narrow alleyway that led to the back of the inn. There, Roland saw a rough shelter, open on two sides but covered from the back of the inn to the back of the establishment which fronted the next lane over. There were a dozen stalls; some already filled with horses, mules and donkeys. Above the stalls was a loft filled with loose hay. A rickety ladder led up to the equally rickety looking hay loft and a trough of water stood near the alleyway on the opposite side. To Roland, who had spent more than a fortnight in the forest eluding capture, it looked like a palace.

"Let's feed and water the animals and rub down Bucephalus. Then we can take a peek around before supper!" said Declan, with glee in his voice.

"Bucephalus?" asked Roland. At that moment, the huge horse swung around and nudged the boy's shoulder.

"Ha! It looks like Buc was just waitin' for a formal introduction!" said Declan. His name is Bucephalus, which—if I understand rightly—was the name of Alexander the Great's warhorse."

"Alexander the Great?" Roland wrinkled his brow. He had never heard of the man. "Was he one of the ancient kings of England?"

"Nay...he was High King of the Macedonians and conquered the whole world a long ways back, he did." The Irish boy was about to continue, but stopped.

"Don't ye know nothin' of the world, my dog-eatin' friend?" he asked gently.

"Not much I'll warrant, but I'll learn," said Roland. He already knew the world was a dangerous place and that he was far from home. He knew that home was now a burned-out ruin and his family dead or in hiding. All this he knew, but if he were to survive and one day return to Derbyshire for the settling of accounts, he had to learn much more and learn it fast. Declan thrust a brush into his hand.

"Rub down your new friend, Roland. Sir Roger expects this horse to get better treatment than we do...or him for the matter. It's probably the only thing he loves as much as his Lady Catherine!"

Roland set to his chore and after a quarter of an hour had passed, he was finished. During that time, Declan had thrown down hay from the loft and taken the mule for a drink. After Bucephalus had his own drink and was safely secured in his stall, the Irish boy turned to Roland with a grin.

"We've at least an hour till supper time! Let's go explore!" He motioned for Roland to follow, and quickly retraced their steps through the alleyway to the Micklegate road and the front of the inn. It was already twilight.

"Which way shall we go?" he asked. Roland could only shrug his shoulders.

"Very well then" the Irish boy said, and spat in the palm of his hand. He took two fingers of his other hand and slapped the pool of spittle. A sizable glob spurted off to the right.

"There's our answer!" he shouted. "Let's go!" The boy turned to his right and headed up the cobblestone street. As Roland sprang to follow, he passed within an arm's length of a man slouching against the corner of the Black Ox Inn. The man watched him intently and absently rubbed a scar that traversed his cheek. He made no move to follow the boys, knowing they would return. He closed his eyes and leaned back against the sturdy wall of the inn.

"Very soon now, me lovely boy." The man whispered to himself. *"Very soon."*

Chapter 7

Assassin

R oland strained to take in the chaotic spectacle that was
York, while sticking close to Declan. The Irish boy
seemed to know his way around the city and Roland feared that if
he lost contact with his guide among the crowds on Micklegate
Road, he would never find his way back to the Black Ox. Darkness
was quickly descending on the town, but street performers and
peddlers continued to vie for the attention of the large crowds
moving along the main thoroughfare. Here and there torches had
been lit and as night fell these cast flickering shadows against the
buildings on either side. The boys had to squeeze through knots of
people who had stopped to admire a juggler or to haggle over the
price of some item.

Weary of fighting the crowds, Declan took an abrupt right turn
into a narrow lane that led them up a gradual slope to the walls of
Castle York, the larger of the two fortifications guarding the city.
The fortress was crude but functional. A steep earthen
embankment, topped by a sturdy log palisade, encircled its bailey.
On the south side of the castle towering over all was a sizable
motte, which provided a clear view of any enemy attempting to
breach or storm the southern walls of the city. From this elevated
mound, archers could rain projectiles down on an attacking force.

Even to Roland's untrained eye, it was a formidable defence.

"They say that King William the Conqueror, himself, had this built," said Declan, surveying the structure, "...and that the lake yonder was made by damming the River Foss. The folks here in York call it the King's Fishpond." Even in the dim light from the torches that illuminated the palisade above, Roland could see that this small lake held no fish or any other live creature by his reckoning. Numberless pieces of flotsam floated in the foul-smelling, scum covered pool. But it was clear that this body of water had never been built with a fish dinner in mind. He looked at the contours of the lake, and saw how it protected two sides of the castle. Whatever else the Normans were, they were no fools when it came to war.

"Sir Roger says the original castle was burnt a hundred years ago when you Danes rose up against William," Declan continued, "but the King rebuilt it on the graves of dead rebels. The Danes did not take the second castle and could not hold the town after seizing it. About here, they call William's retribution the 'Harrying of the North'...and they say the slaughter was terrible. The rivers choked with the dead." The Irish boy seemed falter in the telling of this history. After a long pause, he shrugged and shook his head. "We Irish know something of rebellion and slaughter."

Listening to this tale, Roland again felt the weight of his own ignorance. This history was new to him, but sadly familiar.

"The slaughter of the Danes didn't end a hundred years ago, Declan, nor their rebellion. They rose again, my father among them, not twenty years ago, and were beaten again—but not before putting the fear of the Lord into the Normans!" He blurted this out and then stopped. *Stupid!* He was speaking treason to a squire who served a Norman knight. He considered fleeing on the spot before the Irish boy could raise an alarm but was frozen to the spot. It was full night now and he could not judge the face or the reaction of his companion in the dim light reflected off the murky water. He waited. After several long moments the Irish spoke from the darkness.

"Aye, the Normans can be cruel," Declan spoke quietly, "but so too were the Saxons and Danes when they ruled this land. So too were the Irish when the ruled themselves. In these days it seems all are Christian, but none behave such. It's bad men of all types that make the weak suffer. Were there more like Sir Roger, perhaps there'd be no rebellions…"

Roland had not realized that he had been holding his breath as the boy spoke. He slowly exhaled as it became clear that Declan had no intention of having him seized and turned over to Norman justice.

The boy's words surprised Roland, but they had a familiar ring to them. Had not Tuck told him much the same thing when they had met in the forest? He pondered Declan's claim that all races made cruel overlords, but knew it missed the essential point for him. It wasn't a Saxon a Dane or an Irishman that had destroyed his family. It was a Norman. That was enough for him.

"Your Sir Roger seems a good enough man…for a Norman," he said.

"Aye, he's far and away the best of the lot, Norman or no. Even your beloved King Henry can be bloody-handed—when lesser folk get in his way."

Roland shrugged. Henry was certainly *not* beloved by the Danes, but he had heard his father, and some of the other men, speak of the King with a mixture of anger, fear and respect. It was conceded that the laws Henry enforced were more just than not and that some of the cruelty of the nobles had been reined in under his rule, but Henry was getting old and London was far off. In Derbyshire, Lord Robert did as he pleased. And there was no doubt where the King's loyalty stood in any real dispute between the nobility and the peasants. The men had never spoken much about the uprising twenty years ago, but he understood that it would have succeeded had the King not intervened to crush the revolt.

Declan interrupted the boy's thoughts with a more pressing matter.

"Come on Master Inness, enough of this stirring over old bones. Let's get back to the inn for supper…unless you find these curs around here more appetizing!" He pointed at a mangy pack of stray dogs lying about on the street, hoping for handouts.

Roland was glad of the interruption and fell in behind the Irish boy as they headed back the way they had come. A torch already cast a smoky light around the entrance to the Black Ox when the boys arrived. They snaked their way through a crowd at the doorway and into the murky interior that was lit by dim oil lamps and the glow from a large fireplace. In a corner to himself sat Sir Roger, gnawing contentedly on some obscure chop of meat. As the boys approached, he took a large swig from his flagon of ale and wiped his mouth with the sleeve of his tunic.

"Sit me boys...sit!" he offered loudly, motioning to the serving woman. "Bring these lads some meat, my dear 'fore they waste away!" The woman looked disapprovingly at the two new customers, but moved off toward the fireplace where the indefinable slab of meat was roasting on a spit. She sliced several generous helpings onto a wooden plank and plopped them before the two hungry boys. Declan dove in straight away, but Roland hung back, despite his gnawing hunger.

"What ails ye boy?" asked Sir Roger between bites and gulps of ale. "Eat!"

"Sir, I cannot. I have no money and have accepted enough of your generosity for one day...for which I am very obliged." Roland replied.

Sir Roger studied the boy for a moment, as though really seeing him for the first time.

"So ye've an uncle north of York, who wants to make you rich—as a *pig farmer*?"

"Aye, my lord." Roland nodded.

"Har! And Bucephalus longs to be a plough horse!" Sir Roger snorted. "Do not lie to me boy. Ye've got nowhere to go, do ye?"

Declan O'Duinne raised his head from the chunk of meat he was consuming. He eyed Roland curiously and waited for the boy's answer.

Roland knew Declan had believed his story, but now realized that Sir Roger had seen right through it. He didn't know which was worse—that he had deceived his new friend or that he had failed to deceive his new benefactor. He knew lying was a sin, but telling the whole truth about his crime and flight from Derbyshire would be his death sentence. Sir Roger may be a good man, but he was a Norman, and if he knew that Roland had slain three of the Earl of Derby's men, he would instantly turn him over to the Sheriff of York. The Sheriff would be more than eager to transport him back to face the tender mercies of the Earl—and his son. Deciding which way to flee in the forest from the Earl's men had been much simpler than these choices! He must answer with care.

"Aye Sir Roger. There is no uncle. I've nowhere to go…and cannot go back." Roland dropped his head. He could not look in Declan's direction.

"And why can't ye go back, lad?" Sir Roger asked quietly. "I heard ye telling of yer father and yer farm."

"My father is dead, my lord," Roland answered. He took a deep breath and continued, "killed by the Earl of Derby's men."

Sir Roger de Laval showed no reaction, but Declan O'Duinne choked on his hank of meat.

"And why was he killed?" Sir Roger asked evenly.

"For poaching a deer, my lord" Roland replied. He knew this was still a lie, but it was as close to the truth as he could venture—and survive. Still, he had just confessed his association with a crime against the nobility, and feared Sir Roger's reaction. He tried to appear relaxed, but was poised to bolt for the door if they attempted to seize him.

"They killed him for poaching a *bloody deer*?" blurted Declan. He had been prepared to hear Roland name some truly heinous crime his father had committed. Poaching was, no doubt, a crime, but generally one that would get you a flogging or a stretch in the gaol—not a death sentence.

"Harsh justice, that," said Sir Roger, maintaining his casual tone, "not what I would have expected from the Earl. "He is a hard man, true, but not one to kill a man for a crime such as that."

"It was his son that ordered it, my lord, not the Earl," the boy managed to reply, hanging his head. "He came with men to our farm. They killed him while I hid in the forest. Sir William De Ferrers gave the order. I saw it. I still see it."

Sir Roger nodded. He was a man who had seen much of death and the marks it could leave on the living.

"But why are you fleeing to York, if *you've* committed no crime?" he asked.

Roland knew this question was coming and once more walked the fine line between half-truth and outright lying.

"The Earl has seized our farm and turned us out, my lord. My brother and sister are under the care of the church. I must make my own way."

"And your mother?"

"Dead sir—of the fever this past winter."

Sir Roger took a long moment to consider the boy's story, then turned to Declan O'Duinne.

"Dec, we've been short a squire since Harold took up with that milkmaid in Leeds. This lad doesn't look like much, but I have a feelin' about him. What say you?"

Declan looked for a long moment at Roland, weighing his answer, and turned back to his master.

"He's a liar for certain, my lord, but I expect I might have told a tale myself in his place. And though he's a lyin', meat thievin', spawn of a Viking…he's agreeable company. I suppose he'll do."

Sir Roger nodded and turned back to Roland. "Well then, if Dec can tolerate you…so can I! Shall ye be my junior squire, lad?"

Roland's mind swirled with this turn of events. A moment before, he was sure he would be seized and thrown into the clutches of the Earl of Derby. And now, beyond belief, he was being offered a place in the world—by a Norman. Yet there was something in this man's manner that was at odds with what he knew of Normans. Somehow he knew that this man could not have been a party to the crimes done on Kinder Scout mountain.

"I…I…would be honoured, Sir Roger," he finally managed to reply.

Declan laughed and punched him in the shoulder. "Eat up then dog-boy, for ye're to be my apprentice, and I plan to work ye hard!"

Roland turned back to the mysterious meat on the slab before him and dug in with a passion, as he tried to sort out this strange twist in his fortunes. *Squire to a Norman! What next?* Still, the meat was delicious, whatever its provenance, and the thought of a real night's sleep under a roof, even the rough shelter of a stable would be a luxury.

In a short while, he had eaten his fill and followed Declan through the rear door of the inn to the stables. As they departed, a man sitting near the front door took another deep drink from the tankard of ale before him. He had not been able to overhear the conversation across the crowded inn, but he cared not what was said. It was enough to know that the big knight would be sleeping in the Inn proper and not in the stables with these boys. The man would not interfere with his work. As he watched the boys leave he could see their high spirits.

Lambs to slaughter, he thought.

After an hour, Sir Roger rose from his table and stumbled up the rude steps to his room above. In another hour, most of the patrons had done likewise. The man by the door paid his bill and stepped into the night. The torch was burning low and hazy and barely illuminated the main street. Within a few feet he was deep in shadows and as he entered the alleyway he was nearly invisible. He waited there a moment to allow his eyes to adjust to the night, then moved to a still darker nook where he could observe the stables.

He had not survived dozens of such nights without great skill and caution—and he exercised both here. Simple this kill might be, but he would not be careless. For more than an hour he watched the dark stable across the alleyway in silence, with nothing but one drunken wretch relieving himself in the alley to interrupt his concentration. For a short time he had heard the two boys chattering as they arranged themselves for the night, but they had long since fallen silent. It was a cloudless but moonless night with only the stars for illumination, but that was enough for the eyes of a hunter to adjust to. His finely tuned stalking skills noted nothing to raise an alarm and he started across the alley with infinite care.

When he reached the opening to the stables, he crouched by the first stall and let his senses take in what lay before him. Some of the animals moved restlessly and he could hear one of the boys groan in his sleep from an empty stall half way down the row.

Ivo Brun loved the wealth that his skill brought him, but this—the moment before a kill—was truly what he lived for. Nothing else gave him such excitement, including the Earl's gold. With great care, he moved down the row of stalls toward the sleeping boys. He slid his long dagger silently out of its sheath as he moved like a shadow toward his target.

At that moment, the great warhorse Bucephalus caught his scent and began to move nervously in his stall. Declan rolled over and burrowed further into the soft straw they had laid out for their bed and resumed his soft snoring, but Roland was instantly awake. Weeks of hiding and evading capture in the forests of Derbyshire had honed his senses to a sharp edge and he knew, without knowing why, that danger was near.

As quietly as he could, he slid his hand to the longbow inside its rough cloth wrapping, then lay as still as death. Long moments passed until, through slitted eyes, he saw the outline of a man loom from the shadows and edge through the stall opening. His mind raced. Was this a horse thief come to steal Bucephalus?

The man held something in his right hand—a dagger? He moved into the stall with the slow, deadly grace of a lynx stalking a hare. For a moment, the man's head turned from boy to slumbering boy and back again, as if trying to distinguish one from the other in the near-total gloom. At that instant, Roland knew, without question, that this man was not after Bucephalus. He would not be hesitating thus over which boy to kill first. This man was set upon murder, not theft!

For an instant longer, the man looked from one dark lump on the floor to the other. Finally, he shrugged and moved toward the soundly sleeping form of Declan O'Duinne. He raised his dagger high and brought it forward with killing force.

The blade never reached its mark. With shocking force, a length of iron-hard English yew connected with the man's shin. The dark figure let out a fearsome scream—a combination of surprise and pain. He instinctively halted his blow and grasped his injured leg. Pandemonium followed. Bucephalus snorted and heaved against one side of the stall. Roland leapt to his feet as Declan sat bolt upright. The Irish boy seemed completely confused by the dim scene of a man cursing and hopping around on one leg in front of him. He sat frozen to the spot.

Inside of Roland, a wellspring of tension, built up over a fortnight of flight, was released. He stepped forward, transferring all of his weight from back to front foot, and swung the longbow with all his might. It caught Ivo Brun full on the bridge of his nose. The man's head snapped back and he reeled, his hands flying from his injured shin to this new source of pain. The dagger fell to the floor of the stable. Brun sagged for a moment against the split rail that secured the entrance to the stall, as he tried to gather his wits.

63

Then, with a guttural roar, he leaped forward seeking to grasp Roland by his throat. This was a mistake. The huge warhorse that also occupied the stall was a veteran of many battles and knew what to do if an enemy was foolish enough to approach from the rear. With a quickness that belied his size, Bucephalus cocked a great hind leg and lashed out at the stranger who had invaded his sleep and dared attack his companions. The assassin never saw the blow coming, as he flew across the central aisle of the stable and slammed into the opposite wall.

Declan was now up and fully awake.

Bucephalus was still moving frantically about his stall and the two boys moved to calm the huge animal before it accidentally trampled them.

"By all that's Holy, Roland—what happened?" Declan blurted. It was impossible to make sense of the chaos in the pitch dark stable.

Suddenly, the hubbub arose again, as the back door of the inn flew open and Sir Roger de Laval appeared in his nightshirt, wielding his broadsword in one hand and a torch in the other.

"By God, what has happened here? I could hear the racket in me room!" he shouted. He seemed as confused as Declan for a moment, when he saw the boys gathered around the horse. He rushed over and held the animal's huge head in his hands. "Buc! Are ye hurt old boy? Buc?" He spoke as though he expected the horse to reply.

"He's not hurt me lord," offered Declan, "but I'll wager the man who was out to steal him has had better days! He pointed toward the opposite wall, where the guttering torchlight revealed—nothing.

Roland felt the hairs on the back of his neck rise. In the brief moments that Sir Roger had devoted to checking on his warhorse, their attacker had somehow silently vanished!

"He was there—just now!" Declan sputtered. "Buc sent him flying."

With practiced efficiency, Sir Roger handed the squire the torch and began a careful search of the stables, his sword at the ready. When he reached the alleyway, he lowered the blade and turned back towards the boys.

"Slunk away it seems, and damned quiet in the slinking for certain," the big knight observed as he returned to where the boys waited.

"Declan, tell me what you saw."

"My lord, it was dark and a bit confusing. First thing I see is someone leaping about and yelling. Then me apprentice here gave him a right solid whacking with his staff. I think we'd both be carcasses now if he had'na done it. I could not see the man clear, but clear enough he meant to kill us both and take Buc."

Sir Roger turned his attention toward his new squire and started to speak, but stopped as his eyes were drawn to the object Roland held in his hand.

"And what have we here, Master Inness?" he inquired.

Roland followed his gaze and froze. In the melee with the killer, the rags he had used to conceal his weapon had fallen to the floor of the stall. The boy knew a soldier of Sir Roger's experience would have no doubt what he held in his hand.

"It's a longbow, my lord." Roland answered simply and waited for Sir Roger's reaction. Declan's eyes practically bugged out of his head as he realized what his fellow squire held.

"Can ye use it for more than a cudgel stick, lad?" the knight continued.

"Aye, my lord, I can."

For not the first time this day, Sir Roger de Laval reassessed the young man before him. "No doubt, no doubt, but I'll want to see for meself. It's a skill hard to come by I'm told, but one that would be an *asset* in a squire. Now wrap the thing up before the innkeeper decides to see what's about and get Buc settled back in." The man started back towards the rear entrance to the inn, but stopped and stooped low to rummage through the straw on floor of the stable.

"Seems the fellow left something behind, boys," said Sir Roger, as he bent to pick an object. It was a long, wicked-looking dagger with a single ruby in the handle. It gleamed in the flickering torchlight. Sir Roger handed it to Roland, hilt first.

"I think you've earned this, lad."

Chapter 8

The Test

Roland was up early the following morning. Despite Sir Roger's assurances that the attacker would not likely be back, he had slept hardly at all. More than once he started at some movement by Bucephalus or some unknown sound. Cities like York, he was learning, were very loud places, even in the small hours of the morning. The man who had come in the night had been, without doubt, an experienced killer. It had only been through luck—and the heightened senses of a hunted man—that Roland had heard his near silent approach. He went over the events again and again in his mind. The boy could only reach one conclusion—he had been the man's target.

If the killer had only wanted to silence the boys and steal the great warhorse, he would not have hesitated over which to dispatch first. He had been trying to identify one specific boy to kill and, unless Declan O'Duinne had enemies he knew naught of, it seemed certain that he was the one marked to die. The killer had only gone after Declan because he couldn't tell one boy from the other in the utter darkness of the stall floor.

The boy ran the logic over and over again in his head, but it was hardly necessary. He knew by instinct more than logic that the

66

man in the night had come for him. *Ivo Brun?* Roland shuddered at the thought. How had he tracked him to York? And where was he now? Brun was a name half out of legend and half out of nightmare, but the man was very real. He had heard the men talk of him in whispers and had even heard the women use his name to frighten children. He had never seen this monster, but if half the tales told of him were true, he was indeed a nightmare come to life.

If it were Brun, there could also be no doubt under whose orders he had acted. The hatred of William de Ferrers seemed to pursue him like a hell hound. He thought he would be safe this far beyond the borders of Derbyshire, but now he knew he was not. He saw again the features of the young nobleman, frozen in panic as he sighted his bow for the kill. He knew it was a sin, but he found himself wishing for the hundredth time that his last bolt had reached its intended mark.

Roland studied the long dagger left behind by the assassin. It was beautifully made and lethal looking. It was no doubt worth more than he could calculate, but it would not be for sale. This was a trophy. Ivo Brun had tried to kill him and had failed. *Someday I'll return it to its owner—and not hilt first.*

Outside the stable enclosure, the early signs of dawn were visible and a cock announced the approach of a new day just beyond the city walls. Declan O'Duinne stirred from his slumber and rose up scratching his backside absently. He stumbled to the alleyway to relieve himself.

"So, Roland, me lad," he began between yawns, "did ye sleep well last evening, then?"

"Fine," Roland replied suppressing a grin, "and you?"

"Oh, like a wee babe, I did," Declan replied, while finishing his business in the alley.

"Ye mean you wet yourself and wailed?" Roland inquired.

Declan chuckled and slapped Roland on the shoulder. "Aye, I swear I did both," the boy said, half in jest and half in earnest. "Try opening yer eyes in the middle of the night and seeing the Devil himself a hoverin' above ye." The Irish boy stopped for a moment. "Well, I guess that's just what ye *did* see—and I'm obliged to ye for puttin' yer *staff* to good use on the Devil's own shin…and not wetting yerself as well."

Declan lowered his voice to a whisper. *"Tell me how ye came by this Viking bow."*

Roland glanced about and whispered his reply, *"I made it."*

Declan looked over both shoulders and turned back to his fellow squire. "I suggest ye come up with another tale, friend. 'Tis a crime to make these bows, though odd, since no one seems to know how in the first place!" He spoke quickly, as he continued to keep an eye out for anyone who might overhear. "The few I've seen have been very old. Sir Roger says some were recovered from the Viking raids or seized from rebels during the 'Harrying of the North'. Aye, you'd pay a fortune to buy one, but the lords, they don't want many of these things floatin' around and fallin' into the wrong hands—if 'ye take my meaning. So have a care."

Roland considered his friends warning for a moment. "I found it in a cave," he said, with a straight face.

"Did ye now," replied Declan, with his own smile. "And what a lucky lad ye are, to have found such a treasure." The next hour was spent in preparing Bucephalus and the mule for the day's journey. Declan explained to Roland that Lady de Laval's lands lay less than a full day's journey northwest of York. He had been there once before with Sir Roger for an inspection of the property and was not enthusiastic about the prospect of a return visit.

"Her Ladyship will have a thousand questions," he moaned, "and Sir Roger will have *no* answers! He could count the heifers in a field and forget the number before an hour is passed."

"What good is it to survey the property, then, if he can't remember to report properly?" asked Roland, curious to understand this strange arrangement.

"Well it's no good a'tall, I can testify!" Declan replied. "Ye know, it's not that he *can't* remember. I'll vouch he has a mind sharper than his sword! I've seen the man on campaign remember the most minor details of an enemy's deployments. It's that he cares not a whit for managin' the land. *Whereas*, the fair Lady Catherine…"

"Expects a full accounting!" Declan and Roland whirled around at the booming voice behind them to see the looming figure of Sir Roger approaching.

"Aye, her mind is like a ledger in these matters, and she will get her full accounting…will she not, Master O'Duinne?"

Declan smiled sheepishly and nodded. "Aye, my lord, for she has turned this lion of Erin into a scribbler."

Sir Roger elbowed Roland in the side, and explained. "My lady knows how to read and write and do figures, and she's teaching young Declan here the skill," he said, with obvious pride.

"It's been a marvellous compromise for all parties. I get to travel about in fine spring weather, such as this, while she manages our estates in Cheshire and Dec here pays the price of our adventures by presenting Catherine with what she wants…chapter and verse on her holdings here in Yorkshire! Seems a fair bargain to me." He punctuated his conclusion by elbowing Roland again in the side.

"More a bargain with the Devil," muttered Declan under his breath, but he clearly didn't mean it. Roland was beginning to understand that his fellow squire held Lady de Laval in near as much esteem as her husband did.

The morning's preparations were soon complete and Sir Roger tossed the boys each a generous slice of bread for their breakfast as they departed the Black Ox. They entered the stream of humanity moving along Micklegate and soon reached Bootham Lane, where they swung left and proceeded toward Bootham Bar, which was the gate on the city's northwestern wall. As they neared the gate, Roland was transfixed by a fantastic structure that dwarfed all around it and soared as if reaching for the heavens.

Sir Roger noted the boy's awestruck look. "That be York Minster, lad. A grand cathedral in the Norman style—the grandest, I'm told, in all Europe."

Roland wasn't sure what Europe was, but this was surely a grand structure! It seemed to be crafted by the hand of God himself. The Normans were, indeed, both clever and rich if they erected this. He longed to see inside the massive structure and Sir Roger was in a mood to be accommodating. "Go on lads, have a look, but be quick about it!"

The two boys raced each other up the great flight of stone steps leading to the cathedral entrance. When they reached the great arched doors, they stopped, then proceeded slowly forward into the dim interior. From the shadows of the entrance, they emerged into

69

the nave, which was bathed in the glow of morning light through huge windows on three sides. Roland had never seen such as these. The morning light flowed through sheets of colour that seemed to float in the spaces that divided stone from air. Not just colours, though, images of knights and saints and winged beings seemed to float in the air and glow from within. He could not bring his gaze down from the spectacle of light playing before his eyes.

"What is this, Declan?" he asked in awe.

"'Tis a thing called glass Roland," the boy replied in a hushed voice. "I've seen it once before in Burgundy at a chapel there. It's hard as ice on a winter pond and you can see through it as though through air unless, like these, men have painted them. Those in France did not compare to this!"

Finally, Roland was able to tear his eyes away from the images floating above him and look around. Finely carved benches were arranged in numberless serried rows from where they stood in the rear of the structure to the magnificent altar, clad in shimmering gold.

"By all the saints, these Normans can build a church," he whispered. There were no churches on Kinder Scout, just a few rude stone crosses set in the verge of a meadow where the Christian among the Danes came to worship. His mother had taken him and the other children to that place many times where they had learned about the Christian god and the son he had sacrificed. His father never went to these gatherings and seemed to regard all belief in things unseen as useless.

In his own wanderings through the high country he had seen other sign of the old Norse gods—strange rune stones with symbols and markings he could not fathom. These often had small parcels of food or curious talismans adorning them—offerings to Odin or perhaps Thor. These were the old gods, the warrior gods his grandsire had spoken of when he was a small boy. The rough crosses and the rougher rune stones up in the hills seemed shabby in comparison to this place.

The one god of the Christians or the many gods of the Norse— the boy could not sort the answer, but this place seemed to be divinely inspired. Roland found himself silently praying to whichever god might overhear. For two fortnights he had sought deliverance from his enemies. And, by the narrowest of margins, he had been so delivered—for the moment. For the first time in many days, he thought of his father and his lost brother and sister. He prayed for the soul of Rolf Inness and for the safety of his brother Oren and sister Lorea. He wondered if he would see any of them in this life or the next. He felt tears begin to well in his eyes. The first he had shed since that fateful day that Tuck had found him in the forest. Declan laid his hand on Roland's shoulder.

"Come my friend," he said, gently. "God makes all right in the end, but let's not upset Sir Roger in the meantime."

Roland sniffed back his tears, ran a dirty sleeve over his eyes and followed Declan out of the church and back into the bright light of morning. For a moment, he hesitated at the top of the steps. He looked at the knight sitting astride the magnificent horse on the street below. He looked at the Irish boy bounding down the steps ahead of him. He looked up at the sky.

"Thank you for finding a place for me," he said softly, to whichever God might hear. *"Even if it be with a Norman,"* he added.

***

Miles to the south, a lone figure limped along the road toward Derbyshire. His ribs ached and burned like fire where the cursed horse had kicked him and he could take no breath through his mangled nose. Worse than the pain was the knowledge that he had missed his target. *Such a thing had never happened!* The boy had been awake. The blasted horse had smelled him and fidgeted. All bad luck, but he had been too confident as well. He had hesitated in the dark over which boy to strike first. *A mistake.*

He brooded as he shuffled painfully toward the south. He was in no condition to continue the hunt. The boy was under the protection of an experienced knight and the other boy seemed always to be present. Even if caught alone, this boy might be troublesome for him in his current condition.

No, the prey must go free—but only for now.

Still, Sir William would be expecting results—and the customary proof of his kill. Failure to produce it would mean more than losing the purse of promised gold. It would mean a loss of reputation. In his profession, a loss of reputation was a dangerous thing. He had enemies aplenty and it was fear that kept them well at bay. Should they lose that fear…This he could not allow.

He knew not where the accursed boy was heading with his new companions, but it seemed most likely it was far from Derbyshire. And if none knew his whereabouts then none could gainsay if he was living or dead. Not even the young Lord would challenge Ivo Brun's results—if he produced the proper evidence.

Off to his right, he saw a small plume of wood smoke rising from a patch of woods. He left the road and limped into the underbrush. As he came near, he saw a rather fat merchant fussing over wares that were laid out beside the fire. The man seemed completely unaware of the danger he was in. He reached quietly for his dagger and swore silently as he remembered that it had been lost in the stables. He drew another he always kept in the bag slung over his shoulder and moved toward the man.

For proof, one ear would serve as well as another.

***

The journey to the land holdings of Lady de Laval proceeded uneventfully. Spring was in full sway, and green fields of newly emerged grain swept off in all directions. Low moors appeared on both sides of the road, as they moved away from the valley of the River Ouse. The road they took was more like those in Derbyshire than the fine Roman road they had entered York on—a well rutted path that any Roman would have sneered at. The morning weather was a delight—warm, but not hot—and Declan sang lilting songs as they led the mule behind Sir Roger. Roland's spirits were high, but his caution never left him. From time to time, he turned and surveyed the road behind. It felt safe here, but he knew he could never lower his guard. York had seemed safe as well.

Late in the day, the party arrived at a small manor house set amidst ancient trees. On all sides fields and pastures rose to the tops of the surrounding moors. Roland wasn't sure if he had ever seen a lovelier spot. A great hubbub arose as they approached the house. A peasant, working in a nearby field, saw Sir Roger approaching up the dusty lane and took off like a startled deer to alert others. Roland watched the small puffs of dust rise from his feet as he pounded down the road before them. By the time they arrived, a veritable platoon was assembled in the front of the manor to welcome their master. Sir Roger reined in Bucephalus and was immediately greeted by a tall and exceedingly skinny man who turned out to be the cousin of Lady de Laval.

"My lord Roger! What a great surprise…and greater pleasure!" the man exclaimed. He appeared a bit flustered at the sudden arrival of his cousin's husband.

"I'm certain you will be pleased with our stewardship of Lady Catherine's dowry, my lord. We had an excellent spring lambing and the rains have come at the right time for the crops. I trust my cousin fares well?"

Sir Roger grunted his acknowledgement and dismounted.

"Catherine is well enough, James, and sends her warmest regards. Now, see to Bucephalus, and have food and drink fetched. We've not eaten since York."

James looked a bit askance at the two dusty boys, but hurried off to organize the kitchen servants. Sir Roger passed through the main entrance of the rather modest dwelling, negotiated a long entry hall and proceeded out the back with the two boys in tow. He showed no interest in taking his meal in the dining hall and declared that they would dine under an ancient apple tree that was in full white blossom.

Soon the kitchen servants were scurrying like a line of ants to prepare a place for him. Some rough planks were thrown up between a huge tree stump and a stone fence and benches were quickly provided. The knight and the two boys dug into the proffered luncheon with gusto. For Roland, this was truly a feast. Cold ham, roasted hare, a game bird that Roland thought was a partridge and another he didn't recognize. Declan called it pheasant and seemed particularly fond of it.

Once the meal was completed, Sir Roger called for Bucephalus to be brought from the stables. He was ready to get on with his inspection straightaway. James fussed about and practically pleaded with Sir Roger to take the keeper of the livestock along as a guide, but the big knight waved him off and spurred the horse toward the nearest hill. The two squires had to scramble to keep up. Soon the manor house was far behind and Sir Roger slowed the horse to a walk, so the winded boys could catch up. Presently, they came to a large clearing, planted in barley and surrounded by heavy woods. When Sir Roger reached the middle of the field, he halted and turned towards the boys.

"Stay here," he said, and spurred the horse into a canter. When he reached the woodline he stopped and leaned forward from the saddle to place an object in the crook of a tree. When he turned back to the field, Roland saw that the object was a large gourd. The knight cantered back to where the boys stood.

"Well, Master Roland, I think it's time we see if you can use that thing on yer back for ought but busting shins." He nodded toward the bundle, wrapped in rags and slung over the boy's shoulder. Roland gulped. The thought of unwrapping his bow in front of anyone gave him pause, even though they already knew of its existence. He took a deep breath. If he could not trust these two, he was already lost. He shrugged the bow around to his front and slipped the leather strap over his head.

Roland unwrapped the precious package, being careful to secure the dagger, which now shared the bundle. He held the bow upright and placed one end on the ground, snug against the outside of his ankle. He nimbly stepped over the centre of the bow and braced it against his opposite calf. This created a solid base against which he could exert his weight and strength to string the bow. He grasped the unanchored end with one hand and let his weight start to bend the bow back toward the opposite end. With his free hand, he moved the bowstring up until it slid over the notch. This process had taken the boy but a few seconds to complete. Sir Roger and Declan O'Duinne glanced at each other, then back to the young bowman.

Roland took one of his two remaining arrows and nocked it. He looked up at the gourd, sitting like some ridiculous head in the crotch of the tree, and estimated the distance to be under a hundred yards. He aligned the left side of his body toward the target and drew the bowstring taut. Given the distance, he did not extend the bow to its fullest. His whole body seemed to naturally fall into the familiar pattern of pull, aim, breathe and—*release.*

The arrow leapt across the clearing and pierced the centre of the gourd.

"By the saints!" shouted Declan. "Did ye see that!" He turned to Sir Roger and slapped him on the arm in his excitement. Sir Roger scowled for a moment at the boy's brashness, then grinned himself.

"Aye, Lad. I saw it a'right. The only time I've seen its like was in London, at an archery tournament judged by King Henry himself. The competition was keen, until this young knight steps up with a Viking bow. I'd never seen one before and, plainly, the other archers hadn't either. They were no match with their Saxon and Norman bows. It was no contest. By God, the Dukes and Earls bleated like fleeced sheep over the gold they'd wagered and lost on their own champions, but the King loved it! Can't remember the fellow's name who won—from Nottinghamshire, I believe—but he knew his craft...and so does our young friend here! Roland?"

The two had been talking excitedly and hadn't noticed Roland turn and start walking toward the near side of the clearing where they had entered the barley field. When he reached the woodline he stopped and called to his companions, who were still rooted to the spot in the middle of the field.

"If it's a test you seek, my lord, we should make it a fair one!" he shouted. He nocked another arrow and turned toward the target, which now stood half again as far away. Simultaneously, the two observers in the middle of the clearing realized that they stood directly in the path between the bowman and his target. Slowly, they each edged towards opposite sides of the field.

"Hold steady," shouted Roland, as he drew the bow to its full curve and held it. "I wouldn't want to hit anyone by accident!" The two figures in the field froze. When he released the arrow, there was only six feet separating Sir Roger and Declan. In a blur, the shaft flashed just above and between them, with an audible buzz. Both flinched at the near miss, instinctively turning to follow the flight of the arrow. In less than a heartbeat, it buried itself in the gourd, less than a hand's width from the first shaft.

Sir Roger let out a soft whistle, turning to look at the boy across the field. Roland was running toward them with a half grin on his face. When the boy reached them, Sir Roger held out his hand.

"May I look at yer bow more closely, lad?"

75

Roland hesitated, but for only a moment, and handed the longbow to his new master. Sir Roger held it in two hands and examined its construction.

"What wood is this, Roland? It isn't oak or ash."

"No, my lord. Tis yew. It's hard to find a proper stave, but no other wood serves as well."

The big knight turned the bow vertically and, grasping the centre grip in his left hand, began to draw the bowstring. He was shocked at the resistance. He had never favoured the weapon, but had tried both Norman and Saxon bows on occasion. They were children's play things compared to the power he felt in this longbow. How did this half-starved boy manage to draw it with seeming ease? He turned back to Declan.

"The next time good King Henry calls for an archery tournament, the knight from Nottingham *will* have some competition!" he said, his eyes gleaming, "…and I know where I'll place *my* wager!"

Chapter 9

Shipbrook

S ir Roger did not hurry to complete the inspection of his land in Yorkshire, but spent considerable time dozing under shade trees. Declan and Roland kept busy counting sheep and oxen, stepping off the measurement of grain fields and generally accounting for the assets of the estate. Declan made careful notes with a quill on a small scroll he kept rolled and protected in a leather bag, when not in use. He was determined to be prepared when they reported back to Lady Catherine. He showed Roland the strange symbols that Lady de Laval had taught him.

"She says this be the way the Saracens mark their counting— and this here…" He pointed to the careful circle next to one of the ordinals. "This be a zero, which the Lady says is the key to all this heathen mathematics."

"What does it signify?" asked Roland, curious to learn more.

"Now that's the tricky part," Declan replied. "This little mark can mean ten or nothing a'tall, dependin' on where it's placed."

Tricky indeed, thought Roland. He could count well enough— up to all of his fingers and toes—but on the rare occasions when he had to record such a counting, he merely made the appropriate number of scratches on the ground or scraped them on a piece of bark. This Saracen math was confusing, but he could see its advantage in sheer brevity. This was, indeed, a useful tool his friend had acquired.

At last, every animal had been tallied, every crop estimated and all needed repairs noted. The time had come to leave Yorkshire. James seemed relieved that his guests were departing, but worked hard to conceal his pleasure. On perhaps the hottest day of the spring thus far, they headed south. The week he had spent in the company of Sir Roger De Laval and Declan O'Duinne had been so eventful, that Roland hadn't even thought to ask where they were bound for next. As they headed back down the road they had arrived on, the boy had a sudden horrible fear that they would completely retrace their path, back through York and into Derbyshire.

"Perhaps I should have asked this before," he whispered to Declan, *"but where—exactly—are we going?"*

The Irish boy laughed. "I doubt it matters to you, but we are heading home—to Shipbrook. It's in Cheshire...on the Welsh frontier."

Roland nodded, relieved. *Cheshire...never heard of it...but as good a place as any,* he thought. *And a sight better than some!*

A half-day's journey brought them once more to an ancient Roman road—this one traversing the midlands from York to Leeds and then bending southwest to Chester. Leeds he knew of. It lay just north of the mountains he had been born in, but perhaps far enough clear of the lands of the de Ferres to not be worrisome. The day was pleasantly warm and Sir Roger was in an expansive mood, as he often seemed to be when on the road.

"Wait'll ye see Shipbrook, me lad," he said, turning to Roland. "It's as pretty a little fort as any old soldier could ask for. She sits on a little rise, and from the walls ye can near see the estuary of the River Dee. It's a little arm of the Irish Sea, which brings comfort to your brother squire," he added, nodding back toward Declan.

"Did I tell ye how I came into possession of such a lovely spot?"

"Aye, ye did, me lord—several times," observed Declan, dryly.

Sir Roger swivelled around in his saddle and scowled at the two boys leading the mule behind him.

"*I* haven't heard the tale, my lord," Roland said, quickly. "Please continue." Now Declan scowled, but a large smile split Sir Roger's face, as he launched into the story.

"Well, Shipbrook be one of four holdings I have from the Earl of Chester. Three come down through four generations to me from me ancestor Anton de Laval. Old Anton landed with the Conqueror and fought with valour at Hastings and the Fight at the Fosse. He was the sworn man of Hugh Lupus, King William's nephew and the first Earl of Chester. He fought many a hard fight with the benighted Welsh to secure Cheshire and the Welsh Marches for his liege lord. I'm told he had many scars and killed many men, and yet he died in his own bed of the flux. Hardly a fit end for fighting man, I'd say."

"Shipbrook though, that were given me, *personally*, from the old Earl, Hugh of Kevelioc, *God rest his soul!*"

Roland listened intently, while Declan amused himself by kicking loose stones as they walked. Perhaps he too would grow bored with such stories some day, but for now he had a desperate desire to understand this new world he was entering. The world of lords, ladies and hereditary lands was one he had only observed from a great distance during his childhood. He knew the power of those with rank and titles in the world and the obligations of the peasant, but had never peered behind the curtain into the life of the highborn. For as far as he could see into the future, his fate rested in the hands of the big man on the huge grey horse ahead of him. It seemed prudent to learn all he could about his new master. And Sir Roger seemed more than prepared to instruct him.

"We were hot on the heels of a party of Welsh cattle thieves—and son, *all* Welshmen are cattle thieves. We had already pursued them to the borderlands and in their flight they had abandoned the cattle, so I must admit we were chasin' them for sport as much as anything at that point—when old Hugh orders a halt and goes off to attend to nature." The big knight paused to smirk, then continued.

"While he's squattin' behind a bush a full dozen wild Welshmen come a burstin' into the clearing lookin' for someone to kill! There were only three of us with the Earl, at the moment. One was a Welshman himself, who had fled his clan and had entered the service of the Earl. The other—he turned tail and rode off, without

79

so much as an *adieu*. 'Arise, my lord, the Welsh are upon us!' I shouted, but the Earl replies, 'Just another moment, Sir Roger, if you'll oblige.'" Sir Roger shook his head remembering that day.

"Now, I take second place to no man in appreciating the importance of a good bowel movement, but this seemed unreasonable under the circumstances. These savage Welsh were screaming like demons from the pit and each had a ten foot long poker he wanted to introduce us to! So, this Welshman and me dismounted and stood back to back as they set upon us. It was all we could do to keep from bein' made into pincushions, I'll tell ye. All the while, the Earl was finishing his business up in the bushes. I faith, me sword arm weighed a hundred stone and these pig stickers were not restin' 'till they spilled our guts!" Sir Roger paused and shook his head.

"Just as I was saying me final prayers, Earl Hugh pops up from behind his bush and gives me a big smile and a wave! Well, I would have killed him meself at that moment, but in the next he draws his broadsword and wades into these scoundrels from behind, roarin' at the top of his lungs! 'Tis one of the few times I ever saw the damned Welsh break and run in a pitched fight, but they were so shocked at the Earl's sudden attack, that they fell over each other making their escape. Meself and the Welshman at my back sank to the ground on the spot and nursed the various nicks and cuts inflicted by our attackers. The Earl clapped us on the shoulders.... 'Tis a function requiring peace and privacy, my lads,' says he, 'and I'll not forget that you supplied me with both, when I had a terrible need!'" The knight smiled as he recalled the event.

"When we finally returned to Chester, the Earl granted me the holding of Shipbrook and the Welsh fellow, he dubbed a knight on the spot. By mutual agreement, the Earl and I never told our ladies that Shipbrook was had for the price of a good *crap*!" Sir Roger slapped his leg and laughed until the tears came to his eyes. Roland could not help but laugh at this outrageous tale, though Declan, who had heard it before, just rolled his eyes.

"Sir Roger, what became of the knight who fled?" asked Roland.

"Hanged" said Sir Roger.

On that sobering note, they trudged on to the southwest. For the next four days they made their way slowly through Leeds, Halifax and Manchester. They stayed to the old Roman road where it was still passable and made their lodgings wherever evening found them.

It seemed to Roland that the closer Sir Roger got to Shipbrook and his beloved Lady Catherine, the more intent he became on pushing forward. Late on the second day after leaving Manchester, a dusty and tired party arrived at Chester, the seat of Sir Roger's liege lord, Ranulf de Blundeville, Earl of Chester. It was late in the day, but Sir Roger showed no inclination to tarry in the city. He guided Bucephalus off the main road as they approached the northern gate and skirted the walls of Chester, picking up the westward road that lead to the coast and Shipbrook.

"As vassal to Earl Ranulf, Sir Roger has an obligation to present himself if he enters the city, but we've less than ten miles to home, and the King himself couldn't detain the man now," whispered Declan, as they trudged on into the dusk. "Sir Roger is actually rather fond of young Earl Ranulf, who's but a few years our senior. When his sire—old Hugh Kevelioc—died, the lad was but ten and Cheshire had to be put under the care of his uncle. 'Tis likely the uncle would be Earl now if it had not been for the loyalty of Sir Roger and the other knights of the region. So he may like the noble lad well enough, but he will not abide dallying, with Lady Catherine but a few hours away."

Roland nodded. Although he did not begin to understand the complexities of Norman politics and customs, he did understand the pull of family, and grew melancholy as he thought of his own, now torn apart by the fates. Into the twilight, the party tramped on, and into the darkness of full night. At last, they emerged from a bend in the road to see a torch lit high on a stone wall, looming on a low ridge.

"*Shipbrook*, boys!" shouted Sir Roger, as he spurred Bucephalus forward. "Catch up when you can!" The knight urged the grey charger into a lumbering trot, which quickly left the boys behind. When they finally approached the walls of the small castle, they could see that the gate had swung open and torches were scurrying everywhere. It looked as though giant fireflies were on the loose. A great clamour of excited shouts and barking dogs could be heard coming through the stone arch as they made to enter.

Roland gawked about the courtyard, where stablemen and servants bustled about in a fury of activity. In front of him, loomed the keep, which was more of a stone manor house than fortress. At the top of the considerable flight of steps leading up to the arched entrance to the hall, Sir Roger was standing, holding a tall, slender woman by the shoulders as if examining a fine piece of art. He stood there a moment, contemplating his treasure, then scooped her up in his arms and whirled her around the landing. Roland could hear her shriek from where he stood.

Declan took Roland by the arm and led him up the steps. As they drew near, the Irish boy bowed at the waist and nudged Roland, who quickly copied him. From where they stood they could hear Lady Catherine speak to her husband.

"My lord…" she hissed under her breath, "…have a care! The servants are watching…and besides, I'm no longer a girl, to be tossed about so. You're liable to break something!"

"Ah, Cathy, you'll always be a girl to me," Sir Roger said, as he touched her cheek "…and damned what the servants see—just a man who's missed his wife!" He picked her up again and gave her a rather sloppy kiss on her cheek.

"*Roger!* Really! Stop it," she fussed. Roland glanced up at the scene and could see that she was both laughing and blushing at the attention. Declan caught her eye, and she—somewhat thankfully—turned away from her husband.

"Master O'Duinne, it's good to see you've survived another venture with our lord. I trust you reliably recorded all the necessaries of our holdings in Yorkshire?"

Declan O'Duinne rose from his bow and again Roland followed suit. "All has been inspected, counted and recorded, my lady. I've taken great care with the figures—as you taught me." He withdrew the record he had kept safely in a leather pouch during the journey and presented it to Lady de Laval.

The mistress of Shipbrook unfurled the scroll and gave it a rapid scan. "I'll check these in the morning Master O'Duinne, but you may be commended on the care you've taken—if these prove accurate. Now, who is this you have in tow?" She looked directly at Roland for the first time.

Sir Roger stepped forward.

"Catherine, this is Roland Inness. We lost Harold to a not very pretty milkmaid in Leeds and this young lad turned up at just the right moment. He's to be my new squire.

Lady Catherine looked Roland over sceptically and frowned.

"Where are you from boy?"

"Derby…Derbyshire, my lady," he said. The Lady's examination was making him exceedingly nervous.

She turned and gave her husband a frosty look.

"My lord, his speech betrays him. He's a *Dane*." The Lady of Shipbrook fairly hissed the last word.

Sir Roger seemed not to notice the dark tone that had come into his wife's voice.

"Aye, Cathy, he's a Dane true enough. They do have a strange way they fashion their speech, though he's easier on the ear than Master O'Duinne, 'pon my soul." The Master of Shipbrook lowered his voice so that only his wife could hear. *"The lad has other qualities to recommend him, Catherine. We can speak of this later."*

Her husband's words did little to ease the sudden tension as she turned again to the boy before her.

"I do not trust the Danes, Master Inness. My people, the Saxons, are your enemies of old and much blood has been spilt between Saxon and Dane. I like this not, though my husband will choose whom he chooses."

Roland could think of no reply to give the woman and thought it best to remain still under her stern gaze. After a long moment of awkward silence, the Lady sighed and shrugged.

"How old are you, then?"

"I believe I'm fourteen years of age, my lady."

"Believe? You do not know?

"We had no keeping of the days in the mountains, my lady. My mother told me I was born in the spring and this was my fourteenth. I do not know the very day of it, so, mayhap, I'm still thirteen, but by now, I'd reckon fourteen." Roland felt as though he was yammering like some village idiot, unsure if his answer made any sense.

"That seems to be reasonable figuring to me, boy. Get used to it. Should Declan get his head whacked off on one of my husband's campaigns or…" she arched an eyebrow in the Irish boy's direction, "fall into the clutches of a not very pretty milk maid, I will need someone who can do the figures. God knows, Harold never got the hang of it. Dane or no, you'll have to do—*for now.* Starting tomorrow, you will begin your lessons." Declan sniggered quietly at his side, but Roland was excited. Learning the counting and mathematics of the Arabs would be a powerful skill, and he could use all such as came his way.

"Can you fight, boy?" she asked, her voice still frosty.

Sir Roger intervened.

"He's not polished, Catherine, but I can vouch that he has fight in him. He thrashed a horse thief that was going after Bucephalus in York." The knight avoided any mention of the longbow, still strapped to the young man's back.

"Good! My lord, I'll not have a squire that can't cover your back in a fight. He can be polished up—as long as he has a bit of natural fight in him. Can you sit a horse boy?"

"Never have, my lady."

Lady Catherine sighed. "We've a lot of work to do on this one, my lord."

"Aye lass, but I have this feelin' about the boy. I think he may be worth the effort."

"As you say, my lord," she replied turning a withering look on Roland.

"In matters of this sort, I'll not gainsay my husband, Master Inness, but know this—I do not have his trusting nature. I trust not the Danes nor do I trust some stray that has attached himself to my lord. *I shall be watching you!*"

At that moment, Roland was relieved as a new hubbub erupted from the open door of the keep. A young girl burst breathlessly through the opening and threw herself at a grinning Sir Roger

"Millie!" he exclaimed. "By God, girl, you've grown—in just a fortnight!"

Roland watched, as Sir Roger hoisted what appeared to be a miniature version of the Lady Catherine to his chest and squeezed her as her feet dangled in space. The young girl had thrown her arms around her father's neck and was returning the squeeze, as the knight gently swung her to and fro. Finally, he put the girl down on the landing. From Roland's vantage point, she looked to be perhaps eleven or twelve years old. Like her mother, she wore a flowing gown of some shiny material, but unlike her mother, she seemed uncomfortable in her garments. Lady Catherine looked as if she'd been born in this regal attire. The girl looked as though she'd been forced into them at sword point.

Sir Roger cleared his throat and turned toward the boys on the steps below. "Roland Inness, this is the Lady Millicent de Laval. Millie, this is our new squire, Master Inness."

Lady Millicent drew herself up and nodded toward the boys, who were already bent low at the waist. Once again, Roland feared for his own ignorance, as he tried to mimic the actions of Declan O'Duinne.

"I see Master O'Duinne has returned in one piece. *Pity*." Lady Millicent said sweetly.

"Millicent! I've told you not to tease the squires!" Lady de Laval said sternly. "It's late now. Get to your bed little miss—and Declan, see to Master Inness. You both stink worse than my husband if that is possible. I'll see that hot water and some new garments are provided. Scrub well! You'll both have a full day on the morrow." The Lady of Shipbrook took the arms of her husband and daughter, and led them into the main entrance of the hall.

Lady Millicent peeked over her shoulder at the boys, as she was led away.

"Beware that one, Roland," said Declan, as they watched the family enter the hall. "She has a sweet face, but, Gad, she has an evil mind!"

"The Lady Millicent...an evil mind?"

"Aye. She likes nothing better than to make sport at the expense of us squires—and there's a wicked intelligence behind her jests. She looks for yer *weak spot*, then strikes!"

"Strikes? Whatever do you mean?"

"Well consider this—Ye never met poor Harold, your predecessor. He was a good enough fellow, but a bit...*dense*, if ye take me meaning." He paused to tap his head for emphasis. "The Little Lady recognized this and tormented him with simple jests. 'Fetch me a left-handed bridal for the pony, Harold,' she would say and he would spend the next hour asking all and sundry where he might find one and making a royal fool of himself. And this happened many, many times over. Harold was born a city lad, and, as I said, a bit slow, but he had his pride. I would swear that he took up with the milkmaid in large part to escape Lady Millicent."

"She seems wicked, indeed," said Roland, who was having a bit of trouble suppressing a snicker.

"Aye, she is that and I'll not even tell you some of the dirty tricks she's tried to play on meself! Mark my words, Roland, you are bound to be her next target—so watch your back!

Roland thought to himself, that watching his back was something he had grown rather used to. Perhaps Lady Millicent wouldn't be counting on that. And besides, what did he have to fear from a girl after having escaped William De Ferres and Ivo Brun? Declan motioned for Roland to follow and the two boys made their way to a small room near the armoury.

"This'll be home for as long as we stay at Shipbrook," Declan said, as they entered the cramped, windowless room. He lit a small oil lamp and Roland surveyed the accommodations in the flickering light. There were two straw mats, with a couple of woollen blankets, folded neatly on top. Near each mat, was a small, three-legged stool, and in the corner a chamber pot. Beyond that, the room was bare. Not home, but it would serve.

Moments later a house servant arrived with two large buckets of steaming water and a stack of clean clothes that she placed out in the courtyard behind the armoury.

"Trust me, my friend," said Declan, doffing his tunic and shucking off his breeches. "Lady Catherine will sniff you like a hound on the morrow. So scrub well." He fished a brush and a square of grey soap floating in the water bucket, applied one to the other and began diligently lathering himself. Roland followed his lead. He had never had the luxury of hot water to bathe in before and it was an odd but pleasant sensation.

Roland thought of Lady Catherine and wondered if he should try to scrub off the Dane as well as the dirt. He had known Saxon's in Derbyshire, though only a few, and there was little bad blood between them and the Danes. *Perhaps that was because both were under the heel of the Normans.* Things might be different hereabouts. He would have to learn the ways of Shipbrook, but he could not change who he was and would not if given the chance. The Lady de Laval may be watching him, but he would be watching back.

He followed Declan's lead and poured a portion of the hot water over his head. As he scrubbed at the accumulated grime of weeks on the run, he considered his surroundings. Home this was not, but for a fugitive it would do nicely until he found a way to return to Derbyshire and settle his accounts. He must use this place, this sanctuary, to prepare for that day—whenever that day might come.

Chapter 10

The Jest

William de Ferrers stared at the piece of neatly-wrapped cloth which lay on the table before him. He gently laid back each fold to examine the prize within—a man's severed ear. He found the sight gruesome—and gratifying at the same time.

"Speak," he commanded.

Ivo Brun looked carefully at the man before him. Something had changed in the young nobleman's manner and bearing since last they met. When he had returned to Derbyshire, he had learned that Robert, the old Earl had taken ill and had travelled to London where the King's own physicians attended him. William now ruled in his stead. It seemed to give the man a confidence he had lacked at their last meeting.

For a week Brun had laid up in a hut in the forest recovering from his injuries. Only when he could walk without an obvious limp had he reported to the new lord of Derbyshire. Unlike their first encounter, he no longer sensed any fear in the man. This was bad.

"Trailed him all the way to York, me lord. He'd joined up with a rough lot. Outlaws I expect. Put up a fight, they did."

"I can see they did," de Ferrers interrupted sarcastically. The sight of Brun's swollen nose and the subtle stiffness in the man's movements bespoke rough handling.

"You're quite sure this was the man?"

"Quite sure, my lord. Here's the bow that killed yer men." He proffered the longbow he held in his hand to the nobleman.

De Ferrers took his time examining the bow. He'd seen a few in his father's collection, but had never had much curiosity about the weapon. Men fought face to face, with sword and mace or from horseback with the lance. The bow was a coward's weapon, a peasant's weapon, killing only from afar.

The man wrapped his left hand around the rough leather grip at the centre of the bow's arch and began to draw the bowstring. At the halfway mark of his pull he had to fight against the stiff resistance of the yew. He pulled harder and the bow yielded a little, but by now his left arm was beginning to tremble. William de Ferrers had had no notion of the strength needed to use this infernal device. Even at less than its full draw, he could feel the terrible power of the thing waiting to be unleashed. He quickly released the string and flinched as it raked his silk-clad arm.

He tossed the weapon back to Brun dismissively. From the folds of his garment he withdrew a moneybag and dropped it on the table beside him.

"Take your reward, Brun—and keep yourself available," he commanded. "I have much work to do putting things aright here in Derbyshire. There are scores to settle."

Ivo Brun knew he had passed the test and permitted himself a silent moment of relief. The longbow had been just the right touch—though difficult to obtain. He'd been lucky—the man who had owned this one had been careless. These stupid Normans had no inkling that half the Danes up in the hills had these weapons. *Let the lords sleep well in their ignorance*, he thought. He had no love for Danes or Normans—only for money.

"At yer service, me lord," he answered.

The new ruler of Derbyshire had already turned away in dismissal and Brun silently departed. The relief he felt at his successful deception was already beginning to fade and in its place was a knot of hate and even some fear. *The cursed boy still lived!* And while he lived his reputation and perhaps his neck were at stake. He knew not where the boy or the big knight had gone but someone surely did. England was not so large a country that such as they could go about unnoticed. He would seek news of them in his own way and would find them in time. *Then all would be set aright.*

***

Roland awoke before dawn on his first day at Shipbrook. Rising early was a habit born from years working with his father on the infertile high ground of Kinder Scout. He saw in the dim light that Declan slept soundly curled in his blanket. Early rising was not on the Irish boy's list of habits, perhaps because he loved to stay up late into the evening telling ridiculous tales or singing Irish songs.

Roland had fallen off to sleep more than once in the middle of one of Declan's ballads. Quietly, he slipped from his own blanket and made his way through darkened hallways, past the locked armoury, and into the courtyard beyond. The first hint of dawn was visible over the east wall of the castle as he made his way up steep stone steps that led to Shipbrook's western wall. Two sentries on the east and northern walls observed him but made no move to intercept the boy.

At the top of the steps, he turned to survey the interior of the fortress. The handsome hall, where Sir Roger, his family, the household servants and squires dwelt, was set below him near the western wall opposite the castle entrance on the east. Along the northern wall were additional rooms and barracks for Sir Roger's men-at-arms as well as the armoury. Hard against the south wall were stables for the horses and domestic animals. During a long discourse after the boys had bedded down the previous evening, Declan had explained much about the situation at Shipbrook.

"It's a small place, without even a true keep—but it's more lethal than it looks. The King holds the Earl of Chester responsible for securing the western Marches against the incursions of the Welsh—*may they rot in the pit*—and the Earl has entrusted Sir Roger with this stretch of the border. There be an ancient path that comes out of the high mountains to the west and leads down to the only ford over the River Dee for miles. Since before memory, these Welsh devils have used the ford for raiding into the lowlands of Cheshire, though it's been three years since any chanced it

90

through here. That was a small group, I'm told, but they put up a bloody fight after Sir Roger cornered them out near the bogs. Shipbrook may be on a lovely spot, but it's well situated to bar the door to these raiders and strong enough to hold out against any direct attacks from these bands."

Roland could see the truth of Declan's words as he walked along the parapet of Shipbrook. The wall itself was of native stone perhaps ten feet thick at the base and narrowing to six feet where the boy stood on the wall walk. A full fifteen feet high along the east gate wall, it dwindled to about twelve feet on the other three approaches, but these approaches were protected by the natural contours of the ground which dropped away steeply on all sides. Still on the west wall, the boy peered over the edge and saw a tangle of brambles clinging to a steep slope above a ragged ravine. Even an army would hesitate to fight its way through that.

In the distance, as the morning sky continued to brighten, he caught a glimpse of a small finger of the Irish Sea visible to the west. Declan had said that, properly, it was the estuary of the River Dee, but when the tide was right it was far more sea than river. The boy turned his gaze further west and in the clear morning air, he could barely make out some dark contours along the horizon. These must be the mountains of Wales, whose fierce inhabitants were the reason for the existence of Shipbrook.

The sight of the mountains caused a sudden and unexpected pang of homesickness in Roland. He steeled himself for the memories which came at such times—always bittersweet. In his mind he saw his mother handing a gourd of cold water to his father who leaned on the long handle of his scythe. Behind her his sister crooned a familiar song in her childish voice, but he could not place it. His brother Oren hefted a clod of dirt from the field and Roland knew he was the target. As quickly as the memory came it faded. He could sometimes make them last, but not this one.

He wondered what had become of his family. The strange little monk, Tuck, had gotten them safely away, but were they safe still? He longed to know. The weeks since his flight had been filled with peril and the necessities of survival. He had precious little time to dwell on all that he had lost, but the memories did come, at unexpected times. Alone upon the walls of his new home, his mind again flew back to Kinder Scout and happier times.

An image of his father's face came to him. Rolf Inness was showing him how to hold the longbow for the first time. He was but ten, but eager to learn. His father had been surprised and proud at how quickly he had taken to the weapon. How he missed the man! Like spirited boys everywhere, he had occasionally bridled at his father's authority, but now, more than ever, he knew the debt he owed Rolf Inness. His father had not only taught him the woodcraft that had saved his life during the flight from Derbyshire, but also the need for patience and vigilance in a dangerous world. Vigilance had saved him from an assassin in York, but it had not saved his father in the end. On the walls of a strange fortress, Roland felt only a void where his father's presence had been. For the first time in weeks, he felt the anger start to swell in him again.

"*By every saint, I swear I'll not forget, nor forgive,*" he muttered softly to himself.

"What's that ye say there, lad?"

Roland whirled around to see a burly man watching him from not five feet away.

"No...Nothing...My lord," Roland sputtered.

The man's face was not old, but weathered and betrayed little as he eyed the boy. He was shorter than Roland, but powerfully built. His hair was golden, but flecked with a bit of grey and hung long down his back where it was tied at the ends by a leather cord. He looked like a man not to be trifled with.

"Ah...I see. Talking to yerself. Makes for an agreeable conversation, though some folks might think it a sign of daftness." The man paused for a moment as he continued to survey the boy in front of him. "I'd be Alwyn Madawc, Sir Roger's constable and Master of the Sword hereabouts. Ye can address me as Sir Alwyn. I've not seen you before."

"I'm Roland Inness, my lord. I've taken a position as squire to Sir Roger."

"Ahhh...fresh meat is it? What happened to Harold, the Useless?"

"Took up with a milkmaid in Leeds, my lord," Roland replied.

"Har! I knew that boy had no brains...and now he'll have no peace! I tell ye Master Inness, never take a girl to wife or yer

92

carefree days will be over." Sir Alwyn shook his head sorrowfully. "Aye, I love the lasses, mind ye, but let one get a bridle on ye and yer done."

"I'll remember that sir," said Roland, unsure of where this strange knight's conversation would turn next.

Sir Alwyn seemed to shake himself free of reveries about close calls with the fairer sex.

"But, *fresh meat* ye be, lad, and if ye can survive me weapons instruction—*which I doubt*—yer sure to fall prey to the Little Lady."

"Little Lady, my lord?"

"Aye, the Lady Millicent. She's a *pip,* she is. Watch yer back with that one, lad."

Roland shrugged. This was the second warning he'd gotten about Lady Millicent. Surely, a twelve-year-old girl could not be much of a threat.

"Ye better get yerself down to the kitchen and get a good breakfast, boy. Weapons work begins when the sun crosses over the east wall, which won't be long. Hope you like bruises!" Sir Alwyn gave him a thunderous clap on the shoulder and trudged off toward the armoury. Roland felt a slight twinge in his stomach at the mention of breakfast and decided to take Sir Alwyn's advice. He hurried down the steps and crossed the courtyard toward the smell of baking bread. He was still quite skinny, but had started putting some of his bulk back on, as his meals had become regular. Breakfast would be just the thing to start his first day at Shipbrook.

***

Roland watched, as Declan O'Duinne slowly rose to his feet. A moment before, his friend had been unceremoniously dropped on his backside. The author of this embarrassment was Alwyn Madawc, Sir Roger's Master of the Sword. The Irish boy dusted off his breeches and slowly raised the heavy oak stave, carved to resemble a broadsword, to the guard position.

"Startin' next week, when ye go down, I'll be all over ye like a bad smell!" the big man snarled. "Ye cannot afford to loose yer footin' in close fighting or ye'll be dead before the dust settles. Never...cross...your...feet, Master O'Duinne—too easy to trip."

Lecture completed, Sir Alwyn came roaring in with a huge sweeping stroke of the sword, aimed at Declan's midsection. The boy countered, as best he could, and leapt back, barely avoiding another painful bruise. Then, to the surprise of the Master of the Sword, he leapt forward and thrust his own weapon straight at the man's chest. Had Madawc been a bit slower or less flexible, he would have had his own bruise to contend with. He escaped the thrust by bending quickly backwards.

"Excellent counter, me lad! Excellent!" Now let's see you do it again!" Declan groaned and resumed his guard position, waiting for the next blow to fall. Roland cringed a bit and waited his own turn. Every day for over a week they had been receiving hard lessons from Alwyn Madawc. He was making progress, but was well behind Declan in his proficiency with the sword—and he had the bruises to prove it! After the first day of pummelling at the hands of the weapon's instructor, Roland had questioned Declan about the knight.

"His accent is strange, Declan—a bit like yours, but different. He can't be a Norman, but he doesn't seem a Saxon either."

Declan laughed. "Haven't ye figured it out? His accent is *Welsh*—and it sounds not a thing at all like Irish!

"*Welsh*? Sir Roger trusts a...*Welshman* with the security of Shipbrook? Doesn't he worry, that the man will betray him to his own countrymen?"

"Oh, Sir Roger trusts Sir Alwyn with his life, and, what's more, with the lives of Lady Catherine and Lady Millicent as well. He's depended on the fellow since they first fought together—guarding old Hugh's backside!"

It slowly dawned on Roland that Sir Alwyn Madawc had been the Welshman who had fought back to back with Sir Roger years ago in the service of the Earl of Chester—and had been knighted for his efforts. *So, the two had been together ever since!*

"It is still a bit of a mystery why Sir Alwyn left Wales in the first place," Declan continued. "I have it on pretty good authority, that, as a young man, he fell in love with the prettiest girl in northern Wales. Regrettably, she returned his affections."

"Regrettably?"

"Aye. Regrettable inasmuch as she was already wedded to the

leader of the largest clan in that part of the country. He was not an *understanding* sort of man, and I'm told that our Sir Alwyn barely escaped across the frontier with his life. Perhaps this explains his lack of warmth towards his own countrymen."

"…and his wariness when it comes to females," added Roland, with a knowing nod.

"Wary he may be Roland my lad, but a charmer of the first rank nevertheless," Declan replied with a wink. "On market days you'll find him sampling the wares of the prettiest market maids, and I don't mean their cakes and sundries!"

The two boys had, from the first day back at Shipbrook, fallen into a regular schedule established by Sir Roger and Lady Catherine. Mornings were spent learning the basic skills expected of a squire. This included weapons drills, instruction on the care and use of armour, rudimentary cooking and repair of clothing and harness. Early afternoon was devoted to lessons from Lady Catherine on mathematics, and, in Roland's case, reading and writing.

For Roland, late afternoons were taken up with lessons in basic horsemanship. To his surprise, this instruction was administered by the young Lady Millicent, who turned out to be a fine rider, but a demanding instructor. He was relieved that the young woman appeared to be strictly business when it came to equestrian drill. What torments she did visit on him had solely to do with his woeful riding.

"Master Inness, you are not straddling some log in the forest there! *Sit…up…straight.* How often must I remind you that only ruffians and poor horsemen slouch thus in the saddle!" The young girl seemed genuinely distressed at Roland's ineptitude.

Roland tried to sit bolt upright, but this only made him bounce up and down like a crazed puppet.

"Gad, Roland. You look like an idiot, with a branch up your backside! Take some weight on your stirrups. Flow with the horse's gait." The instructions flew continuously—to little avail. After his fifth lesson, she spurred her own mount forward and grasped the bridal of Roland's horse, reining it to a stop.

"Perhaps you Danes are better suited to the deck of ship, for I fear you shall never be a horseman," she said with a combination of frustration and resignation.

Roland was ashamed of his poor performance, but bristled at her reference to his people. He held his tongue, but refused to hang his head. He looked at Lady Millicent. She seemed born to this infernal mode of travel. She was tall for her age, but still seemed to be dwarfed by the magnificent horse she handled with such assurance. The girl did not, however, appear frail. She sometimes rode in breeches that would have been suitable for any boy. Her hair was cropped short and her cheeks were browned by the sun and wind. When she was galloping across the fields of Shipbrook, Roland could see the sheer joy on her face—so different than the terror he imagined marked his features when his horse moved beyond a trot.

Roland looked about him and was, once again, taken with the beauty of the countryside around Shipbrook. Stretching away on all sides of the castle were alternating fields of barley and stands of old hardwoods, some of which covered several square miles. The winter barley was well along in ripening and the woods in June were in full leaf.

It was to these woods he repaired late each day to gather cuttings from the ash trees to replenish his supply of arrows and to hone his skills with the longbow. This he did at Sir Roger's direction, and only Declan and Sir Alwyn knew of this secret drill. On occasion, the Irish boy came along, but, more often, Roland practiced alone. It was the favourite part of his days. In his flight from Kinder Scout he had had no time to dwell on the beauty of the forest. But now his love of wild places came back to him.

This was the world he had been raised in. The world he understood and took strength from. It was as close to a homecoming as he was likely ever to get. As one summer day drifted into the next he explored far and wide, running along deer tracks and savouring the sights and smells of the forest. *There* lay the scat of a passing fox, *there* the crushed grass where a deer had passed the night. In his wanderings he could have taken any number of rabbit, deer or grouse, but he required none for food and thus, let them pass undisturbed.

Above all, he loved to handle the longbow. At times, it served as a connection to the memory of his father. At other times, in the taut bend of the wood and tension of the cord, he felt some reflection of his own situation. Despite the comfort of his new life he felt like a drawn arrow, ready for release—but at what target and to what purpose? He knew not.

For the most part, he simply enjoyed the mechanical drill of repeatedly drawing, aiming and releasing. His father had told him he had a natural talent for the bow, but he had never felt it fully until these long afternoons at Shipbrook. As he had grown stronger with the passing weeks of regular exertions and regular meals, the bow in his hand seemed to become a part of him. He felt as though he could not miss and yet he was never quite satisfied with his results. During his hours at solitary practice, he maintained an urgent and strict discipline. Bolt after bolt flew true to his aiming point and tight clusters of arrows, like some strange nesting bird, blossomed where they struck. He may be a dolt on a horse and a menace to himself with a sword, but woe unto an enemy if he had his bow in hand!

"Roland! Could you stop your wool gathering a moment?" It was the voice of Lady Millicent ending his daydream.

"Nice to have you back with us," she said, with a slight arch to her eyebrow. "Now, I've completely forgotten to tell you about the masquerade Mother has arranged for this evening, and we're bound to be late, unless we hurry. Mother has prepared costumes for each of us, and I can show you yours." She dug her heels into the flanks of her thoroughbred and waved to Roland to follow. The boy kicked futilely at the sides of his own, less regal, mount and succeeded only in accelerating to a bouncy canter.

"My Lady, what in the world is a…a…*masquerade*?" he yelled.

"Oh, you'll see! *Your costume* is quite wonderful!" she yelled over her shoulder, as she disappeared in the dust ahead.

Roland arrived back at Shipbrook to find the young Lady de Laval waiting beside her horse with a broad smile.

"Why Roland, I think that's the fastest you've gotten old Bones to move—ever!" She smiled and clapped. "Now come on, we'll be late to the party." She grabbed Roland's hand and fairly dragged him up the main steps and into the front entrance of the hall.

"But...but...my lady, I know naught of...costumes...or..."

"Parties!" she cut him off. "Well it's high time you did, Master Inness. I know you are of peasant stock, but even the peasants have their celebrations, do they not?"

Roland thought for a moment, as the young girl continued to lead him up various stairs and down unknown hallways. He did remember the occasional gatherings of the Danish peasants, but these had been few and he had been young. He vaguely recalled music and dancing, but could conjure up no details.

"Will Declan be there?" he asked.

"Why of course. All the household will be there and each in *fantastic* costume! Wait 'til you see!" The excitement in the girl's voice was starting to become contagious. Perhaps this would actually be enjoyable, Roland thought to himself.

At last, they reached a room at the end of another hallway, which Lady Millicent entered with a flourish.

"*There it is!*" she exclaimed proudly, pointing at what appeared to be a sizable dead deer draped across a fine bed. Roland had never seen anything like the bed and was, briefly, fascinated by this small glimpse of the luxuries enjoyed by the gentry. He could not, however, ignore the deer carcass, which seemed entirely out of place against such finery.

"We're all to go as animals, Roland, and you seemed like such a creature of the forest, I had to claim this costume for you." She lifted what appeared to be some sort of garment, constructed from the head and hide of a stag. She held the costume out proudly to the boy. "Everyone loves to be the stag, but I saved it for *you*," she continued, with a conspiratorial wink. "Poor Declan got the rooster suit, which, frankly, will look a bit ridiculous on him. Oh...try it on!" She handed the strange garment to the befuddled boy.

Roland held it by its head, which was complete with impressive antlers and looked at the sleeves which had been fashioned from the front legs of the beast and which still had the tiny hooves attached.

"Go ahead and put it on," insisted the girl.

With some reluctance, Roland slipped the sleeves over his arms and slipped his legs into the breeches fashioned from the rear legs of the deer. The fit was actually quite good. The deer's head had been contoured to fit over the crown of a man's head, which would allow him to see clearly and even eat if he was of a mind to. The entire ensemble tied up neatly with deer hide thongs in the front. When complete, Lady Millicent clapped her hands and fairly bounced with excitement.

"Oh, you look magnificent! I feel rather sorry for Declan and the others, left to wear the trappings of barnyard animals."

By now, Roland was feeling rather satisfied with himself. He could not help but be drawn into the excitement of the event. He tentatively touched the antlers he now sprouted from his head.

"My lady…what shall you wear?" he asked.

"Oh, I actually will go as the doe. Not nearly as impressive as the stag costume, but it does fit me! Roland, I must be off, for we should have been there long ago. Please go ahead to the banquet hall and tell Father and Mother that I shall soon attend them. Just descend the steps at the end of the hall and enter through the double doors straight ahead." Finished with her instructions, Lady Millicent hurried from the room.

Roland took a moment to get used to moving in the somewhat cumbersome costume, but soon felt ready to proceed. He exited the bedroom, taking care not to snag his antlers on the doorway and proceeded as Lady Millicent had directed. He was a bit anxious to see how the others looked in their costumes, but was secretly sure that his stag suit would be the best. He smirked a bit to himself, as he tried to picture Declan in the rooster suit. He found his way to the great double doors of the banquet hall and pushed them open. He dined in the hall quite frequently for the evening meal and was familiar with the surroundings. On this occasion, however, he could immediately tell that something was dreadfully wrong.

All members of the household were in their usual places. Sir Roger and Lady Catherine sat in the place of honour at the centre table. Sir Alwyn sat to Sir Roger's right and Lady Millicent to Lady Catherine's left. Declan was in his usual place with some of the other members of the household staff at a side table. All was as it should be, with one exception. No one was dressed, evenly vaguely, like an animal.

"Ho, there, Sir Stag!" cried Sir Alwyn, upon catching sight of this strange apparition entering the hall. I thought we slew ye last winter, but now I see ye must have survived!"

"Lovely antlers ye have there, Master Stag," added Sir Roger. "Try not to stick anyone with them when you reach for the mutton…Har, Har, Har!

Declan O'Duinne was at a loss for words. "Roland…?" was all he managed.

The boy stood there turning several shades of crimson.

"*Millicent?*" interjected Lady Catherine, severely eyeing her young daughter. "Are you responsible for this?"

"Mother? Whatever do you mean?" Lady Millicent asked sweetly. "I think Master Inness looks magnificent!"

Gathering the tatters of his pride, Roland managed to address the head of the table. "Begging your leave Sir Roger, I seem to be wrongly dressed for this…*party*. I must be excused."

"Yes…Yes…" managed Sir Roger, as he wiped tears of laughter from his eyes and tried to stifle another outburst. "But do be careful, Roland. There are *hunters* in these parts." Sir Roger and Sir Alwyn lost what little control they had and dissolved into loud gasping laughs. Roland turned on his heels and, with what dignity he could muster, left the hall.

***

Later that night, two boys looked at each other over a flickering oil lamp.

"Are ye sure about this, Roland?"

His companion nodded, grimly. He knew this to be a grave risk, but he had had a stomach full of the arrogance of the Normans and would not let this humiliation pass. His cheeks still burned as he recalled the amused look of innocence on the face of the girl when he had entered the hall. She was one badly in need of a comeuppance and he would find a way to supply one.

"Dec, you had best stay clear of this. I won't ask you to risk your position."

Declan looked at him gravely for a moment then broke into a slow grin. "Did I ever tell ya of the time the Little Lady convinced me that …Well it hardly matters what she convinced me of. Suffice it to say my dignity was no better served than a Dane in a deer suit. In this matter, I am your sworn man—but God help us if it goes awry."

He spit in his palm and the two boys shook. *Now all that was needed was a plan.*

Chapter 11

Payment in Kind

Devising a plot went slowly over the following week, as the boys proposed and rejected one idea after another. Lady Millicent was not just a Lady, she was—more importantly—the beloved daughter of their master. This would have to be done *very* delicately.

"There must be no large audience," said Roland, "for a public humiliation, though it be tempting, may not sit well with Sir Roger."

"Or, more particularly, Lady Catherine," supplied Declan.

"Still, it must be *reasonably* mortifying and, above all, she must know that she's been had by her own victims."

"She'll be on guard," said Declan.

"Yes, but not truly. For all her dishing up of jest, she's never been the victim of one—has she?"

"Not to my knowledge," said Declan. "Neither I, nor Harold had the nerve, to be honest…but I'm wonderin', why ye're so intent on this. I know you've reason enough to want to give back to the Normans, but Sir Roger has done you no harm. Are ye truly *that* angry at the girl?"

"No! Well, at first I was… I mean…she seems a decent sort—for a girl." Roland stuttered, as he tried to form an answer to Declan's question. In truth he had no good answer. Perhaps, after

102

all the blows he had suffered, he simply didn't wish to be trifled with. Yet he knew that had he been made jest of by anyone other than Millicent de Laval, he would have long since shrugged it off. He did not understand what it was about the girl that compelled him, but he could not let the matter go. Finally he shrugged.

"Decent or no, the girl deserves back some of her own."

Declan looked at his friend and reluctantly nodded. "That she certainly does," he said.

In the days that followed, the boys continued with their rigorous schedule and could scheme only at odd times. Despite a steady accumulation of bruises, Roland began to feel more at ease with the use of a sword, albeit a wooden one. He had yet to land a solid blow on Sir Alwyn, but he had come very close and the stocky knight had begun to note his progress.

"By Gad, Roland, ye may get lucky someday and actually nick someone with one of these pig stickers," he said. He paused for a moment, leaning on the hilt of his sword. "Listen to me, lad. Your skills are improvin', but when swords are crossed ye'll need more than skill. Ye must…and I mean *must* have the will to destroy the other man—or he will certainly destroy you. Ye're gaining the control ye need, lad, but ye're holdin' back. Ye lack the *battle fury*, the spirit that drives a great swordsman. Technique alone will not save ye from a man who has it. I'm Welsh by birth, lad and we Welsh have the fury—oh we have that in *abundance*—though most of my kinsmen lack the control. Did ye not say your great grandsire was a Viking, boy?"

"Aye sir," answered Roland, who was listening intently to the words of his teacher.

"Then why do ye fight like a *priss*, lad! What does it take to rouse that old Viking blood? Was yer sire not a fighter? Ah, but I hear the Danes have lost their old berserker rage these days and have been broken to the plough."

Roland knew full well that Sir Alwyn was purposely goading him, but that knowledge didn't help. His anger rose at this slur on his father and on his fellow Danes. Slowly, he lifted his weapon to the guard position. Sir Alwyn sneered at him and did the same.

"Come on little Viking…or do I *scare* ye?"

Roland ignored the taunt. He moved forward hesitantly. Sir

103

Alwyn shook his head at this timid display of aggression.

"Boy if that's all you have..."

His words were cut short in mid sentence, as Roland launched a furious assault on the older man. The boy first leapt forward, with a slashing attack aimed at his instructor's head. Taken off guard, Sir Alwyn barely managed to dodge a blow that would have split his scalp. As he recovered, Roland lunged forward with a straight thrust at the man's mid-section. The Master of the Sword leapt back, while striking downward with his own weapon just in time to deflect what would have been an incapacitating blow to his gut—but he was not yet out of danger. His moves to avoid Roland's onslaught had taken him across the courtyard and hard up against the stone wall of the manor. He had nowhere left to dodge. He set his jaw and went on the attack.

Roland was prepared for this move and gradually gave ground to the older, more experienced swordsman. Slowly, a grin of triumph crept across the face of the Welsh knight.

"Nice try, lad...but...it'll be another day...before ye best...Alwyn Madawc!" he said, between gasping breaths. Then, he raised his heavy oak sword above his head and bore down on the young squire with a roar.

"Arrrrghhhh!"

To his surprise, Roland made no move to retreat. As Sir Alwyn swung his weapon downward, the boy lunged inside the arc of his blow and thrust his stave straight forward, sinking it painfully into the charging man's belly. Roland felt the impact all the way to his shoulder, and barely missed being buried under the falling weight of his foe. Sir Alwyn had crumpled in a heap directly before him. Instantly, Roland leapt to his feet and thrust the point of his oaken sword under the burly knight's chin.

"My Father *was* a ploughman and he k*illed* better men than you, sir," the boy said, between his gasps for breath, "...and my great grandsire—the Viking—would have killed you now—even with this piece of wood."

Sir Alwyn looked at the boy, whose face was still twisted with rage and managed a weak smile between gasps for breath.

"Aye, I expect he would have, Master Inness...but what of *you*? Will you kill me?"

The man's response seemed to snap the momentary spell Roland had been under. After a moment, he lifted the sword from Sir Alwyn's neck and considered his instructor, on the ground beneath him.

"Not this day, Sir Alwyn, but I'd settle for a passing mark from the Master of the Sword!" he said, and extended his hand to the older man.

Sir Alwyn grasped it and dragged himself to his feet, limping to a nearby stool where he sat and massaged his aching stomach.

"That, ye'll have, my lad," he said, beginning to laugh, wincing in pain. "Though I think it was you that administered the lesson, not I! Now, dismissed—the both of ye."

He watched as Roland and Declan made their way toward the kitchen, looking for their usual mid-morning handout from Cook. He rubbed his chin with the hand not rubbing his injured belly. What had the boy said about his father killing men? Perhaps, it was a boast. Or perhaps there was more to this peasant boy than met the eye. It would bear watching.

***

"What about a dead toad in her porridge," suggested Declan.

"Not bad, but difficult to manage. Cook keeps a sharp eye on everything transpiring in her kitchen."

"Or put it in her slipper!" Declan continued, warming to the basic notion of a dead toad.

"You'd have to be a phantom, to get into her room unnoticed."

"Well what, then?"

"I don't know, Dec...but it'll come to us."

***

Early afternoon found Roland in his regular session with Lady Catherine. The Arabic mathematics was beginning to come easier to him and Lady of the manor, while maintaining her icy distance from this new addition to her household, seemed pleased with his progress.

"Master Inness, you've a quick mind. With a little more drill, these things will be as second nature to you," she said. "Now, thirty-one remove seven," she quizzed.

"Twenty-four," he responded promptly.

"Which is?"

"Two dozen."

"A pound has how many ounces?"

"Sixteen, my lady."

"...and one quarter of a pound is?"

"A very small portion indeed, my lady"

Lady Catherine frowned.

"You've a quick wit and a talent for jesting, Master Inness. You remind me a bit of Millicent."

Roland blinked at that. Lady Catherine allowed just a hint of a smile, as though expecting his reaction.

"You object to the comparison, master squire?"

"My Lady...I...I...she's a little girl!" he blurted.

"And growing fast, lad. Perhaps, a bit too fast, I fear. She grows more full of herself every day, but for all of that, she has a good heart and quick mind.

Lady Catherine continued to survey the boy carefully as though trying to see inside his own heart and mind.

"I understand you had to flee your home and you lost your father to the Earl of Derby's men. It's a hard thing, lad—but we live in hard times. We must all act with caution when needs be...and boldness when caution fails." Lady Catherine paused for a moment, her gaze drifting far away.

"I am Saxon by birth, Roland, and the great granddaughter of Edric the Wild. I know something of crossing purposes with the Normans."

"Edric the Wild, my lady? I know naught of him."

"Aye, few do these days. In the time before the Conquest, Edric held wide lands south of here and protected the Saxon regions from the incursions of the Welsh. The Norman Earls, installed by King William in the Welsh Marches, continually encroached on his lands, until he could stand it no more. He allied himself with his old enemies, the Welsh, and rose against the King. As luck would have it, the Saxons and the Danes rose at the same time and the Norman power was very nearly overthrown." She paused a moment, as though savouring what might have been.

"Ah, but William was not known as the Conqueror for nothing, lad. He personally led a great army north to York, which the Saxons and Danes had seized, and recaptured the city—with much slaughter."

"The Harrowing of the North..." Roland muttered. Lady Catherine nodded.

"A bloody harrowing it was, too. One hundred thousand dead they say, hundreds of villages burned and the fields salted so that others would starve. So many bodies thrown into the rivers they became clogged and overflowed their banks. When he was done with your people, he marched across the mountains to the east of here and drove Edric and his allies back across the border. The Welsh turned on Edric and handed him over to William—who had him imprisoned in London, till his death." Lady Catherine paused in her discourse, then continued.

"We Saxons and you Danes are a conquered people, Master Inness, but the wheel always turns. For me, I care not for Norman, Saxon, Dane or Welshmen. As a race I trust them not. I put stock only in good men of any race—of which there are precious few in these lands."

"Sir Roger," volunteered Roland.

"Is one in truth," she said and smiled. "And what sort will you become, Master Inness?"

Roland did not know how to answer the question.

"Time will tell, I suppose," she answered for him. "I was impressed with the amount of...dignity you managed the other evening when Millicent made jest of you. And I hear you gave Sir Alwyn a buffeting. This is all to the good, but in these times you will surely face sterner tests. The first will be your loyalty to my husband. I shall reserve my judgment until I can be certain on that point."

That night the boy lay long awake on his straw mat thinking of what Lady Catherine had said. It seemed to be the opposite of the advice that Tuck had given him, but nevertheless it arrived at the same place. Tuck found some good in all the races of men and Lady Catherine found much to distrust in them all. Both seemed to say that lineage mattered not and perhaps that was so. He had been at Shipbrook long enough to observe that Sir Roger did not abide mistreatment of the peasants who worked his lands. For their part, the locals seemed content with their lot. They turned over part of their bounty to their master and he, in turn, protected them from all who would plunder them—or worse. It seemed a fair bargain in a world where little fairness prevailed.

He listened to Declan O'Duinne snoring beside him. Irish... and Alwyn was Welsh and the Lady Catherine Saxon. It was an odd stew, but one that seemed to be working here at Shipbrook. He knew nothing of the sort was the case in Derbyshire. There it was a foul pond with the green scum at the top choking out all below it. He also knew the day would come when he would return to stir that stinking pool.

***

Roland awoke groggily the next morning to Declan shaking him.

"I have it! Gad, Roland, I have it!"

Roland looked at his friend and rubbed his eyes.

"Have what?"

"A plan you dolt! What have we been chewing on the past weeks? A plan for her Little Ladyship's comeuppance."

Now Roland was fully awake.

"Tell me."

"*Little people!*"

"What?"

"*Little* people! Roland, Lady Millicent has a very vivid imagination. It's part of what makes her so lethal at these jests. We shall use that against her! I have often told tales of the Little People, back home in Erin—and Roland, she *believes*!

"She believes in Little People?" asked Roland, incredulously.

"Aye, she fair loves the idea that the Little People live in the earth and hide away their treasure from men."

"Tell me more of these little folk, Declan."

"Well, there are hundreds of tales—and to be honest—I half believe them myself, though I've never really seen any of the race." Declan proceeded to tell Roland several stories of how the crafty Little People played on the greed of men to trick them. Declan's idea was beginning to have great appeal.

"So how would you use the Little Lady's belief in Little People to our advantage?" Roland asked.

"We help her catch one!" Declan replied in triumph.

For the next two days, the boys made their preparations in secret. In a small glade, Roland lead Declan to a partly concealed burrow on the side of a shallow ravine near where he practiced with his longbow. In his months roaming these woods he had found many such, but this one seemed well suited to their purpose. At the entrance, they constructed a small porch of twigs, complete with a miniature thatched roof. Declan carefully carved a tiny bench, which he positioned under the shade of a nearby bush. The boys finally stood back to admire their work.

"A right cosy little burrow, I'd say!" offered Roland.

"Just the kind of country place, the Little People would favour," agreed Declan.

"Let's bait our trap," said Roland.

The two boys returned to Shipbrook by a different route and arrived in time for a mid-day handout from Cook. After eating generous portions of black bread dabbed in a bit of honey, they loitered near the stables. It would soon be time for Roland's riding instructions. As the time approached, the two boys moved to a corner of the stables and began an animated conversation, speaking in hushed voices, though loud enough to carry some distance. Occasionally they glanced over their shoulders to see if they were being observed. All in all, it looked convincingly suspicious—which is exactly what they hoped for.

Lady Millicent rounded the corner and immediately spied the boys. She was close enough to pick up a snatch of conversation...

"If we can catch him, he's bound to tell us where his treasure is!" whispered Declan, just loud enough to be sure he was overheard.

"But they're not that easy to capture," hissed Roland in reply. *"We may need hel..."* He stopped abruptly, as Lady Millicent approached. She could not conceal the look of interest on her face.

"And what are the squire's whispering about today?" she asked brightly.

"Nothing, my lady," answered Declan. "I was just going out for a ride in this the fine weather."

Lady Millicent gave him a sweet smile. "It is lovely, isn't it?"

She turned to Roland. "Are you ready for your lesson, Master Inness?" she asked.

"Aye, my lady, I'm ready."

While the stable man ran to fetch Millicent's mount, Declan hurriedly climbed on his pony and, giving them a wave, clattered off across the courtyard and out the gate. Soon after, the groom appeared leading Lady Millicent's beautiful bay mare, as Roland turned to the complicated task of properly saddling his own, less magnificent mount.

Over the past month, he had learned how to properly cinch up his rig and there had been no further embarrassing slides under his horse's belly. He pulled the last cinch rope tight and mounted. In a moment, they were through the gate of Shipbrook and cantering along a riding trail that led up into the surrounding hills. They had hardly gotten out of sight of the castle, when Millicent swung her horse about and blocked the path.

"Roland, you will tell me instantly what you and Declan have been up to!" she said, in her most commanding voice. She had learned well the air of authority expected of the gentry. She now employed it fully on Roland.

"My lady, I cannot," said Roland hesitantly. "I can't betray Declan's trust."

Sensing that the boy was uncertain, the girl pressed harder.

"Roland, I overheard most of what was said, so you'll betray next to nothing. On the other hand—should you keep silent—I can make these riding lessons truly unhappy experiences for you." This last, she said with a clear threat in her voice.

Roland squirmed in his saddle. "Do ye promise not to tell, my lady?"

"Oh, I'll tell no one, Roland. I swear it! What is it you two are trying to capture?"

"It's hard to believe, my lady."

"*It's one of those Little People, isn't it?*" she burst in.

Roland let a look of amazement creep over his face.

"Why…yes…yes it is, my lady. How could you know?"

"I heard you speak of treasure, and it's well known the Little People always have a bit of gold hid away. I've always wondered if they lived only in Erin or if, perhaps, some had travelled—even here to Cheshire. Now it seems, we have the answer. Tell me more!"

With some show of reluctance, Roland spun the tale of how he and Declan had been walking in the woods—farther up into the hills—when they saw something rustle in the bushes. Thinking it a rabbit, or some other small animal, they approached cautiously, but found only tiny prints in the soft earth—boot prints that looked all the world like that of a man, shrunken down to the size of a housecat.

"I've spent many a day in the forests, my lady and I know all of the sign left by the creatures there, but none were like this. So we followed, even more cautiously."

Lady Millicent hung on his every word. He told of how they followed the trail into a small ravine and there, in the side of the embankment, was the neatest little cave—complete with front porch! The boys hid in the tall grass on the opposite side of the narrow cleft and waited. To their astonishment, a tiny man appeared, dressed in greens and browns that blended almost completely with the surrounding vegetation. He took a seat on a small bench, shaded by a mulberry bush, and whittled away on a twig with a tiny knife. Whatever object he may have been fashioning was too small for the boys to make out, but he remained at his labour for the good part of an hour. When he'd finished, he held something up—as if to admire it in better light—then returned to his burrow. The boys watched for another hour, but the little man did not return.

"Oh, it *must* be one of the Little People!" exclaimed Millicent. "There can be no other explanation!"

"Declan said the same, my lady...and he is intent on capturing the fellow and making him reveal the whereabouts of his treasure."

"I knew it! I knew it!" the girl squealed. "Roland, you must take me to this place at once!"

"But, my lady, Declan..."

"Will do as he is commanded!" Millicent completed his sentence. "Regardless, I heard you say you might need help to capture the fellow. I can be of help!"

Roland sighed and shrugged his shoulders. "As you wish, my lady."

The boy gave his horse a kick and started back up the trail into the hills. They rode in silence for most of an hour before Roland stopped and dismounted. He turned to Millicent and held a finger to his lips.

"Hitch the horses here, my lady," he whispered. *"We must be very quiet and careful, from here forward."* Millicent looped her horse's reins over a branch and silently followed Roland up the forest path. At length, they came to a small glade, which shaded a narrow ravine that ran up the side of a hill. On the far side, they could see Declan, lying on his stomach, peering over the edge of the embankment. Roland turned to Millicent and again put his finger to his mouth. She nodded and followed. It took them several minutes to cover the distance to where the Irish boy lay in the tall grass.

Declan looked completely shocked to see Millicent walking behind Roland. His brow furrowed in irritation as he pointed at the young girl then looked inquiringly at Roland. Roland could only shrug his shoulders in silence. Declan eased backwards, still on his stomach, to where the two stood and motioned them to follow. After a few minutes they were back across the glade near where the horses were tethered.

"What is *she* doing here?" Declan whispered fiercely and pointed at the girl.

"She overheard us, Dec. She knew we were on to something…She made me tell," he concluded, weakly.

Lady Millicent stood by, with a small, satisfied smile on her face during this exchange.

"Like it or not Master O'Duinne—we are in this together," she hissed. "I'll help you capture this thing, but I share the plunder as well." This she said with complete finality.

Declan shook his head and kicked at the dirt of the trail, but it was clear he was beaten.

"Very well then," he said. "Seems we have no choice." He motioned them closer.

"The little fellow was out for a few moments, just before you arrived. He seems completely unaware that his hideout has been discovered. I think we need to act now if we are to capture him."

Roland nodded and Lady Millicent could hardly contain her

excitement.

"I've scouted about, and there are two other ways out of that burrow, both on the opposite side of the bank from the main entrance. Here's what we must do..."

In time, all preparations had been made. Declan led Roland and Millicent back to his vantage point overlooking the ravine. Each boy held a long, supple willow shaft and the girl held a large leather sack, with a drawstring at its neck. Millicent lay flat and looked below. The scene was amazing. Such a snug and cozy house the little man had! She could see the little bench where he had done his carving. It was just as Roland had described it. She could hardly breathe from the excitement! Declan pointed to the main entrance and looked at Millicent. She nodded her understanding of her role in the plan.

The two boys moved off silently, in opposite directions, to position themselves at the other entrances. Millicent counted to one hundred, as she had been instructed to do then slipped silently over the embankment and moved to the entrance of the burrow. Kneeling down, she opened the broad mouth of the sack and positioned it firmly over the hole, all the while admiring the workmanship of the little man's porch.

After a moment, she observed Roland and Declan approaching from different directions. The two boys moved to their places on the other side of the embankment. As agreed, Declan raised his willow wand as a signal. Millicent gave a swift nod and braced herself. The two boys plunged their branches into the holes before them.

For a moment, nothing happened. Millicent looked up to see Roland and Declan working their wands back and forth as they pushed them deeper into the earth. Then, something exploded out of the hole in front of her and barrelled into the bottom of the leather sack. Reacting quickly, Millicent pulled the drawstrings, closing the trap. As she lifted the bag, there was a frightful squirming and hissing inside! *They'd caught one of the Little People!*

"*Roland! Declan! I have him! I have him!*" she shrieked, holding the bag high. The two boys scrambled over the embankment and gathered near, as she sat the bag on the ground.

Every few seconds, the sack would explode in frenzied movement, as the occupant sought to escape.

"Let's take a look at him!" Millicent exclaimed breathlessly.

"*No, No!*" commanded Declan. "These creatures are as wily as a fox and as quick as a snake. He'll be out and over the hill, before you could lift a finger! No, we must get him back to Shipbrook, so we can release him in a place where he cannot escape us. If the tales are true, he will trade his treasure for his freedom!"

Roland and Millicent nodded their solemn agreement with this plan. The two boys mounted, one behind the other on Roland's horse, and Millicent tied the squirming bundle to her saddle, as they set off for the castle. When they arrived, Millicent immediately dismounted and started up the steps of the manor house.

"Where are you taking him?" Declan asked urgently.

"Father must see this!" the girl replied. "He made great fun of me for believing in such creatures—and I shall make him regret it!" She fairly whooped in triumph. "Don't worry boys, I'm certain that Mother's study is secure enough to contain this little creature." The two boys had no choice but to follow as she disappeared into the hall, the squirming bag flung over her shoulder.

Sir Roger was seated in the great hall playing with one of his hunting dogs when his daughter burst in.

"Father, you must come at once to Mother's study. I've a great wonder to show you," she said, with a gleam in her eye as she rushed past her sire and up the near staircase. The burly knight looked quizzically at the two boys following in her wake. They shrugged their shoulders in unison and continued to follow the young girl. His curiosity aroused, Sir Roger did the same. When they arrived in the small study where Roland took his mathematics lessons, they found Lady Catherine staring bemusedly at her very excited daughter. The two boys and the Lord of Shipbrook crowded around. Lady Millicent turned to her father in triumph.

"You said that the Little People Declan spoke of were a fairy tale, Father...but I knew different! Now, we shall soon have a treasure—when our little friend here buys his freedom! With a dramatic flourish, she undid the drawstrings of the bag and upended it on the floor.

From the open mouth of the bag, emerged a very confused and

surly hedgehog. Surveying its surroundings and seeing no means of escape, it instantly rolled itself into a ball. Sir Roger looked entirely befuddled by this strange sequence of events. Lady Catherine, on the other hand, quickly covered her mouth and looked away to stifle an irresistible urge to laugh. Lady Millicent turned a livid shade of red and cast a furious glare at the furry ball on the floor, then turned on the two squires who stood before her.

"My lady," said Roland gravely, "our little man seems to have transformed himself into a...hedgehog." The girl gave him a withering look.

"It's well known the wee folk have magical powers," added Declan sincerely.

Sir Roger, gauging the imminent explosion about to engulf his wife's study, gave a quick jerk of his head toward the entrance. The two squires needed no further urging and beat a hasty retreat. As they clambered down the stairs, they could not help but grin at each other. Who knew what the payment would be for this uprising of squires? But for this moment, it felt like victory and worth whatever the price might be.

Chapter 12

The Abduction

In the days that followed, the two squires kept as much out of sight as their duties allowed. Among the populace of Shipbrook there was much talk of the Little People and the prank—though always discreetly—and much speculation on the fate of the two boys. All waited for retribution to be meted out, but days passed and none came.

The confused little hedgehog was kept as a pet and named "Little Man" by Sir Roger—much to the consternation of his only daughter. Lady Millicent continued to fume, but, had apparently been forbidden to retaliate. Roland remained on guard each day during their riding lessons, but there was no hint of mischief. Whereas before, Millicent had cultivated a superior and bemused air as she instructed him, now her manner was frosty and businesslike. But it is not in the manner of the young to long maintain an unnatural artifice and in time her embarrassment and his caution gradually dispelled. For Roland and his master's daughter there seemed to be an unspoken understanding that accounts had been settled.

It was early July in Cheshire and the days were becoming longer and hotter. The countryside about was in its full summer lushness and the crops looked to be bountiful. The spring barley was high and green and the winter crop was being harvested. Men with scythes and women with large baskets brought in the sheaves as their fathers and mothers before them had. It was a pleasant time for Roland. Each day brought some new knowledge and a further expansion of his horizons. Weapons instruction continued daily, as did his riding lessons with Millicent. In each, he was making progress, though it was clear he would never be a first rate horseman or an expert swordsman.

His skill with the longbow was another matter. On occasion, Sir Roger would accompany the boy to the remote clearing where he practiced his craft. His initial appreciation of the boy's skill was undiminished, as he watched him continue to extend his distance and hone his accuracy. The regular and abundant feeding Roland had received since arriving at Shipbrook had erased all evidence of the gaunt boy the knight had taken on in Yorkshire. His ribs no longer poked out and his shoulders seemed to have broadened. Sir Roger noted with amusement the first hint of fine, downy hair on his squire's chin and upper lip. The boy was not a man yet, but he wasn't far removed either.

"So, tell me Roland, how are ye with a moving target?" Sir Roger inquired one hot afternoon during a practice session. "Ye can hit a fly in the eye standin' still, at most ranges, but what if yer target is movin'? Most enemies I've faced aren't inclined to stand still while ye take aim."

Roland paused in mid draw and eased the tension from his bowstring. His master's question was a fair one. He had brought down a running buck more than once with his father's bow, but he'd had some misses as well. He had also missed some rabbits on the run—but no man could move with the speed and elusiveness of the deer or rabbit, even on horseback.

"I can say with certainty, my lord, that within one hundred meters I can hit a man running or a horseman at a gallop," he answered truthfully—and hoped he didn't sound boastful.

Sir Roger smiled at his squire. There was no mistaking the boy's confidence in his own abilities, and this was good. But everyone needed a goad from time to time...

"Well what about a target...on the wing?"

"Pardon, my lord?"

"A bird, boy! Could you hit a bird on the wing. I'm right fond of quail and the occasional duck when on campaign. Could ye take one of them in flight?" The big man fought hard to suppress a grin.

A bird in flight? The boy hadn't been sure he'd heard his master correctly. Shooting a bird in flight had never occurred to the boy, though he'd once struck a fat goose as the bird was alighting on a small marsh. Striking a bird in full flight seemed near impossible. Still, he hated to disappoint Sir Roger.

"I...I'm not sure, my lord."

"Well, let's have a go then," the knight said with a grin.

Sir Roger foraged about on the forest floor, picked up a medium-sized limb recently fallen and not yet rotted. It was nearly two feet long and thicker than a large man's arm. He nodded toward the boy. Then, with a great heave, he sent the limb soaring into the blue July sky. Roland drew, hesitated a moment to draw a bead on the tumbling target, and released his shaft as the limb reached the peak of its arc. The arrow missed its mark by more than a foot and the target tumbled unharmed to the ground.

The boy's face flushed red with embarrassment. He had not wanted to fail at the one thing of value he could do—not in front of his master. Sir Roger watched the boy's reaction and was satisfied with what he saw.

"I'll give ye leave to use Master O'Duinne as your tosser—if ye think ye can master this drill."

Roland nodded. Sir Roger wanted him to take birds on the wing? *So he would!*

Sir Roger nodded and changed the subject. "Sir Alwyn says you right near ruptured his gut in weapons drill a few weeks back."

"It was a lucky blow, my lord. I still have much to learn."

"Aye, that's a fact, lad," Sir Roger said and clapped him on the shoulder, "but yer getting' there...and it's well ye are."

The knight sat down in the cool green grass of the clearing and beckoned the boy to join him. "I love this place, Roland," he said gazing around him. "Times like this are sweet when the sun is warm, the grass is green and all around men go about their living in peace—but it won't last...can't last."

"Can't sir?" the boy asked.

118

"Nay lad, men both high and low are fools. They want what they do not have and will take what they do not own. Peace does not suit us Roland. It has been ever thus. In these days and these parts, peace never lasts for long. Be it the Irish, the Welsh...or the heathen Saracens in the Holy Land, there will always be enemies. I fear it cannot be long before ye'll be sighting yer bow on something more than a stick. Will ye be ready for that, boy?"

Roland did not answer for a long moment. He had thought long about the men he had slain those months ago on Kinder Scout and was at peace with his actions, but his sleep was still disturbed at times by the memory. In truth, he had no wish to sight his bow in anger...ever again. Still, he had accepted a position as squire to a knight. This came with the understanding that his master was a warrior and that, if called upon, he must be as well. It was his duty.

"I'll be ready—as needs be, my lord."

The big knight grunted his satisfaction and left the boy to his training.

***

Two days later, Roland was returning to Shipbrook from his late afternoon bow practice astride the pokey and slightly sway-backed horse Lady Millicent had assigned him.

"You suit each other," the girl had said, with a slight sniff.

For such a sleepy summer day as this, the boy thought his mount was perfectly suited as he guided the horse slowly down a small path through a patch of woods. Declan had had other chores to attend to this day and he was alone. As was often the case when he rode through the countryside, he let his mind wander, taking in the beauty of the day and the smell of the forest. At Shipbrook he was not far from wooded hills, but having grown up in the heart of the wilder glens of Kinder Scout, it sometimes seemed that he was. The hours he spent among the trees were his most peaceful. On this day, however, his reverie was shattered—by a high pitched scream.

Roland immediately snapped his mind back to the present. The scream had stopped abruptly, but was nearby—perhaps no more than a hundred yards from where he sat his horse. He knew he was near one of the main riding trails that he and Lady Millicent used during equestrian lessons. Something terribly wrong was happening on that trail! Roland started to spur his horse forward, but checked himself. He knew not what he would face ahead and trusted his legs more than the skittish horse he rode. He slid off the horse and tied the reins to a bush. He would proceed on foot.

Silently, the boy made his way along the faint trail he had been following, toward the larger path below him. As he neared the trail, Roland slipped off the connecting path and into deeper underbrush. He moved with ever greater care, examining each spot before placing his next step. The boy dare not alert whoever was ahead of him by the snap of a twig as he passed. *Another scream*, more muffled than the first came from just ahead and he fought the urge to leap forward to find its source. Moving with all of the stealth honed by years of stalking game, he was finally able to slip into a concealed position that gave him a view of the small clearing ahead.

Seven men were moving about the clearing. Three held the reins of a string of rugged little ponies, one was trying to calm a rearing thoroughbred and one more seemed hunched over a figure on the ground. Two men seemed to be posted as guards along both approaches on the trail. By their dress and the arms they carried, Roland could see that these were not local peasants. Their rough garments marked them as woodsmen and each had a sword or dagger belted to his waist. One had a broadsword hitched over his back and two had bows.

It took no expert to know that these were hard and dangerous men. They seemed intent on conducting their business quietly, but at this close range, Roland could catch snatches of their hushed speech. It was in a strange tongue he had never heard before, but he instantly recognized the accent and rhythm of speech from his many hours in the company of Alwyn Madawc. *These were Welshmen*! Roland had hardly a moment to absorb this information when his stomach twisted at the recognition of the thoroughbred one man was trying to calm. It was Lady Millicent's favourite mount, the bay mare!

He turned his gaze to the figure crouching at the edge of the trail. The man rose abruptly and Roland's worst fears were realized. There, her arm grasped roughly by a man twice her size, was Millicent! He was close enough to see the fear in her eyes—even though the young girl held herself proudly erect. Her hands were bound in front of her. Roland's mind raced. He reached for his longbow, but hesitated. He could surely drop several of these fellows from where he sat, but his nearness presented problems of its own. They would quickly discover his position and be on him before he could take them all with the bow. Beyond that, he was armed only with the dagger he had claimed from Ivo Brun in York. Not a fit weapon to counter swords at close range. Yet, if he could gain more distance, he was not certain he could dispatch them all before they might turn on the girl. With great reluctance, he stayed his hand and watched.

The man holding Millicent dragged her roughly to one of the small ponies and fairly threw her into the saddle. He motioned to the other, and all mounted quickly. The man who had bound the girl confirmed his position as leader by leaping on the back of her thoroughbred. With hardly another word spoken, the group spurred their mounts and headed back down the path towards Shipbrook. The reins of Lady Millicent's pony were held firmly by one of her captors, who led her down the trail. Two other riders followed, clearly positioned to prevent the girl from bolting from the saddle and attempting to escape into the woods.

As the last rider disappeared around a bend, Roland sprang back along the path and leapt onto the back of his horse, which had been contentedly munching grass. To the horse's surprise, his rider dug hard heels into his flanks and smacked him on the behind with a length of rein. Unused to such treatment at the hands of the boy, the startled animal bolted forward down the trail, moving faster than he had in years. Roland urged the horse onward, determined not to lose the girl or her abductors.

Looking down, he could read their trail as clearly as a ploughed furrow. Tracking them would be easy—but they must not know they were followed! Roland reined in the horse. He could not afford to burst upon them if they stopped for any reason. He must keep his distance and follow. The urge to sprint for Shipbrook to summon Sir Roger, Sir Alwyn and the men-at-arms was strong. There was no way he could fight his way through seven men to free the girl. He had to have help, but he could not afford to lose the track.

He glanced at the sky and grimaced to see the approach of dark thunder clouds blowing in from the Irish Sea. A thunderstorm would make this easy track a quagmire and wash away signs of the passing of these men. No one at Shipbrook could follow a track like he could. They had not been trained to it as he had, but if he returned to get help, even he might find the track too washed out to follow. Then all hope of rescue might be lost. It was a risk he could not take. He must hang to their trail, for if they disappeared into the wilds of the Welsh borderland, and their trail lost, there would be no easy salvation for the girl.

Roland settled the horse into a steady trot and unwrapped the longbow from its rough cloth and slung it over his shoulder. He secured his quiver of arrows to the pommel of the saddle and the dagger, he tucked in the leather belt around his waist. He knew not where this trail would end, but he knew his duty to Sir Roger and to Lady Millicent. So help him, if they harmed a *hair* on the Little Lady's head…Roland forced the thought away. As he tracked the Welsh raiders, the first fat drops of rain began to strike about him. The storm was coming.

***

Ahead, the group of horsemen also felt the first drops of rain. The leader, astride the fine Norman courser, smiled. He didn't expect his captive to be missed for a few hours and, if anyone at the castle was capable of tracking them, there would be little sign left after the storm did its work.

This foray across the border was to have been a simple probe. It was three years since they had last come this way into Cheshire and that raid had been a bloody disaster. Sir Roger de Laval, the local Norman knight, had laid a trap for them, and they had ridden directly into it. They were lucky to escape with half their numbers. *But three years is a long time.* Fear, and the vigilance that goes with it, can fade. *Perhaps, the owner of Shipbrook castle had grown lax.*

He had convinced his clansmen that the time was right to test the Normans. The man glanced over his shoulder at the girl. Stumbling on her in the forest had been a stroke of luck. The quality of her mount marked her as gentry and she was almost certainly from the nearby castle of Shipbrook. As such, she would bring a rich ransom—but he was a man of vision and he had already devised a bolder plan.

For generations, the men of his clan had grown wealthy and powerful from their frequent raids into the rich lands of Cheshire. The coming of the Norman lords, with their chain of castles protecting the Welsh Marches, had made raiding a risky business. A party bent on plunder might slip by these fortified posts, but any attack on a settlement instantly raised an alarm. With knights and men-at-arms alerted, it was no sure thing that the Welshmen could escape back across the border with their lives—much less their booty. Without the wealth brought from raiding, the clans of the borderlands were growing weak—and weakness, in the land of Wales, was a very dangerous thing.

Why exchange this girl for ransom, when, if held hostage, she could open a permanent gate to all of Cheshire? Surely the Lord of Shipbrook would see the wisdom of turning a blind eye to certain travellers from the south passing through his lands, rather than hazard the life of his kinswoman. The man looked at the young girl trailing behind. This was probably the daughter of Sir Roger, judging from the quality of her dress and, more importantly, the quality of the mount he now rode. Would this Norman betray his duty for a daughter? The man thought that he might. A flash of lightning flickered across the dark clouds that had rolled in from the Irish Sea and were now almost overhead. As the rumble of thunder rolled across the darkening hills, the rain came in all its fury, drenching the party and making visibility difficult.

On a small highland pony Lady Millicent de Laval bent her head forward against the downpour. As they moved through the storm she glanced backwards down the trail. *How long would it be until someone discovered her missing?* She had free run to ride these hills in the afternoon and her absence would not typically be noticed until the evening meal. Even if the storm prompted a question as to her whereabouts, it would be assumed that she had taken shelter somewhere to wait out the worst of the rain. No…pursuit would take hours to begin and, by then, much of their trail would be washed away.

In the driving rain, she knew that her movements were less visible, even at close quarters. Carefully, she let her bound hands slide down and felt the hard lump of the small dagger which her father had insisted she fasten beneath her garments whenever she went riding alone. Such a weapon was useless against this many assailants and so she had kept it concealed. Thankfully they had thought her so insignificant a threat that they had not searched her person. Perhaps the weapon would find a use later.

Now she was intent on leaving some sign for those who would surely follow. She eased up the hem of her riding dress and tore off a small piece of fabric, letting if fall to the trail beneath her. The rider behind her showed no sign that he had seen this, as his own mount plodded stolidly past the point where the cloth had fallen. *If nature would leave no trail for her pursuers to follow, she would!* She could only pray that someone would have eyes sharp enough to see such a tiny marker in the murk and the mud left by the growing storm.

***

Roland reined his horse to a halt. The rain still fell in sheets and he had to use one hand to shield his eyes so that he could make out the increasingly faint trail. He had almost missed it, but there, unmistakably, was something floating in a puddle that didn't belong there. He slid off his mount and picked the tiny piece of material from the muddy water. It was a piece of cloth, ripped ragged along one edge. Even covered in muddy water, its colour could be made out. It was the same as that worn by Millicent.

Roland let out a quiet whoop. *The girl was planting a trace!* Whatever his past feelings about the sometimes-arrogant young woman, he had to admire her resourcefulness. Dragged through a blinding storm by strange abductors, she still had the presence of mind to mark her trail! The girl had spine—and brains.

He remounted his horse and continued along the trail, keeping a close eye out for new fragments on the muddy path. He was not disappointed. With steady regularity he found another piece of cloth every half mile or so. At one point, where the trail branched, Millicent had been quick enough to drop a marker near the fork on the correct path. He only hoped she didn't become too bold and risk being discovered when the cover of rain lifted. It was beginning to slack and, as quickly as it had come, the rain stopped. Clouds still scuttered about overhead, but the sky was growing lighter. With the end of the downpour, the trail left by eight hurrying horses slowly became more evident. As if on command, the tiny fragments of clothing ceased to appear.

The trail led southwest out of the low hills and into a marshy section of land that bordered the estuary of the River Dee. It was unfamiliar to the boy, but it was clear they were heading towards the ford of the river. It was the only place the Dee could be crossed for miles and the most direct path to the frontier. These lowlands were not far from Shipbrook, but Millicent had steered clear of them during his riding instructions. He knew that a false step in these bogs could quickly trap and sink a horse and rider.

The men ahead of him seemed to know these marshes well, as the trail showed no signs of riders searching out a path. It plunged right into the tall grass and Roland could see that, though overgrown, it had been used before. Traversing the marshes after the storm had passed made for slow progress. From time-to-time, shore birds sprang from their hiding places in nearby pools at his approach. Seeing this, the boy halted, and raised himself high in his stirrups. He looked ahead to where the marsh melted into the river and, sure enough, saw a small flock of frightened waterfowl take wing less than a mile away. He was closing on his quarry!

Roland had only taken his eyes off the trail for a moment to look ahead. It was a costly mistake. Rough hands grabbed his tunic and dragged him from his horse onto the boggy ground. The boy was already twisting violently away from his attacker, as he landed on the spongy turf and sprang to his feet. It was just as Sir Alwyn had taught him. His quick reaction broke the grip of the man and left the two standing, facing one another on the mucky path. Silently, Roland cursed himself for failing to foresee that the raiders would leave a guard on their back trail. He had ridden right into the trap!

His horse had skittered a dozen yards away taking his quiver of arrows out of reach. The boy eased his longbow off his back and tossed it aside while never taking his eyes off his attacker. The man he faced was bulkier than Roland and very much intent on killing him. The boy was scared, but offered a quick prayer of thanks for the hard lessons Sir Alwyn had been drilling into him.

The Welshman launched himself at Roland with a guttural oath. To his surprise, the boy took a quick step forward and drove the heel of his hand into his chin, twisting away to the right in the same motion. The man's head snapped back and he lost his footing in the muck. He was down in an instant, but whirled around like a cat before Roland could move in for another blow. He rubbed his chin and spat in the brackish water by the path.

"What be ye doing in these swamps, boy?" he demanded. His accent was so thick Roland could barely understand him. The man circled slowly to his right.

"Come to get the girl," Roland replied simply. He saw little purpose in lying—either he or his attacker would be dead in but a short while.

"Har! Yer a bold lad, but I'll be spillin' yer guts for yer trouble. The girl is gone and no one comes back from the Clocaenog Forest without our leave."

Roland still had difficulty with the man's dialect, but he recognized one word—*Clocaenog.* He had heard both Sir Roger and Sir Alwyn speak of it in dark tones. It was at the edge of this trackless forest, years ago, that his master had earned the keys to Shipbrook by defending his liege, the Earl of Chester. Clocaenog had been the stronghold of some of the fiercest of the Welsh clans for decades. The Saxons and the Normans, each in their turn, had sent large contingents of troops into these woods to root out the clans. Few of these men ever returned. This complicated his task immensely. He had to act, before Millicent was beyond all help in that distant forest.

All of this calculation took place in but an instant of time. The initial blow to his chin had enraged the larger man and his eyes now blazed with fury as he lowered his head and charged forward, intending to overwhelm his smaller foe. Roland was reminded of Sir Alwyn's words about the Welsh. They had the fury, but lacked control. Roland sidestepped deftly and drove his fist into the man's ear as he slid by. This made his attacker roar in even greater anger. If he ever laid hold of Roland, he would surely tear him apart.

Roland had no intention of letting that happen. More was at stake here than his own survival. *He must live for the sake of Lady Millicent.* Nothing else mattered. As the man turned to launch

126

another charge he stopped as though reminded of something. A leering grin split his face. He reached over his shoulder and slowly withdrew a large two-handed broadsword that had been hitched to his back.

"If ye insist on hoppin' about like a frog, boy, I'll be giggin' ye like one!" he said, and laughed at his own joke. With the sword held in the guard position, he advanced steadily toward Roland. The boy scrambled backwards, frantically trying to think of a way to defend himself. His bow had been flung aside in the tall grass and the sway-backed horse had retreated a safe distance up the trail when his rider had been unseated. Then he remembered the dagger at his belt—the gift of Ivo Brun. It was a decent weapon, if you could grapple with a man, but the wild Welshman advancing toward him would never let him get close enough to be effective. He'd use the reach advantage of the broadsword to run him through. He could think of only one desperate ploy, and he had to use it quickly, as the man was almost on him.

Roland counted on the man's anger overcoming his good sense. If he figured wrong, both he and Lady Millicent would be lost. With feigned clumsiness, he let his rear foot slip in the slimy mud and went down on one knee. Seeing an opening, the man leapt to seize the advantage and finish this pesky boy. Rather than simply stepping forward and ending the struggle with a straight thrust, he swung the great broadsword high over his head to bring a crushing blow down on Roland's skull. Spurred by his anger, he sought to not just kill the boy, but to cleave him in two. He had not seen Roland gently slide the dagger from his belt as he slipped to the ground. When he did see it, it was too late.

The boy who knelt helplessly before him suddenly exploded forward. The great broadsword was fully extended behind the man's back and could not be brought into play. With a straight thrust, Roland sank the dagger into the Welshman's groin. The man uttered a wrenching scream, as he let the broadsword tumble into the mud. He stumbled backwards and fell to his seat in a puddle, clutching his wound.

Roland wiped the blade of his dagger on his pant leg and retrieved the sword. Just as he had done to Sir Alwyn, he nudged the point of the weapon under the sitting man's chin.

"Tell me where they go, or you're a dead man," he said.

Between groans, the man spat on the wet ground.

"Ye'll no doubt kill me anyway, pup. I'll not say," the man managed.

"I'll not, and that's my word—but I will if you don't tell me the truth." He pressed the blade forward slightly. The man squirmed.

"Awright then...they go to Clocaenog...like I said. They'll hold her there.

Clocaenog. He had feared this and now his fears were confirmed. Roland was painfully aware that, with each passing moment, Millicent was moving closer to that dread place.

"Where in Clocaenog.man!" Again he increased the pressure of the blade on the man's neck.

"At Bleddyn's keep," he blurted. "Won't do ye no good t' know."

He could spare no more time questioning this scoundrel. He withdrew the blade tip from the man's throat and, stepping forward, drove the butt of the weapon against the man's temple. He was out before his head hit the ground. Roland ripped open the man's breeches and examined the dagger wound. It was deep, but seemed to have hit no major organs. With luck, the man should survive—if the bleeding stopped. The boy ripped a section of fabric from the man's tunic and wadded it tightly against the wound. It was a rough dressing, but it would have to do.

He retrieved his bow and walked back up the path until he encountered his poor horse, looking frightened and confused. He steadied the horse and, with his dagger, hurriedly etched a message on the leather of the saddle. Thank God Lady Catherine had taught him his letters. He was far from sure that the words *Clocaenog* and *Millicent* had been properly fashioned, but he was certain they were close enough. Sir Roger would understand the meaning of this message, if, as he prayed, this stupid horse could find its way home. He turned the beast to face back along the marsh trail that led to firmer ground and, beyond that, to Shipbrook. He gave it a sharp slap on the backside and watched it step lively back down the path.

When the horse was out of sight, Roland turned back and secured his weapons. Without further delay, he broke into a steady trot along the marshy path. The trail was easy to follow now. From the time he was ten, he had helped his father chase down deer in the mountains and he knew he could sustain this pace for hours, eating up the miles. Though his quarry was mounted, he did not think they would gain much distance on him in this marsh and in the hills to come. Somewhere ahead, he had to overtake them—somewhere before they reached Clocaenog.

Chapter 13

Pursuit

Sir Roger de Laval was troubled. Both his daughter and his squire had been absent from the evening meal and it was unlike either to miss a feeding. Millicent was known to sometimes lose track of the hour when out riding. This was often the case in the summer months, when the light lingered well into the evening—but there had been a storm. He would have expected her to return once the rain had ceased.

The Lord of Shipbrook had summoned Sir Alwyn and Declan O'Duinne to join him as soon as the meal was finished. They would ride out to find their wayward charges and again warn the headstrong Millicent not to stray too long from the castle. It had been three years since they had turned back the last raiding party from the Marches, but this was still a rough frontier.

The two knights and the squire were just leading their mounts from the paddock when a lathered, sway-backed horse trotted into the courtyard and immediately stuck his nose into the water trough. All recognized that this was Roland's horse. Sir Roger felt his level of alarm rise higher. The group gathered around the tired horse and searched for some clue as to the absent rider.

"Roger, look here!" exclaimed Sir Alwyn. He pointed to a spot near the edge of the saddle.

Sir Roger flinched as he made out the rude message.

"*Clocaenog*! My God, Alwyn, Millie's been taken!

"It'd have to be Bleddyn's men if they come from the Clocaenog," Alwyn said, grimly. "I thought he'd left us be for good, after we bloodied his last raiding party."

Roger De Laval thought back to his last encounter with Bleddyn and his raiders. He and Alwyn had cornered them against the River Dee and there was much slaughter, but the leader had managed to swim his little pony across the channel as his men covered his escape with their lives. Bleddyn was not the only raider from the west, but he was the most savage. Rarely satisfied to plunder, he and his men thought nothing of butchering defenceless peasants and burning a hamlet as they fled back across the border.

"Aye, Alwyn, it may be Bleddyn, but may God have mercy on whoever it is," Sir Roger said, with finality, "for I shall not!"

"What of Roland, my lord," asked Declan.

"Perhaps, taken as well, or killed," Sir Roger stated bluntly. "Don't know how he managed this message—but it had to be him. He's a brave lad. I hope he lives." The big knight mounted Bucephalus and motioned to a house servant.

"Tell Lady Catherine what has happened when she returns from Chester. Tell her to remain here. I *shall* return with our daughter." The servant bowed in acknowledgement. Bucephalus, sensing his master's urgency reared in excitement.

Sir Roger whirled the great warhorse around to face Sir Alwyn and Declan. By now a half dozen men-at-arms had gathered with their own mounts. "Follow me, lads! We go to hunt the Welsh!" He gave Bucephalus a sharp dig with his heels and led his men into the gathering dusk.

***

Less than ten miles away, Roland knelt in the cover of the tall grass which grew along the main channel of the River Dee. He faced a dilemma. The ford was an obvious place for the raiders to leave another guard on their back trail. A man concealed on the south bank could spot anyone trying to cross the river. The tide was up and the ford would be at its deepest now. Roland had spied a heavy branch snagged on the bank when he had reached this point half an hour before. It was just what he needed to float across the channel, but he had resisted the urge to plunge in. Instead, he focused all of his hunter's skills on scanning the opposite bank. He would give it a few more minutes and, if nothing was revealed, he would make his way down to the river bank and resume his pursuit.

There! It had been a small movement, of dark against dark, but it was not the natural sway of the marsh grass. Something had moved on the opposite bank. It could have been some creature of the bogs, but Roland knew it wasn't. It was one of the raiders, watching for a pursuer entering the river. Roland exhaled slowly and again calculated his options. He would have to make his way upstream, through at least a mile of swamp, to find a place to cross without being seen. There was no time for such a manoeuvre. There seemed but one solution, short of giving up his attempt to follow Millicent. He must eliminate the watcher on the other bank.

Having made up his mind, the boy wasted no more thought on the decision. He drew an iron-tipped shaft from his quiver, nocked it and smoothly drew the bow to its full arc. The shot was less than a hundred yards. If the man had not moved again, he would not miss. He released the shaft and focused intently on the far bank.

There was a moment of silence as sound took its time crossing the distance. Then, Roland heard a shriek and a man half rose from the grass by the water's edge. The boy could see his shaft sunk deep in the man's chest. The raider tumbled headfirst down the bank and sank into the muddy water. Roland made a swift prayer to God, to again be understanding, plunged down the riverbank and pushed his makeshift raft into the current.

He did not know how to swim and had never been in water deeper than the shallow mountain streams that ran off the slopes of Kinder Scout. He had crossed the Aire River with Sir Roger and Declan, but the water had hardly reached his waist. Here, the water came up to his neck, even near the shore, and further out the bottom was quickly lost. He was petrified. He flailed his legs, in part to propel himself toward the far shore and, in part, out of fear that some unknown creature from the depths of the river might seize him and drag him under. He had never been so happy as when his feet touched bottom on the opposite bank and he scrambled back

132

onto the marshy ground.

The boy checked his weapons and turned to see what had become of the man he had shot, but the river had already claimed the body. Roland turned back to the muddy trail, which headed through the marsh and toward the high ground visible in the distance. He resumed his steady trot, determined to gain ground on the little Welsh ponies ahead of him. It was now starting to get dark. He didn't expect Millicent's captors to rest and neither would he. He ran on into the night.

***

The boy had been smart to send the horse back with his message. Roger De Laval hoped it had not cost him his life. Knowing Millie was being taken to Clocaenog narrowed their search. There were few approaches to the River Dee ford where the boggy land was firm enough to support horses, and the Dee must be crossed to get to the borderlands. These paths had been used by raiders for as long as men had plundered across these wild lands and Sir Roger knew them by heart.

The first path they struck had shown no evidence of any passage but as they approached the next the knight noticed Bucephalus' ears prick up, and reined in the grey destrier. He had learned long ago, to trust the instincts of his horse in hostile territory. Here they discovered a faint trail left by the men who had taken Millie. Much of the sign had washed away, but enough marsh grass had been uprooted to indicate that horses had recently passed this way.

There was no sign of the boy, and this did nothing to ease Sir Roger's anxiety. He urged the horse slowly forward, looking for what had alerted Bucephalus. There, to the side of the muddy trail, sat a man in rough dress, leaning against a weathered stump. He made no move to flee as Sir Roger dismounted, drew his broadsword, and approached.

"You there. Tell me what ye know, and tell it fast or ye're a dead man." No one, looking into the knight's eyes, could have doubted his sincerity.

The man struggled to speak, grimacing and clutching his groin. He held up his hand, signalling a need to catch his breath. Sir Roger waited, idly swinging the broadsword in his huge hands.

"Ye...be the Lord...of Shipbrook?" the man managed.

Sir Roger stepped forward and placed the tip of the blade on the man's breastbone.

"*I ask the questions here!*" he said, with barely controlled rage. "Now speak!" By this time, the rest of party from Shipbrook had gathered near.

"The girl...is unharmed," the man gasped. "Taken...taken to Clocaenog. Will be held...held in safety there."

"*Taken by whom? Held by whom?*" thundered Sir Roger.

"Bleddyn."

"And what will be the ransom, you son of a Welsh dog?" Sir Roger asked quietly, but with clear menace in his voice.

"Bleddyn says she's t' be held safe as...*guarantee.*"

"Guarantee? Guarantee of what?"

"Free...free passage...to raid...Cheshire" the wounded man managed.

Sir Roger and Sir Alwyn looked at each in consternation. This was unexpected.

"Impossible!" Sir Roger sputtered. "We could not betray our own folk, thus!"

Sir Alwyn grasped his friend's arm.

"Roger, it's *Millicent* yer talkin' about here. If we can't get her back...betrayal may be our only choice."

Sir Roger's shoulders sagged, as he realized the awful decision he might be forced to make.

"Then we must get her back, Alwyn—we must!"

From behind Sir Roger, Declan O'Duinne stepped toward the injured raider. He could not wait a moment longer to speak. He grasped the man by his rough tunic and pulled his face close.

"What have ye done with Roland, dog?"

"Roland?" the man shook his head in confusion.

"The boy! What of the boy? Is he dead?

The man's head turned to the side and spat on the ground.

"He will be dead...if I get another chance at him! Gave me this...he did." The man nodded toward his wound. "Tricky, that one...but ye'll no doubt find his body further along. One of our lads...he'll get him sure!"

Declan let the man fall back and turned to Sir Roger.

"He lives, my lord! And he's on their trail!" he fairly shouted.

"By Gad, Roger. He did learn something in me classes!" added Alwyn.

Sir Roger said nothing for a moment, but his shoulders no longer sagged in resignation. Millicent may be in the grasp of his enemies, but she was not totally alone out there. There was a boy— a damned resourceful boy—dogging her trail. There was hope.

It was growing very dark now. He motioned to one of his men-at-arms. "Take this trash back to the castle and secure him," he said, nodding toward their captive. "Have his wound tended to. We may have more questions for him. If we do not come back within the week...*kill him*."

***

Lady Millicent clung to the saddle of her pony as it steadily climbed the low range of hills that she could barely make out against the night sky. For not the first time since her capture, she wondered at the stamina and agility of these tough little mounts. She wouldn't trade her Norman thoroughbred for one, but if chance ever allowed, she would be pleased to own one of these rugged Welsh steeds.

She knew they were now climbing up into the Clywdian Range, a rampart of high hills that ran from the west coast of Wales clear to the border of Cheshire. She had never been allowed to venture here, but her mother was familiar with these lands and had included them in her lessons on geography.

"Geography is fate, child," Lady Catherine was fond of saying. "We Saxons ventured across the narrow sea to the east into these lands in a time before reckoning. We were protected for eons by the sea, but then the Norse and later the Normans used it as a highway for invasion. The Scots and the Welsh have been more fortunate. Their lands are mountainous and rugged. Nor are they so rich as to tempt a conqueror. You will be Lady to a Lord someday Millicent, but you must not be ignorant of such things. You may be the *servant* of your husband—or his ally. It's your knowledge that will make it one or the other."

Millicent had sniffed at this. "I'll be servant to no man,

135

Mother…and since *you've* married the only man in England worthy to be a husband—I expect to be a spinster!"

Lady Catherine smiled at her daughter. "Aye, lass, I caught a good one, but I have high hopes that you will as well."

Millicent's thoughts were jerked rudely back to the present when a low-hanging branch gave her a stinging slap across her face. The little pony was changing directions, and had started up the next leg of a winding switchback trail. Now that it was dark, she resumed her cautious marking of the trail. Someone would be following, sooner or later, and by now her father would have raised the alarm and would be searching the lands around Shipbrook for her. She only hoped that he would strike her trail and follow it through the marshes and hills. She must have faith, for beyond her wits and the little knife under her skirt, she had little else.

***

In the darkness, three miles behind, the boy maintained a steady trot as he followed the clear track of eight horses across the narrow coastal plain. The moon was just rising over the approaching hills and it easily illuminated the track churned up by the ponies in their passage. He had even spied another small piece of Lady Millicent's dress and took comfort that she was still alive and keeping her wits about her. Roland knew his pace would have to slow in the hills, but so too would that of his quarry. He picked up speed, as the high ground loomed nearer. High ground was all that he had known his whole life. He would feel at home on the slopes ahead—even though it be in enemy country.

As the night advanced, Roland ran steadily uphill. His lungs ached and his legs felt heavy and leaden. He had run without pausing since leaving the marshes behind and the last miles had been steep ones. Judging from the contour of the land, the crest of the ridge was near. This was confirmed as the steep slope began to flatten.

The track suddenly emerged from deep woods onto a high, treeless area choked with heather and gorse. In less than a minute, he had reached the summit and could see what lay ahead. By now the moon had risen to the point that it cast an extraordinary illumination on the descending slope and on the broad valley far below. Boulders around the ridgeline cast eerie moon shadows around him. In other circumstances, he would have thought it beautiful.

The floor of the valley was a mix of forest and a few scattered meadows and, far off at its centre, was the silvery strand of a river. This must be the Clywd. Lady Catherine had spoken of this river during her lessons. No point of light shone in the lowlands ahead. This was indeed a wild borderland. He could vaguely make out a dark plateau that rose on the far side of the valley that extended to the horizon. It was Clocaenog.

The path was now downward and Roland let his body lean forward as he picked up speed. With luck, he hoped to catch the raiders in the valley below, before they crossed the river. There would be only five left now and he might have a fighting chance of taking most of them with his bow. If he did not catch them there, he knew he would have to follow them into Clocaenog. The thought made the hair stand up on the back of his neck. He ran faster.

At length, the slope became less steep and the woods thinned. He was nearing the river valley. To his surprise, he noticed the sky to the east was now showing the first hints of dawn. He had lost all track of time during the long night of pursuit. Now, he would have to be more cautious. It took hardly more than an hour for him to cover the level ground that led down to the river. He now saw that some of the meadows were actually small cultivated fields and he could only hope that the peasants who tilled them would not be stirring this early.

Moving slowly through a light fog that clung to the low areas near the river, the boy came to an abrupt down slope that led to the meandering channel of the River Clywd. The signs on the muddy bank showed that the horses had crossed here. Exposed rocks in the slow current confirmed that it was a ford.

Roland observed all this, from the concealment of thick brush near the water. The river was the last natural barrier before the forest itself. He knew there was a chance that this crossing was being watched, but he could no longer afford to wait or detour. He prayed the raiders felt secure this close to home and splashed into the shallow river. Roland held his longbow, quiver and the broadsword he'd taken over his head, as he crossed. No one challenged his passage.

On the far bank, he took a moment to survey the land. The track of the raiders resolutely followed the trail to the limits of his view, where it disappeared into a dark mass of woods. He had lost the race. He would have to follow them into the Clocaenog.

Chapter 14

Clocaenog

It was mid-morning when the raiding party arrived at the fortress. Millicent had not slept in over twenty-four hours and had ridden hard for the past eighteen. She was exhausted, but forced herself to pay attention as they passed through the massive timber gate. Any detail noted might be important when the time came to make good her escape—*and escape she would!* She knew her father would somehow find her trail and would follow her to this place. She must prevent that, at all costs. She had watched the terrain carefully since her capture and had come to the painful realization that only an army could force its way into the Clocaenog. But her father would try, and would certainly die in these dark woods if she could not get herself free. Without appearing obvious, she scanned every detail of the fort, before she was roughly pulled from her saddle.

The leader of the raiding party had turned her bay mare over to a servant to be fed and watered and was splashing his dust-streaked face from a horse trough. Several men crowded around him as he squeezed the water out of his long, black hair. The man was half a head taller than any of the other Welshmen and had the unmistakable air of command about him.

"What prize have ye brought here, me lord?" said one man motioning toward Millicent.

"A valuable one, I'm thinkin'," replied the leader, with a broad smile. "Bring the girl here!" He took a seat at the top of a flight of steps leading to the entrance of the single large dwelling within the enclosure and continued to smile as the girl was dragged across the dusty courtyard. The man's smile had no mirth or warmth behind it and Millicent did not try to resist.

"You're a fair rider, lass. Tell us your name," he said to the young girl.

"Millie Brown, my lord," Millicent replied, meekly, trying to appear cowed in her captivity.

"Millie Brown? I think not, my lady. Ye are daughter, or perhaps niece, to Sir Roger de Laval, are ye not?

"Oh no, my lord," she replied with her head hung low. "I'm the daughter of the laundress at Shipbrook—*And I'd drown you in a wash pot if I could*," she thought to herself.

"Ho! The scrubwoman's daughter!" The man seated before her hooted and slapped his knee. "That's a good one lass, but never has one so low born worn such a fine dress and ridden such a fine mount!" The men on all sides of him hooted and one stepped forward to sample the fine cloth of her dress, only to retreat when he saw the black look on his chief's face.

"So tell me, scrubwoman's daughter, how passes Sir Roger and does he ever speak of his old friend, Bleddyn?" the leader asked after the laughter had died down.

Millicent knew full well they did not believe her lie, but was determined not to give them the satisfaction of admitting her identity. She was also determined to convince them that she was too frightened to cause any trouble.

"The Lord of Shipbrook seems in good health...my lord and I know naught of ...Bleddyn or other of the Lord's...friends." Millicent replied, in a quavering voice.

"Well *know* this, child of Shipbrook," Bleddyn said, his voice grown suddenly harsh as he stood and stepped forward. He grasped her tangled hair and twisted it in a single rough hand. His foul breathe gagged her as he used her hair to pull her face close to his. "I have been too long from Sir Roger's acquaintance and cannot wait 'til we meet once more. He shall pay dearly to have ye back, I'm wagering, and if he will not, well, I will think of something amusing to do with you."

Millicent did not have to play at being frightened. She could see that there was no hint of mercy or pity in the man's face. *"You will not find it amusing when my father comes for me!"* she thought silently. Bleddyn released her and motioned to a couple of his henchmen that he was finished with the girl for the moment. As she was being led away toward a side entrance to the dwelling she glanced around and saw that her horse had been secured in a small paddock on the same side of the building. She also noticed that the gate to this fortress appeared to be routinely left open, at least during daylight hours. The lookout, perched high above the compound could easily spot any approaching trouble in ample time to sound the alarm and have the gates secured. The beginnings of a simple plan took shape in the girl's mind.

***

Roland moved with great care, picking his way through the underbrush where it existed, and darting from tree to tree where the forest floor was clear. As he had moved deeper into this ancient woodland, the trees had grown larger and taller. At times they so blocked the sun that he had trouble reckoning a direction from the scattered light. In the larger stands of oak and chestnut, there was little cover—save for deadfall—as the brush could not grow in the sparse sun. There were game trails aplenty, and Roland kept to these as long as they meandered near the path he was following. From time to time, he would stray from cover to make sure the pony track was still there. He worried that his need for stealth was forcing him to fall further behind, but he had little choice. The Welsh must not know he was here or they would be on guard. He could not afford that.

For all that morning, the land had risen gradually, then plateaued. There had scarcely been a clearing in the miles of unbroken forest. The boy had known little but the ways of the forest his whole life, but the gloom of these dark woods unsettled him. As midday approached he began to pick up the distance sounds of some sort of settlement—the high yip of a dog and a faint but steady sound of metal on metal, perhaps a smith. At last he reached the edge of a clearing that had been made by men, not nature. For many acres around, the trees had been felled by the ax. From a point, out of sight over a small rise, a thin ribbon of wood smoke rose above the tree line. The trail of the ponies disappeared over that rise. Here was where they had taken Millicent.

With even greater care, Roland began to circle the clearing. The familiar noises that indicated the presence of men became more distinct. He caught the high pitched squeals of children at play and thought he heard a rooster. Finally, he arrived at a vantage point where he could safely view the source of these sounds. He lay flat on his stomach, a yard in from the edge of the wood line and surveyed the scene. In the centre of the clearing was a rough wooden palisade, with a single high timber tower inside. The roof ridge of some sort of dwelling could be seen above the sharpened logs that made up the fortress wall. Bleddyn's keep was a rude fortification, but effective enough. A force of any size, seeking to invest this place, could be harassed and ambushed at a hundred different points along the trail. No stone castle was needed here. The forest was enough.

As the sun reached its midpoint, Roland eased back further into the brush and considered his options. The trees had been cleared for hundreds of yards in each direction from the fort, so approach by day was impossible and by night, risky. Approach he must, though. There could be no doubt that Millicent was being held here, and a way must be found to free her.

Just then, the boy froze. A sizable group of men had issued forth from the single gate in the wooden wall and were moving rapidly across the clearing. Each man was armed with a bow, as well as various blade weapons. No doubt, this contingent had been dispatched to lay in wait for any possible pursuit from Shipbrook. This added a new complication for the boy to consider. If he could not get Millicent out of here before Sir Roger arrived—there being no doubt that he would be coming—the rescue party from Shipbrook would be cut to pieces in the depths of these woods, long before they reached this place.

"So it must be soon," he said, grimly to himself. He was frightened, but pushed that aside. The boy settled down to watch

the fort from his invisible vantage point. He must study every inch of the place and find a weakness—if there was one.

***

Sir Roger de Laval said a prayer for the long twilight of summer. There was just barely enough light to ford the River Dee and he had ordered torches to be lit. Moving through the marshes on the other bank in full dark would be suicidal.

"Sir Roger, look there!" Declan O'Duinne shouted over the splashing of the horses. There was a section of the approaching bank off to the right where the torches revealed tall marsh grass had been crushed downward. Something large had obviously slid down that bank into the water. What drew the Irish boy's attention was the trail of blackening blood on the bent stems. Once again, Sir Roger could barely take a breath. *It could not be Millie!*

"Declan, go look," the big knight said. He could not bring himself to see what may lie at the end of that bloody slick. The squire spurred his horse downstream along the bank and around a small bend. The waving green grass quickly obscured him from view. A moment later a shout was heard and he came splashing back.

"Sir Roger, Sir Alwyn, you must see this!" he called excitedly.

The two knights turned their own mounts and followed the boy around the bend. There, half submerged in an eddy, was a body—floating face down. The dress was not that of Millicent or Roland, and Sir Roger let himself exhale.

"Turn him over," ordered Sir Alwyn.

Declan dismounted, as did one of the men-at-arms. They grasped the man and turned him face upwards. The body had started to swell a bit, and they were struck by the surprised look on the man's face. The source of that surprise was evident in the flickering light of the torch. From his chest protruded an arrow. Declan grasped the shaft and pulled it free.

"My lord, as sure as Patrick is a Saint, this is Roland's arrow!" he exclaimed, after a moment's examination.

Sir Roger had already dismounted and he made his way through the sucking muck of the river bottom to where Declan stood, brandishing the shaft. He took the arrow and held it before him with two hands. He looked at Sir Alwyn and the Welshman scowled.

"He must have dropped this fellow from the other bank," he said, surveying the distance of the shot. Only one thing could do that. "Ye told me the lad had a bow, but neglected to say it was a *longbow*."

"I was going to surprise you," Sir Roger said sheepishly.

"I had no idea the boy was this lethal, Roger, but thank God he is."

Chapter 15

Escape

Sir Roger looked up at the sun and fretted. They were nearing the crest of the Clywdian range as midday approached. Though they were making haste, he knew they would not reach the Clocaenog until dusk. Entering that forest in daylight was hugely hazardous, at best, but entering at night would be suicidal. They would have to make yet another camp before they could follow this trail to its end! His instincts as a father were to ignore this fact and press onward. His daughter was in the hands of his enemies, and it was up to him to extract her! His experience as a soldier, however, kept him in check. He knew he would be leading these men to their death, if he proceeded in darkness—and dead, they would do Millie no good. He sighed and kept his own counsel.

***

During the course of the long afternoon, Roland moved methodically around the wood line, observing the fortress of the Welsh raiders from every angle. To his dismay, he saw no obvious weaknesses. Nowhere had brush been allowed to grow in the cleared ground. The closest thing to cover was a small streambed, which issued from underneath the west side of the wooden palisade. They must have built this structure around a natural spring, and this was the small channel it had cut over eons of flow.

He guessed that Lady Millicent was being held in the large dwelling, but could not be sure. The boy groaned in frustration. There seemed to be no strategy that would get him in and out of that fortress alive, much less affect the rescue of the girl. By his own reckoning, any force coming from Shipbrook would probably reach the fringes of the Clocaenog by dusk and, as a veteran campaigner, his master would have the good sense to wait until light before trying to enter. What came after could only be calamity. He must act, even if he had no good plan.

Roland resolved to use the cover of darkness to work his way up the streambed to the base of the wall. From there he would find some way to gain entrance to the place. Once inside he would hide himself and watch. With luck, there would be some sign of where Lady Millicent was being held. *Without luck, I'll be dead before I ever reach the wall,*

***

The night seemed endless to Millicent. She had been placed in a small room that was designed to hold Bleddyn's prisoners. There was a small window, barred with weathered oak that was as strong as steel. The door was heavy oak as well, and was secured on the outside by an iron latch that lowered into a slot on the jam. She had observed this as she was being shoved inside. For most of the afternoon and evening, she had lain on the one piece of furniture—a rough plank shelf—and whimpered, just loudly enough for the guard to hear. To any observer, she was a very frightened and heartsick girl. In truth, she was all of that—but not helpless and despairing.

After long hours, she crept to the small window and peered out. As she hoped, the guard was sound asleep. She returned to her rude bed and reached under her long skirt. Why they had not searched her, she did not know. Perhaps, they would not expect a mere girl to be armed, but in this, they were mistaken. Her father had insisted and Lady Catherine had agreed that, if she were to be allowed the freedom to ride in the miles around Shipbrook, she would have some small protection. The girl's hand closed on the handle of the small dagger. Removing it, she went to the door and traced her finger along the narrow crack between door and frame.

She had already determined that the door fit snugly into its opening, but there was a tiny space there. Carefully, she forced the blade of the dagger into the hard wood, at about the level of the outer latch. With luck, she could widen the crack enough by dawn to slip the blade through and lift the latch from within. If she succeeded, she was certain she could be out the door and on her horse before the guard could bar her way—even if he were awake. If she could clear that gate on her thoroughbred, they would have a devil of a time catching her with those scrawny little ponies!

She must be ready, and prayed that she would hear the sound when the main gate was opened in the morning. She had listened intently, as full dark had fallen, and had heard a faint groaning and scraping sound that she was sure was the heavy gate being closed. She was counting on catching a similar sound when it opened. That would be the moment to act!

***

Night took long to arrive in midsummer, even in these gloomy woods. Roland had little choice but to burrow down into a thicket and wait until full darkness fell. As he waited he continued to watch, but saw nothing that would gain him any advantage in approaching the fort. It was a clear night and warm. There was only a thin sliver of a moon and a few stars that shown through a thin layer of clouds.

He wished for another storm to roll in and mask his movements, but none came and, as the evening advanced the sounds from within the enclosure slowly quieted. He could see a guard in the tower near the main gate and another, faintly, along the back wall, but save for the occasional whinny from a horse corral somewhere inside, all was quiet. He reckoned that most within were now asleep.

Carefully he slipped out of his secure hiding place in the thicket and slid down to where the stream passed from the cleared expanse and into the woods where he had been hiding. He reached down and scooped clay from the bank of the small stream and rubbed it over his face and neck. It was a trick his father had taught to conceal himself from game as he waited in ambush. He would be very exposed as he crossed the open area. This might help. He made sure the longbow was secure across his shoulder and over his back and slid into the water.

***

Dawn was well advanced when Roland watched the heavy gate of the fort being swung open. It had taken him most of the night, crawling on his belly through mud and over mossy rocks in the stream bed, to reach the base of the wall. From there, entry into the fort had been easier than expected.

The place where the stream issued under the wall was carefully blocked by iron bars secured to the wooden palisade, but the palisade itself had proven vulnerable. For a nimble boy, there were more than enough handholds in the upright timbers where limbs had been sheared off to allow him to hoist his way up. Near the top, he paused for long minutes waiting for a cloud to fully obscure the crescent moon, then slipped over the barrier and on to the wall walk. The lone guard in the watch tower faced the main gate and saw nothing.

The boy dropped to the ground and found cover in what appeared to be an empty pig sty. It stunk horribly, but was uninhabited. The sty stood between the gate and the main dwelling. It was foul, but was as good a vantage point as he was likely to find. He settled in to wait for dawn.

He still had no plan beyond locating the girl and creating enough havoc to escape in the confusion. A poor plan it was, but he could think of no other. Before it got light, he had unslung his longbow and took half a dozen arrows from his quiver. He did not expect to live, and silently asked God to forgive him his wicked deeds. He also sent a quick prayer up to Odin. On this day, all divine intervention would be welcomed.

As dawn approached people began to stir within the fortress. The boy held his breath as girl of about his age stumbled sleepily from the large hall and headed toward the sty where he hid. To his great relief, she tossed the contents of a chamber pot into the already foul muck near the sty and stumbled back toward the hall.

Two men crossed her path and offered some jest. The offended girl motioned as though to toss the contents of her pot on them and laughed as they scattered. Together, the men heaved up the great crossbar which secured the main gate. With a good deal of grumbling, they slowly swung the gate open.

Roland watched intently as two more men came from a rough barracks near the back wall and headed through the gate carrying axes and with bows and quivers slung over their shoulders—no doubt off to collect the day's supply of firewood. After this brief flurry of activity at the gate, all grew quiet within. The boy was hoping to see some sign that might point him to Millicent's location, but nothing moved for long minutes. He had resolved to risk seeking another vantage point when a mighty uproar burst forth inside the walls.

"What now?" the boy whispered to himself, and sank back into the muck of the pig sty.

***

Millicent, like Roland, heard the groan of the great gate being swung open. Through the small, barred window, she saw that dawn had arrived and heard the steady snore of the guard. She would wait just a few moments for the men attending the gates to move on to other duties, then she would flip the latch—and hope for the best. She saw that her horse was still in the small paddock nearby. Though its saddle and bridle had been removed, she was not daunted. Since she was quite small, she had ridden bareback—and even without reins on a few occasions. She had no doubt she could keep her seat and control the big animal.

She steadied her breathing and moved to the door. A small mound of wood shavings lay on the floor at her feet, evidence of a long night of labour. She peeked through and could see faint daylight on the other side and the dark outline of the latch cutting horizontally across the crack. She slid the dagger into the space she had made and hooked the tip under the latch. Slowly, she lifted, until the latch was free of its cradle.

She took one last deep breath and burst through the door. The guard was half awake and startled, but he was quick and recovered his wits just in time to seize the girl by the arm as she tried to squirm past him. He raised a meaty fist to teach her a lesson she would not soon forget. To his shock, the girl twisted towards him and rammed the dagger he had not seen into his chest. Weakly he released her and sat back into the chair he had occupied all night, staring dumbly at the hilt of the weapon protruding from just above his breast. He reached for it, then toppled to the ground dead.

"The girl...the blasted girl is loose!" someone shouted from across the way. Millicent was focused only on the great horse, which was nervously prancing around its small enclosure. Behind her, she heard other shouts, but did not pause to see from whence they came. Hardly breaking stride, she vaulted over the top rung of the paddock, grabbed the long mane of the horse and swung her slender body upwards. She had never tried this kind of mount, but it proved effective. Within a second, she was astride the thoroughbred and was tightly grasping the mane with both hands.

"Close the gate!" Someone shouted behind her. Using all of her strength, she swung the horse's head about.

"Come on girl, come on!" she whispered urgently in the bay mare's ear. *"Show me your breeding!"* Then gave her a sharp kick in the haunches.

The horse sprang forward with a snort. It cleared the top rung of the paddock by a foot, with Millicent hanging on for dear life. The mare needed no guidance where to head next. She bolted toward the open gate and began to gain speed. One man ran from near the entrance of the dwelling and tried to turn the horse, but the girl urged the animal on, and he was knocked senseless in the dirt of the courtyard.

Two other men had reached the gate and were straining to close it before she could escape. Her heart sank, for there was no way to close the distance in time. But now a new danger caught at the edge of her vision. She whirled to see a nightmare figure, covered in mud and slime, draw a bow and take aim. She steeled herself for the terrible impact of the arrow as the horrible archer released the shaft. To her amazement, no impact came. Instead she heard the angry buzz of the shaft as it sped by her ear. For a moment she was convinced he had missed his target, but a scream from the gate revealed a Welshman sinking to his knees with an arrow in his back. Before she could gather her wits another bolt flew and the second man at the gate fell face forward in the dust.

For a moment she froze as the archer swung to his left and elevated his bow. The guard in the tower had also taken aim with his bow and the two released in the same instant. She heard the sickening sound of both arrows strike flesh, one in the thigh of the man on the ground and one in the heart of the man in the tower.

Everything now happened too swiftly. The Welshman in the tower was still clutching his bow as he toppled from the tower and hit the hard earth of the courtyard with an audible thud. She turned to look at the strange bowman behind her. He had sunk to a sitting position on the ground and stared for a moment at the shaft protruding from his leg. His head flew up and he looked directly at the girl. He was a hideous sight, covered in mud from head to toe, his face completely blackened. Who—or what—was this creature aiding her escape?

"Lady Millicent!" The figure sitting in the dirt shouted at her and frantically waved toward the gate. *"Don't stop. For the love of God—ride!"*

Millicent didn't move. She recognized that voice, but could hardly believe her eyes or ears. The strange bowman was...*Roland Inness!* She would have been no more surprised if King Henry himself had popped up in this forsaken place, but there was little time to ponder this miracle, as three men, led by Bleddyn himself, came bursting out of the hall with drawn swords. Millicent quickly regained her wits and whirled the horse around to where the boy sat.

"Roland! Up! I shan't move an inch without you!" the girl shouted down at him, in her most commanding voice.

The swordsmen were no more than thirty yards from them now and closing fast. Roland knew enough of the girl's stubbornness not to attempt to argue. He struggled to his feet and swung his bow towards their pursuers, which froze them in their tracks. They had seen this mud covered bowman drop three of their number.

He looked back at Millicent as the girl extended her arm. He grasped it and heaved himself upward. He had not yet felt any pain from his wound but only a strange weakness. Still, he was able to pull himself bodily up behind the girl. He had hardly grasped her around the waist, when she dug her heels once more into the thoroughbred's flanks and they were off. As they burst through the gate, Millicent shrieked with the release of tension, and the sheer joy of gaining her freedom.

Roland could barely stay astride the animal as it plunged forward. He clung to the girl like a drowning man clings to a branch. Glancing over his shoulder, he groaned. Bleddyn and fully a dozen of his men were hurriedly saddling ponies to give pursuit. But the big Norman thoroughbred was reaching full speed now and Roland knew that no Welsh pony could hope to catch them. For the first time, he began to have hope that they might win free.

From a tree line ahead of them, two men appeared. These were the men Roland had seen leaving at dawn to cut wood. They must have been aroused by the alarm from the fort, and were now running toward the trail—but the distance was too far. They would never reach the path in time to cut off their escape! But the boy saw something that made his stomach sink. One of the men slipped something from behind his back—*a bow*. He drew an arrow from his quiver, nocked it, sighted and released the shaft.

Roland could not see the arrow's flight, but heard it strike home. It had missed him and Lady Millicent but had sunk deep into the haunch of their mount. The horse squealed and instinctively kicked out with its hind legs but continued to run. A moment later a second arrow buried itself in the horse's shoulder and the girl fought to keep him moving forward.

At last they reached the relative cover of the woods, and Millicent eased the wounded animal back from a full gallop. Bright blood now streamed down the chest and rump of the bay mare. Roland could see the horse's eyes were wide with fear and pain. He marvelled that the animal kept moving, but knew she couldn't last long. Millicent bent forward and spoke softly to the horse, urging it onward. They had to put distance between themselves and the pursuit which would surely come.

The girl was still stunned by the squire's sudden appearance. Had he not arrived when he did, she would surely have been caught —or taken an arrow in the back—before she had fairly begun her escape. She turned to speak, but her words caught in her throat. The arrow was still buried deep in the boy's thigh and even though his rough trousers were wet and covered with mud, the bright stain of blood could be seen soaking through to below the knee. She instinctively pulled back on the big horse's mane, and the animal slowed to a trot.

"Roland, does it hurt much?" she blurted. She felt like she hadn't breathed since bursting out of her cell. Roland tried to grin, but it was closer to a grimace. The initial shock was starting to wear off and the pain was becoming intense.

"Ride on, my lady...not bleeding too badly," he managed, through gritted teeth. "They'll be... coming...."

Millicent knew the boy spoke the truth. They could not stop now to tend the wound, for if they were overtaken, Roland would surely be killed outright and she would, at best, be a prisoner once more. They must get clear of Clocaenog, to have any chance at all. Reluctantly, she urged the horse forward into a moderate trot. She knew each bounce had to be agony for the horse and the boy clutching her waist, but there was no help for it. *They must move!*

For half of an hour, they continued through the winding forest trail while both the boy and horse continued to bleed. Millicent recognized this trail as the one she had been led along during her abduction. Before noon, they should be free of this dark and fey wood, but the girl knew the horse could not last another hour—and perhaps not the boy. She also suspected that somewhere ahead, more raiders lay waiting to ambush her father and they were in danger of riding right into their hands.

She halted the animal at a bend in the trail and slid to the ground. The horse's breathing was now ragged. As gently as she could she grabbed the boy's tunic and slid him off the animal's rump. Roland could not suppress a groan as he tried to rest some weight on the injured limb. The girl forced him to sit on the ground while she walked forward and took the horse's head in her arms. She caressed the animal's neck and thick jaw and whispered in its ear, then walked back and slapped him on the rear. Obediently, the horse trotted off down the path. When she turned back to the boy, he could see that her eyes were shiny with brimming tears. He had never seen Lady Millicent cry.

The girl sniffed and dried the wetness in her eyes as she turned to the wounded squire. *She would be hanged if she let this stupid boy die after following her all the way into the Clocaenog—and saving her skin!*

"Let me see this, Roland," she said, with both gentleness and urgency in her voice. She knew a bit of the healing arts, thanks to her mother's insistence that she be trained in a host of disciplines that might, one day, prove useful. She took Roland's dagger from his belt.

"Quite a weapon, Master Inness. Where did you come by it?" she asked brightly, while slitting the fabric of his trousers near the protruding arrow.

"Gift...gift from a friend," the boy managed, as he gritted his teeth.

"A friend? Who?" she replied, trying to distract the boy from the wound, while she examined it.

"Brun...Ivo Brun." Roland answered. "I...I intend to return it to him...one day."

"Hilt or blade first?"

Roland snorted. He knew she was trying to take his mind off of the incredible jolts of pain that now were coursing through his thigh—and he appreciated it. She completed her examination and turned to the boy.

"Roland, the arrow missed the bone and any major vessel, but almost pierced the thigh entirely. I can see the shadow of the head, just beneath the skin on the inside of your limb," she explained rapidly. "We have little time, do you understand?"

The boy nodded.

"They are coming. I cannot pull this out like it is. It would tear a much greater wound in your leg and we must move. The horse is gone. We must go on foot, and you cannot do it with that arrow inside of you. Do you understand?"

Roland nodded again.

"I will push it through the other side and remove the point, then I can pull it free and bind the wound," she continued.

Bracing himself, he gave the girl a wan smile.

"Do it!"

She did not hesitate. In one swift motion she shoved hard on the imbedded arrow. Roland stifled a scream, as the pain seemed to overwhelm half of his body.

"It's free," Millicent reported. She reached forward with the dagger and made two deep cuts in the shaft just below the exposed iron head. With one hand she grasped the shaft, and with the other, the bloody arrow head and snapped it off. She tried not to move the arrow inside the boy's leg, but it was impossible. Roland groaned between clinched jaws.

"Take a deep breath, Roland," she commanded. He obeyed and, without hesitation, she drew forth the arrow with one quick pull. Roland thought he would faint, but fought the urge.

"There!" said Millicent dropping the bloody arrow on her patient's chest, "a keepsake." She continued to move swiftly, ripping a length of fabric from her underskirt and binding it around the boy's leg. She pulled it tight and secured it with a hasty knot. The girl stopped and tilted her head sideways, seeking to locate their pursuers. The sound of hooves could now be heard, and dangerously close. They must move—now!

"Can you walk on it?" she asked.

"I'll run if needs be, my lady," he croaked, struggling to his feet. His face was white with pain, but the girl could see determination in his eyes. "Let's go," he said, and limped into the underbrush with Millicent at his heels. She had proven her abilities on horseback; it was now his time to use all of his skills as a woodsman to see them both to safety. Horseless, they could not outrun their enemies, but on foot they might yet outfox them.

Roland knew the Welsh would follow the trail of the riderless horse for some distance before realizing their error. In truth, the path down which they had fled would have ultimately led them into the ambush party lying in wait for any force from Shipbrook. He preferred their chances off the trails.

He stopped for a moment to look up at the dense canopy of the trees above them. The morning sun was not visible, but he could roughly make out its position from the scattering of the light. They would move east and north using that light as their guide. Eventually they would emerge from the Clocaenog, perhaps a league or more to the east of the main trail. He fretted about the fate of Sir Roger, should he fall victim to the ambush he knew lay on that path, but they had little choice but to look to their own escape.

They soon struck a game trail that ran roughly northeast. He led the girl along this trail as fast as his aching leg would allow, using his longbow as a staff. The wound still hurt like the devil, but he saw that the bandage had staunched most of the bleeding. Every few moments he halted to listen for pursuit, and, to his dismay, he heard it sooner than he expected. These Welshmen were skilled woodsmen and had not been led astray for long! He could hear the sound of men moving through the brush less than half a mile behind them. Once again, their situation looked grim. With his leg thus, they could never outdistance their enemies. As he led Millicent onward he searched frantically for some stratagem that would confound those who followed, but could devise none. Steadily, the sound of pursuit grew behind them. He stopped and grasped Millicent by the shoulders.

"My lady…we cannot outdistance them." he said, between rasping breaths. "We must turn and fight. I don't fancy being run to ground like a rabbit. I have six arrows left. It may be enough…if no more than that follow." He unslung his bow as he spoke. "Get yourself behind that log, and keep down!"

Lady Millicent considered the boy in front of her. Could he be serious about turning to fight these men who pursued them? She had seen a dozen or more gathering to give chase back at the fortress. Who knew how many now were approaching through the woods?

"Roland, they will have bows as well."

Roland held the longbow before her. His face showed a grim assurance.

"They have bows, my lady, but *none* like this!" he stated simply.

There was nothing about the strange, roughly made bow that inspired confidence in the girl, but she had seen this boy shoot, back in the fortress. Three men dead in but a few seconds. She looked at him for another long moment.

"Then shoot straight, Master Inness, or we are lost."

The boy managed a weak grin. "I know of no other way to shoot, my lady," he replied.

Millicent moved behind a large fallen log a few feet away. For the first time she noticed that her hand still clutched the jewelled dagger she had taken from the boy to cut out the arrow. Roland eased himself up a slight rise to the right, until he found another deadfall that gave him a decent view of the surrounding area. He took his six arrows and stuck them, point first, into the soft ground beside him. He withdrew one and fitted it to his bowstring. All that remained was to watch and wait, and he knew the wait would not be long.

Roland saw the first man far off to his left, and could hear others closer to his position. He held his shot, hoping to catch sight of at least one other potential target before he revealed his presence. An instant later, a second man appeared, much closer to him. This one moved with his head down, concentrating on following their track. Roland aimed, released and the man pitched forward without a sound.

One down.

Without hesitating, he notched his next arrow and dropped the man farther off to his left. He never saw what hit him, but let out a squeal as he died.

Two down.

Suddenly it grew very quiet as nothing stirred in the woods to his front. They knew he was here now and had turned to fight. The boy cursed softly. Surprise was gone and they would now approach cautiously. He would have to wait patiently for one of his enemies to make a careless mistake, but doubted they would.

Already he could hear them off in the distance to his left and right moving to outflank him. When they had him and the girl surrounded they would move in. Once they had closed the distance, he would lose the advantage of range he held with the longbow as he had already lost the advantage of surprise. It appeared that Bleddyn had brought all of his pursuing party with him. There would be far too many to take with the four arrows he had left.

Roland's mind raced, as he pondered their plight—but there seemed little hope. As if to seal his dark thoughts, an arrow struck the log where he was concealed, not two inches from his cheek. His position had been ferreted out and already flanked! That shot had come from his right rear! The boy dropped to his knees and scrambled back through the cover of the brush—to where Millicent lay concealed.

"My lady…they've flanked us," he gasped, as he came to rest

beside the girl. "More than six…perhaps a dozen. Can't…can't hold them long."

The girl nodded her understanding.

"You must flee. I…I can delay them…for a while—then I'll follow."

"I shall stay with you," she replied, quietly.

"*You shall not!*" This time it was the boy's voice that took on a commanding tone. "Do not be a fool. If they take us, I am a dead man and your staying won't change that. But for your father's sake, flee. Do not let these men use you."

For a long moment, Millicent stared at the boy, torn by the truth of what he said and her determination not to leave him. To Roland's surprise, she flung her arms around his neck and hugged him fiercely. When she spoke, she could hardly get the words out.

"I …I shall go…but Roland…if you die—*I shall never forgive you.*"

She gave the flustered boy no opportunity to speak, but turned and ran, crouching low to the ground. A new crashing sound to his right drew his attention as she disappeared into the underbrush. He rose with his bow drawn and dropped a rash attacker not twenty yards from where he stood. Then to his left and right, Welshmen seemed to spring out of the ground. A wild cry rose from their lips as they bore down on him. Behind them he could see Bleddyn approaching more deliberately as he swung a broadsword lazily from side to side. No more time now for arrows. He slid his hands down the longbow and prepared to use it as a cudgel.

"*Get down boy!*"

The voice behind him was like a physical force which froze him in place. He turned in time to see Sir Roger de Laval sweep by, shoving him to the dirt like a child's toy. The knight wore chain mail and a battered helmet and carried a scarred and dented shield before him. In his right hand a great battle axe rose, its blade honed to a razor edge that glinted in the odd twilight of the deep woods. Close behind him came Alwyn Madawc, his face glowing with the joy of battle. The men who had been charging the boy hesitated, stunned by the sudden onslaught. It was a fatal mistake.

From that day forward, Roland Inness would never forget the sight of the Lord of Shipbrook in a full battle rage. For a man of his bulk he moved like a panther and was upon the Welshmen in a moment. Two tried to slash at the knight with their swords. He met them with shield, axe and a guttural roar. These men had laid hands on his Millie. *They would pay.*

Both were down in seconds as their two companions turned to flee, but for these men there would be no escaping the fury of Roger de Laval. Overtaken, they turned and tried to attack the knight from left and right. He effortlessly parried their frantic thrusts. Raising the lethal axe above his head, he made a wide sweeping slash toward the man on his left, who barely avoided the blow. The man to his right saw his opening and closed for the kill. But the great sweep of the axe had not stopped as it missed the first man. In fact, the blow had never been intended to land, but was designed to draw in the other man. Too late, he saw the knight pivot on his heels and continue the blurring sweep of the axe in his direction. It landed with a sickening crunch and the man simply folded up and collapsed in a heap.

Ripping his hand from the axe cord, Sir Roger sprang on the remaining raider with nothing but his shield. It was the only weapon he needed. The man tried to stand his ground, but was overborne by the Norman who used the shield as a bludgeon. The man went down and did not rise.

Sir Alwyn had taken the group to Roland's right and waded into them with a fury worthy of the Welsh. A frightening war cry rose from his lips and in a moment one man was down and two more were running for their lives.

Slowly, the boy arose and looked at his master standing over the slain raiders. Sir Roger had removed his battered helmet and was surveying the dead. His mail shirt was bloody. He called to Alwyn. "Where is Bleddyn?" He is not among this lot."

"There!" Alwyn pointed in the direction of the main trail. Through the big trees, near the top of a long slope, they could see the leader of the raiders fleeing well ahead of his men. Once he had made it over the rise he would only have a short way to go to where his horses were surely tethered—and from there, back to the security of his keep. Sir Roger wheeled around.

"Roland, have you a shaft left?" he shouted.

"Aye, lord," the boy shouted back.

"Then take him."

Roland steadied himself, pulled his final arrow from the ground and notched it. He felt dizzy but fought off the feeling. He could see Bleddyn pounding up the rise. It was a long shot. He took a deep breath, exhaled slowly and released. An urge to escape with some pride intact before the few men he had left must have seized the raider. He turned and raised his unblooded sword high. He saw the party from Shipbrook had not moved and gave a quick sigh of relief. He would live to...

The arrow struck him in the throat. He pitched backwards and lay still.

Roland lowered his bow. His head was swimming. He sat down.

"No time for sitting down on the job!" A familiar voice came from his right. It was Declan. The Irish boy wore a broad grin, but Roland could see there was blood on his broadsword. A moment later, Sir Alwyn appeared from the same direction. With him was Lady Millicent. Up the slope, Sir Roger dropped his shield to the ground.

"Millie..." He said her name softly, as though it were a prayer. The girl ran to him and leapt into the big man's arms.

Roland turned to Declan. "How...?"

"Did we come to be here? Oh, Sir Roger assumed there'd be a welcomin' party skulkin' about on the main trail off to the west and decided it would be a wise thing to just go around. Didn't count on running right into you and the Little Lady! Don't think these Welshmen counted on running into us either!"

Roland turned back and watched the father and daughter embrace and thought, for the first time in days, of his own father—but the thought would not keep. Somehow, everything seemed to be growing confused, and even Declan's face seemed to go strange and distorted. His friend, and the forest around him, faded into black.

***

"Roland?...Roland?...*Roland!* Wake up!" The voice seemed to come from a deep well. Roland wanted to sleep some more, but the voice was insistent. Slowly, and a little painfully, he opened his eyes. Everything was blurry for a second, then the world snapped into focus. Lady Catherine de Laval was staring intently at him and over her shoulder, Lady Millicent held him in a solemn gaze. He recognized that he was in Millicent's room, and could see daylight out the window. How had he been so instantly transported from Clocaenog to Shipbrook?

"My lady?"

"You've been sleeping for two days, Master Inness. They brought you here strapped to a travois. You've lost a lot of blood, but it looks as though you'll survive, and probably be good as new in a month. But there will be an excellent scar you'll have there on your leg to brag upon when you are an old man!"

"I'm hungry," he said a bit sheepishly, as his stomach commenced an audible grumbling.

"There's a good sign!" Lady Catherine said, with a beaming smile. "I'll send for a meal." With that, she rose and left the room.

Millicent sat down in her place. Roland could see that she was no longer the dirty and dishevelled girl he had fled with through the Clocaenog. Her hair was clean and shining, and she looked every inch the daughter of Lady Catherine.

"We thought we would lose you," she said.

"You told me you'd never forgive me if I died, my lady."

The girl smiled.

"Roland, when we are alone, I shall no longer be addressed by you as 'my lady'. You shall call me…'Millie'".

Roland started to protest. The distance between peasant and gentry, squire and lady was wide—and breached only at peril—but one look at the girl told him any protest would be useless. And in his heart, he knew that a protest would be false. Something had changed between them in the dark forest of Clocaenog, but he was far too weary to sort it out just now.

"Millie it is, then," he sighed and closed his eyes once more.

Chapter 16

The King is Dead

Mid-summer hung over Shipbrook like a warm blanket, relieved only by the occasional breeze coming in from the Irish Sea. Dust hung in the air whenever horses came or went, and the drone of insects filled the night. It was a lazy—though somewhat painful—time for Roland Inness, as he recovered from his foray into the Clocaenog. The wound had knitted nicely, with no infection, but the torn muscle and flesh stilled ached and his skin itched fiercely as it healed.

Being unable to ride for several weeks left Roland with an excess of free time. The Lady of Shipbrook filled much of the surplus with new lessons and he filled the rest with his determination to master the wing shot with his bow.

"Roger, are ye ever gonna' tell the boy it's a joke?" Alwyn inquired one day as he watched the two squires leave for their afternoon drill.

"Joke? Indeed it isn't a joke!" The Norman knight shot back. "The boy needed a challenge. God knows he can hit anything standing still upon the earth."

Declan O'Duinne complained bitterly when Sir Roger's appointed him "master of the flock" and directed him to toss as many targets into the air as Roland should desire. The Irish boy

162

tried to convince his friend that their master could not be serious about shooting birds on the wing, but Roland would not budge. For hours each day, he shot until his callused fingers blistered. With painful slowness his accuracy improved. It was all a matter of judging speed and trajectory. He could place an arrow at any spot he chose, but judging if the target would arrive at the same spot and same time was the challenge. As summer wore on, his ability to track and hit the various objects Declan flung into the air improved steadily, but still, many targets fell to earth completely unscathed.

Lady Catherine took a particular interest in the boy during this period. To Roland's surprise, he was actually making good progress in learning to read. This was a skill usually reserved for churchmen and clerks. Few noblemen or gentry could read, including Sir Roger, and it was even rarer that a woman could—but Lady Catherine was the exception.

"My people have always valued the learned arts, Roland," she told him one day. "I was a lucky lass to have a mother and sire who provided us with a tutor when I was young. Have no doubt, Roland, this knowledge will serve you well…better perhaps than your skill with the bow."

By now, his prowess with the longbow was a poorly kept secret at Shipbrook. To hear some of the exaggerated tales, he had slain half the raiders in Wales, as he fled the Clocaenog. He shrugged off these silly stories and felt a bit uncomfortable with all of the attention being shown him by the household servants. They were obviously devoted to Lady Millicent, and treated him as though he had single-handedly rescued her from Bleddyn. *In truth, she had done as much to rescue him!*

He and Millicent had spoken little of their escape since returning to Shipbrook, but the experience had changed them both. She was, once again, the pampered daughter of the Lord of Shipbrook, but Roland knew well her depths. He recalled the look of absolute determination on her face as she spurred her horse toward the closing gate of Bleddyn's fortress, and her composure when they had been run to ground. She may be pampered, but the warrior's blood of Sir Roger de Laval ran in her veins—and perhaps a dash of Edric the Wild!

She was still the high-spirited young girl Roland had met when he arrived just a few months ago, but she had gained a new measure of gravity in her bearing. The girl still had a fondness for jests, but he saw that she now showed a bit more gentleness when she sprang one of her traps.

"Millie, how old are you, exactly," he asked her one day as they walked along the battlements of Shipbrook.

"I shall be thirteen on the first day of fall…and what of you?"

"Fifteen…sometime in the spring."

"Do you like it here at Shipbrook? Will you stay?"

"Aye, for now. Your sire is a good man and the Lady de Laval has…has shown me great kindness. I think she may even trust me!" he said and the girl giggled. It was well known that the trust of Catherine De Laval was hard won.

"Besides—I have nowhere else to go." Millicent paused in her stride and turned to the boy.

"I know of your father's death, Roland, but what of yer mother…and I believe you have a brother and sister?"

"My mother died of the fever last winter and now Oren and Lorea are hidden…and protected by the church. I…I have a promise… from a monk." Saying it out loud made the Tuck's promise seem unconvincing, but there had been *something* about the little churchman that gave him confidence.

"You miss them?" she asked, gently.

"Aye, I do. My mother was a strong woman—like your own…and proud, though she be a peasant. My father was a brave man and more than that—he was a good man. I miss him every day."

"Can you never return to your home then?"

"Never is a long time and in truth I've made an oath to myself that I will return, but not while I'm hunted by the Earl of Derby," he said, and stopped. *He had spoken too much!* Sir Roger knew only that he had fled because the family's farm had been seized. He did not know that he had slain three of the Earl's men and was a fugitive. It was a lie of necessity and one he had now tripped over!

Lady Millicent was quick to catch the import of his statement.

"You are hunted? For what offense?" she asked, suddenly very serious.

"I cannot say, my lady." He could not lie to Millicent.

"Cannot or will not?" she questioned sharply.

"Will not, my lady..."

Millicent looked at Roland with anger in her eyes. She turned away with arms crossed, then turned back, still angry.

"You will not...understand me, *not*...address me as 'my lady.' I had thought we had that clear between us!" she said, and poked the boy in the chest with her finger. "Answer me only this...this...*thing* that you did, crime or no in the eyes of the Earl, was it an *evil* thing?"

Roland hesitated under the unflinching eyes of the young girl. How could he answer?

"My la...um, Millie, I am not the one to judge. My father was an innocent man and the Earl's son killed him with no more thought than swatting a fly. I...I struck back. Men died. 'Twas a deed that sometimes troubles me...but I would not see it undone. The monk who has sheltered my family said God would understand. I ...I cannot sort it."

The girl looked at him for a long moment.

"I've seen you kill, Roland Inness, but you are no murderer—and I'm well aware of the manner in which some of the *nobility* deal with the peasants. I'll not ask you to explain yourself further. If a crime you committed, you must have had cause. This will always remain a secret...between us."

Satisfied, she looped her arm around the boy's and resumed their stroll along the battlements of Shipbrook. Once again a confusing mix of feelings that had plagued him since he had awoken alive at Shipbrook returned. The girl looked no different than she had a fortnight ago, but now, the sight of her face caused a curious restriction in his throat and a warm ache in his chest. He looked at her from the corner of his eye. She was two years his junior, but somehow seemed older than him at such times. Declan had once referred to her as a "gawky colt," but now, as he secretly studied her face, he thought her...rather...*pretty*. The notion terrified him. He felt himself flush.

"I think we should be getting back now," he stammered. "My leg..." She looked at him curiously, but nodded.

As they approached the gatehouse, Millicent pointed into the distance. A cloud of dust was rising over the near wood line, where the Chester road ran out of sight. This could only be a rider approaching at considerable speed. A moment later a man on horseback emerged into view at a full gallop. He only reined in his mount when he had clattered across courtyard below, the horse's iron shod hoofs sending sparks across the cobbles as it came to a sharp stop.

Sir Roger and Sir Alwyn had already been alerted by the guard in the gate house and hurried down to where the dusty rider stood, holding his horse's reins. Roland and Millicent followed, as fast as his healing leg would allow, to see what news the man brought in such haste. When they arrived, he had already begun his report to the two knights.

"...died two weeks ago—in Chinon. I've come from the Earl...in Chester. The Duke...Richard...is to be king." The man was fighting for breath, after his frenzied ride. "Church bells throughout the realm are being rung this day, with muffled clappers. None can believe he's really...*gone*. The Earl...is much distressed. King Henry was like a father to him. He knows naught of Richard, other than he's a fearsome soldier."

"Aye, he is that," interjected Sir Roger, "sometimes to his royal sire's woe! I've been on campaign with the Duke. There be no better field commander in Christendom."

By now Declan had joined Roland and Millicent. The import of this amazing news was just beginning to sink in. King Henry II had been monarch of this land for longer than any of them could remember, longer than any of them had been alive!

The messenger had little additional information to offer other than the Earl wished to counsel with his knights in three days at Chester. He asked but for water and a little bread, as he had to deliver the message to other vassals of the Earl along the Welsh Marches.

"Henry...*dead!* I can hardly believe it," Sir Roger said, shaking his head. "I must tell Catherine. Alwyn, you and Declan will accompany me to Chester. Roland," he turned toward the boy, "keep an eye on things here...and get that leg well! I have cause to think you'll have need of it soon. Millie, come with me!"

The tall knight made his way up the stone steps to the manor house with his daughter trailing behind. In his wake, the news was

166

spreading, as stable hands, smithies and men-at-arms gathered in small knots to discuss the development.

"Looks like you'll be missin' Chester again, Roland me lad," said Declan, draping an arm around his friend's shoulder. "Pity. Some of the performers in the streets are marvels—once saw a man juggle three piglets!"

In truth, Roland was disappointed to be left behind, but knew the leg needed a few more weeks to fully recover. Two mornings after receiving the summons, Sir Roger, Sir Alwyn and Declan departed for the day's journey to Chester. Roland and Millicent watched them disappear into the far tree line. It felt odd to watch his master and friend leaving without him. It left him in a melancholy mood.

"Roland, Mother wishes to see you," Millicent said, as the party disappeared from view. Roland looked quizzically at the girl, who just shrugged her shoulders. He knew it was best not to keep Lady de Laval waiting, and hurried to the chambers where he had been receiving his lessons. Lady Catherine was waiting for him. She motioned him to sit across from her. As soon as he had settled, she spoke.

"Roland, we...Sir Roger and I...owe you much for what you did for Millicent." Roland started to protest, but the woman waved him to silence. "Yes, I know your account of events," she said, and began to mimic the boy, "Lady Millicent rescued *me.*" Aye, she may have given you a ride, but how did you come to be inside that horrible place to begin with? Sir Roger figures you had to run steady for many leagues through rough country to be in that pig sty when Millie made her escape." The boy again started to speak, but the woman scowled at him and he remained silent.

"You've shown yourself brave and resourceful, and beyond that...*deadly*, with your longbow. A time of trouble is coming, Roland, and I would value a boy with these virtues by my husband's side. I trust Alwyn and Declan with Sir Roger's life. I believe I can trust you as well."

"Aye, my lady, you can."

"*Good*...for there is another matter that I would attend to. I have watched you in your studies. You have a quick mind—which may serve as master to your other virtues—but you are sorely lacking in your understanding of the world beyond these walls. Here you've come to know every tree and animal and where danger might lie. Soon you will be entering a world much different. The danger out there comes on two legs and you must be on guard. We shall take these days to come to complete your education, Roland."

The boy knew how ignorant he was of the world of the nobility, the world he had only just started to enter. "I will learn, my lady," he said.

"Excellent! Now, why shall Richard be King?"

Roland thought for a moment. This, even a simple peasant knew.

"He is the eldest son of King Henry, my lady," he answered with confidence.

"Wrong, master squire! Aye, he is the eldest son since the death of his older brother Henry many years past, but that alone would not give him the throne. Nay, Roland, Richard will be King because he controls the provinces in France and because he is ten times the soldier that his brother is *and* because *the Queen* will be backing him!"

"The Queen, my lady?" He knew that Henry had a queen, but little else.

"The Queen, Roland. Eleanor of Aquitaine—a most formidable woman. She was once married to the King of France, but spurned him to marry Henry. Almost half the lands Henry ruled came to him from her holdings. For many years, she had great influence over the king, but, alas, she made one mistake."

"A mistake, my lady?"

"Aye, she backed her eldest son Henry when he rebelled against his father," Lady Catherine continued. "The King forgave his first born, at least at the time, but never his wife. She's been locked up for these past fifteen years!"

"The queen is a prisoner? This seems most strange to me, my lady." The boy shook his head. He was just beginning to grasp the depth of his ignorance.

"She shan't be a prisoner for long now that Richard is to be crowned. Henry was king for thirty-five years. Certain men grew wealthy and powerful in his reign. Others suffered and grew impatient. Now, all will be in flux. When the crown changes heads, all men must look to their interests—and to their own heads, for it is a most dangerous time. The more you understand the danger, the better you can watch my husband's back!"

Roland could see the wisdom of her words. He nodded for her to continue.

"Sir Roger has faith in Duke Richard as a war leader and hopes he will also prove a just king, but time alone will tell. What preys on my mind are events far from here that may draw us all into the whirlwind. You know of the Holy Land, Roland?"

"Aye, my lady, 'tis where Jesus was born, died and rose again," Roland answered promptly. His mother had made sure he knew the basic story of the Testaments.

"Aye, lad, but did ye know 'tis also sacred ground to the Muslims, and that not two years past they seized it from the Christian King?"

"No, my lady," Roland answered. He thought he had heard *something* about trouble in the Holy City of Jerusalem, but wasn't sure what.

"Perhaps you've heard of the 'Saladin Tithe,' then?"

"Oh, aye, my lady," the boy replied eagerly. "I've heard of this. 'Twas a new tax levied by the Earl. We couldn't pay the old, much less the new!"

"This tax was not levied by your Earl, but by King Henry," Lady Catherine explained. "It is to raise money for a great crusade to oust the Muslims from the Holy City. Saladin is their leader and, by accounts, a great general."

"Will King Richard continue this tax, my lady?" the boy asked.

"I've little doubt of that, Roland. But unlike old King Henry, young King Richard will be eager to spend the money he raises. I fear he will call for a crusade—as his father did—but that he will be in earnest, which his father never was. If it is so, then your master must go."

Roland digested this news.

"Why must Sir Roger go, my lady. Who will guard the Welsh Marches?" he asked.

"I know not who will keep the raiders at bay, for no doubt there were ten waiting to fill Bleddyn's boots when he fell. But most of the experienced soldiers will be expected to follow the

King, and Roger is one of the best. Duke Richard will know this—from their service together." The distress in Lady Catherine's voice was painful for Roland to hear. "He will go. He *must* go…and I will hate it. Lesser men will stay safe here in England, and create mischief," she sighed. "I care nothing for some dusty ground a world away, but everything for my husband! You understand that, do you not Roland?" her voice held a plea that could not be ignored.

Roland nodded gravely. Lady Catherine had said the Queen was a formidable woman. No more so than the woman who sat before him, he thought.

"I shall watch his back, my lady," he said. "I shall watch it well."

Chapter 17

To London Town

Sir Roger returned from his counsels with the Earl of Chester after three days. Roland couldn't wait to pull Declan aside for a full accounting of the visit.

"Tell me everything that happened! Are we to go on Crusade? What is Earl Ranulf like? What of the coronation of Duke Richard?"

"Full of questions aren't we?" Declan asked, as he beat some of the dust of the highway from his tunic. "This will teach you not to go about getting shot in the leg and lazing about the castle for weeks on end!"

"*Declan!* What news?" Roland begged.

"Well, take a load off that leg of yours and I'll tell ye, me lame friend." The Irish boy pulled up one of the three-legged stools in their room. Roland did the same.

"First—and just between us—Earl Ranulf seems a most unhappy sort, for all of his wealth and power. Sir Alwyn, of course, blames his wife, Lady Constance. She's the widow of King Henry's son Geoffrey, and quite wealthy in her own right, but just a bit...*unlovely*," Declan said, diplomatically. "She's also ten years his senior, and appears to loathe the Earl. We squires sat against the walls of the dining hall during one feast and I observed that she hardly looked at him—save to stare daggers. Alwyn says this is why we must avoid marriage at all costs. It always ends badly!"

Roland snorted, "One look at Sir Roger and Lady Catherine disproves that point."

"Said the very same thing, I did," Declan replied. "Sir Alwyn says the rarity of that union only proves his case."

"Perhaps," said Roland, sceptically, "but continue…"

"Ahhh…ye should have seen the *food*! Roland, I've never eaten so much in my life. I thought my stomach would burst like a ripe seed pod!"

"*Hang* the food, Declan. What of the coronation?"

"Oh, of course, the coronation. It's to be the third day of September…at Westminster, in London. We will accompany Sir Roger, who attends the Earl."

Roland whooped with excitement. The forests of Kinder Scout had once been his whole world, but in the past months he had travelled far and seen much. He hungered to see more. *London!* The largest city in the realm and its centre of power—and he was going there. Against this, York would seem to be little more than a country village. It made his head spin.

"When do we leave?" he said, clutching Declan by both shoulders. The Irish boy looked at him askance.

"Steady, boy. Don't want to wet your breeches, now."

"Declan!" Roland fought the urge to strangle his best friend.

"Alright!" Declan laughed. "No need to get so worked up. We leave in three weeks. The journey to London will require perhaps a week or more and the Earl wishes to spend a week in the city before the coronation. His Lordship seems to have a great deal of politics to attend to and wants his vassals about him. Sir Roger hates these sorts of things, but will be required to attend. My guess is he will not want us underfoot, so we shall have a great deal of time to explore the city."

Roland felt his excitement rise. *Free to roam in London!* He couldn't wait.

***

"*It's a ridiculous expense!*" Sir Alwyn muttered, as he checked the belly cinch on his horse. He looked at the two squires, who were grinning sheepishly while securing their own saddles. "It'll cost an extra pound to stable the mounts for these pups in London."

"Got to maintain appearances, Alwyn," Sir Roger de Laval said. "Don't attend a coronation every day!"

"Squires riding! Roger, we'll spoil these boys."

Roland and Declan had long since finished checking their horses, but continued to fuss with their bridles and saddles, while listening with amusement to Sir Alwyn's lamentations. The great day had arrived. They were off to London!

"My lord," asked Declan in an innocent voice, "did you *never* ride as a squire?"

"Never *was* a squire," Sir Alwyn growled. "—not in the way of the English. All the lads of my clan learned to fight and became soldiers by your age. We walked, 'til we were skilled enough or lucky enough to acquire a horse—Usually, obtained from some stupid Saxon or Norman knight who got lost along the border!"

"Sooth, but boys must have been of sturdier stock back in those days!" Declan replied sincerely.

"Aye lad, we were tough as the hide on a wild boar. Had no need to ride!"

"And in that *far away* time—when you were a lad, did …ogre's and giants yet roam the land?" Declan inquired, sweetly. Roland snickered, despite himself.

Sir Alwyn turned with a dark look on his face and advanced on the Irish boy.

"Alwyn! Temper, man!" Sir Roger roared, trying to suppress his own laugh. He walked over and draped a long arm over the man's shoulder. "It's a sure sign that you'll soon be doddering, when you speak thus of your youth—and besides, what's this about *'stupid Normans?'"*

Alwyn hesitated a moment then looked up at the Norman knight, who towered over him. A small smile creased his face. "Didn't say they were *all* stupid."

"Right then!" Sir Roger exclaimed, slapping his companion on the shoulder. "Let's be off. Catherine! Millie!"

The two Ladies de Laval made their way down the stone steps of the manor. Lady Catherine managed a smile for her husband.

"They say the ladies at court have an eye for knights newly come from the country, my lord. *Do* take care."

"Oh, Cathy." The tall knight chuckled and pulled her to his chest. "I've no doubt those powdered up tarts are bored with the fancy fellows at court, but *you'll* always be my lass."

Lady Millicent stood by, with a rather sour look on her face. The big knight released his wife and turned to his daughter.

"I know ye want to go Millie, but London will be packed with barons and their followers. I'll practically be sleeping in a stable meself—and the boys will be!" The knight pointed to Roland and Declan. The young girl thrust her chin forward and scowled at her father.

"My lord, you know I can sleep in a bog if I have to, and certainly a stable would suffice," she said.

"Aye, lass, I know ye could also thrash half the squires sharing your quarters—but that's not the point, Millie. It would be unseemly for a daughter of the gentry to sleep thus, and besides, it would be completely impossible for you to go without your mother, and she must tend things here." He said all this gently. "Now, say your good byes."

She couldn't stay angry with her father, and hugged him tightly around his neck. When she released her grasp, she turned to the two boys and looked directly at Roland. Something had passed between them in this past month, something that she could not acknowledge—but for the flush in her cheeks.

"Mind his back, Roland...and you as well Declan," she managed.

The two boys bowed simultaneously and—for once—there was no artifice in the gesture. There was nothing more to say. The two men and two boys mounted their horses and clattered across the courtyard and out the gate. They would take the well-known path from Shipbrook to Chester—there to join Earl Ranulf—and thence, southeast down Watling Street to London.

"Why do they call the highway to London 'Watling Street', my lord?" Roland shouted to Sir Alwyn above the jangle of the horses.

"'Tis the old Roman road to Chester and it begins at Watling Street in London," the Welsh knight replied. "Londoners, in their arrogance, think this whole great country serves only as the outskirts to their city, and for some reason we country folk go along with the conceit. So even as far as Chester, it's known as Watling Street."

Pleased with Sir Alwyn's ready knowledge of the countryside, Roland peppered him with questions as they rode through the growing heat of the day. The Welshman seemed to be a fountain of knowledge about London and its inhabitants and was willing enough to share his information with the young squire.

"Terrible place for a city, even if it was chosen by Roman engineers for their capital," the burly knight pronounced. "Fog thick as river water—worse than the bogs down by the Dee. Provides good cover for the thieves, of whom there are legions about the city."

Roland was fascinated by Sir Alwyn's knowledge, until Declan edged up quietly beside him and leaned in close to his ear.

"Sir Alwyn has only been to London, the once" the Irish boy whispered, *"and that time he got lost for half a day."* Roland snorted, and left the Welsh knight to his discourse. Sir Alwyn hardly noticed the boy's departure, as he continued his lecture on the perils of the great city.

For the rest of the day, Roland and Declan rode together. In high spirits, they jested with each other and the two knights, until suddenly the afternoon was fading and the walls of Chester came into view. Sir Roger guided Bucephalus into a small meadow half a league from the old Roman bridge which spanned the Dee and led to the city's southern gate. By now a steady stream of travellers of high station and low filled the road. He turned to Sir Alwyn.

"There'll be no room within the walls tonight--even in a chicken's coop. Camp here. I'll go pay my respects to the Earl— you mind these boys."

Roland was again disappointed that he would not see the sights of Chester, but Sir Alwyn soon had them busy tending the horses and gathering forage, so he had little time to complain. Besides, with London in the offing, Chester no longer seemed as interesting. When finally their chores were done they lounged around a small campfire and watched the last groups of pilgrims entering the city. The nobles were easily identifiable by the size of their contingents and the splendour of their clothing. The simple traveling clothes the party from Shipbrook wore seemed shabby by comparison.

"What must all of this clothing cost?" Roland whispered to Declan.

"More than Sir Roger collects from his lands in a year," the Irish boy replied wistfully. "I told you our master was a poor knight, at best, though a fine man and great soldier. The last time the man had any surplus money was after King Henry rewarded him for his services in Ireland."

"Perhaps there will be a reward if King Richard leads us on Crusade," Roland offered.

"Well, I should hope there'd be more to gain than redemption for our souls!" the Irish boy said. "They say the Saracens wield wicked curved swords and delight in the lopping off of Christian heads. To face that, I'd expect a little jingle in our purse at the end of the day!"

Roland shrugged. Money seemed not to move him in the same way it did his fellow squire. He hoped that one day his friend would gain his fortune. At least Declan knew what he wanted. Roland was sure of nothing, save his loyalty to the big knight. He still found it passing strange to find himself sworn to be loyal to a Norman, but these were strange times he was living in. He still loathed the heavy yoke the Norman lords kept on the necks of his own people, but Roger De Laval had taken him in when he had needed sanctuary and had given him a new life. His loyalty was a small price to pay in exchange. The day would surely come when he would avenge the death of Rolf Inness, but if Sir Roger must face the Saracens on some far off field—he would be there. He had given his word to Lady Catherine to guard her husband's back, and he would keep it.

***

The departure for London was a disaster. All of the knights attending their liege lord were jockeying to have a place of honour near the Earl, as the entire entourage sought to leave the city by the East Gate. Curses echoed off the ancient walls, as horses, riders, grooms, servants, squires, and pack animals all became entangled in the narrow streets. Taking one look at the mess, Sir Roger chose to rejoin his party on the opposite side of the Dee and proceed east along that bank, untroubled by the uproar on the other. This would require recrossing the river farther on to join the Earl, but the knight appeared in no hurry to do so. As they proceeded leisurely southeast along a dirt road, he was in high spirits.

"Look there," he pointed across the river. From their vantage point, they could see a vast and tangled parade of squires, baggage carts, cursing knights and harried servants, all trying to move forward along the choked Roman road. Some of the curses could be heard clearly from across the river in the early morning calm.

"Earl Ranulf had best not stop sudden, lest he be trampled by his admirers," Sir Roger observed, acidly. "Ye lads should have seen the spectacle that grown men made of themselves this past night. They'd have kissed the Earl's arse—had he but presented it!"

Soon the tangled mess on the far shore was left far behind. The companions-in-arms and the two squires enjoyed the fine summer morning in relative peace. They reached a ford in the Dee by midday, and stopped briefly to dine on bread and sausages, packed two days before by Lady Catherine. Crossing the shallow ford, they proceeded slowly, reaching Whitchurch by early afternoon. The party stopped here, having covered a little over twenty miles.

"The Earl will be lucky to reach here by nightfall," Sir Roger said. "We'll find some quarters and await his arrival."

Declan edged up to Sir Alwyn. "The day is still young, my lord. Why don't we press on?" he asked.

"Oh…on the march, we have ample excuse for not being at the Earl's beckoning, but should he wish to speak to Sir Roger in evening quarters, it would be…*awkward* to be elsewhere," the Welsh knight said. "It's why it's called 'attending', and—while our master would rather talk to his horse than to the Earl—it is part of his duty. As you've noticed, no one attends to his duty more loyally than Roger de Laval."

Having arrived well in advance of the Earl's party, they had no problem finding modest accommodations in the village. Lodging secured, they watched, with barely concealed amusement, the arrival of the main body. It was a ragged group that finally entered Whitchurch as evening approached. Tunics, which had been so bright and dashing in the morning, were now sweat-soaked and dusty. Tempers were clearly frayed. One of the arriving squires confided to them that there had been several incidents during the long day where swords had actually been drawn. Only the intervention of the Earl had stopped potential bloodshed. Roland and Declan had new reason to appreciate the wisdom of their own master in avoiding the entire affair.

Sir Roger was not summoned that night or on any other on the journey to London. As the week progressed the caravan centring on the Earl gradually sorted itself into some sort of rough order and fell into a daily rhythm which managed to cover upwards of thirty miles each day. As the days passed, the road to London was now filled with travellers headed to the coronation. It looked like all of England was turning out for a glimpse of the new monarch.

On the final night of their journey, Sir Roger halted his party at a small village just beyond St. Albans. Here, the crowds were a bit smaller, and they were less than fifteen miles from London proper. As they had done for the past several nights, the squires tended to the feeding and watering of the horses and fended for themselves for a place to sleep.

Sir Roger and Sir Alwyn had managed to procure a single small room at the local inn, and were lucky for that. It was likely that Earl Ranulf was evicting some of the lesser nobility from worse quarters a few miles back in St. Albans. Sir Roger had concluded that if the Earl had not sought his company throughout the journey, he was not likely to this night. Roland was surprised when the knight invited his squires to join him, after they finished with the horses.

"I'll buy ye both a meal and a pint of ale, boys. Celebrate our last night, before we get all cramped up in London," he said as he turned the reins of Bucephalus over to Declan. The boys hurried through their chores, eager to sample the fare at the inn. They had finished off the perishables Lady Catherine had packed days ago and were already weary of the crude rations they had been scrounging on the road.

It was full dark when they entered the interior of the place. The yellow light from oil lamps gave it a warm glow, and something in the cook pot suspended over the fire was producing a delicious smell. Sir Roger and Sir Alwyn were seated at a rough table on the far side of the large room and they beckoned for the boys to join them.

"Lass, bring these two whelps a mug of ale and a bowl of that stew!" Sir Alwyn said to a passing serving girl, punctuating his order with an affectionate swat to the girl's bottom. She turned on him, a serving ladle raised to strike, but seemed to be mesmerized by the broad grin on the Welshman's face. "You're even prettier from the front!" he declared and she blushed. The burly knight patted his stomach and lifted his own empty bowl to the girl. "I'll have another as well." Roger de Laval shook his head and sighed.

The girl returned with four pints of ale and three steaming bowls of stew, all balanced on a plank of wood. She gave Sir Alwyn a winning smile, which he returned with a wink, then ignored her to return to conversation with Sir Roger. As the boys dug into the hot food, Sir Alwyn launched into a long and slightly confusing tale of how he had narrowly avoided marriage through the years. Roland half-listened to this familiar story between bites of stew and draughts of ale. He felt warm and contented as he finished the bowl and turned to summon the serving girl to fill his empty mug. Across the crowded inn a sudden movement caught his eye. Was it his imagination, or had someone ducked out of sight when he turned?

He tried to dismiss the notion. Surely his enemies could not have tracked him to this inn. He doubted that after four months he was being tracked at all, but he had sworn that the new security he had found in Sir Roger's household would not dull his vigilance. He was unsure of distances, but they must be a good ways from Derbyshire. It was probably some patron leaving for the night, just as he happened to turn. He was unused to crowds and would have to temper his alertness in the crush of people he would encounter in London. He could not bristle like a cat every time someone left a room! *Still*...few men died from being on their guard. Casually, he leaned over to Declan.

"Dec, I will be leaving in a few moments to return to the stable," he whispered. Someone may be watching me and may follow. Will you wait a short while and see who may be on my backtrail?"

Declan was momentarily confused by his friend's request.

"Watchin' ye? Who'd be watchin' a squire?" he whispered

back, a little too loudly for Roland's comfort.

"Shhh!" he cautioned the Irish boy. "If you be my friend, trust me. I will explain, but Declan...*take care.* If I am followed, it won't be by a gentle man."

Declan hesitated a moment and looked keenly at his friend, then nodded.

"Laugh, as I rise to leave," Roland whispered, and rose to his feet.

"Ho ho ho," Declan mimicked a belly laugh. "It appears to be past young Roland's bed time!" he said loudly, as he slapped his fellow squire on the back. "Sleep well, and don't hog my blanket. I'll be along in a bit." The Irish boy turned back to his stew and to Sir Alwyn's story—which was still underway. Roland turned and walked wearily toward the door, stifling a yawn. Through heavy lids, he intently surveyed the crowd as he passed through, but no one appeared to be at all interested in a sleepy squire retiring for the evening.

As he left the confines of the inn, he stopped for a moment to stretch his arms and yawn again. He delayed his departure from the relative security of the crowded inn until his eyes adjusted to the dark. There was no moon, and clouds made the night even darker than usual, but he could see well enough after a moment. He patted his tunic. He felt the hilt of the dagger hidden underneath the material and hoped he would have no need of it.

Maintaining the appearance of a weary boy seeking his bed, he started down the narrow lane that led to the stable. As he passed each dark corner or shadowed gap between dwellings, he steeled himself for a possible attack, but none came. His fellow squire should be on his trail soon, and watching his back. The stable was only a hundred more yards away, and he was beginning to feel a bit foolish. How was he going to explain his actions to Declan?

Undisturbed, he entered the dark confines of the stable and found the spot where he and Declan had laid their bedrolls. He reached inside the tattered cloth he still used to conceal his longbow and withdrew it. He would rather use the bow as a bludgeon than fight with a dagger if it came to that. He sat quietly, waiting for Declan to join him. Minutes passed and his friend made no appearance. Had he misunderstood Roland's whispered instructions? The boy began to worry. Quietly, he rose and slipped out the back entrance to the stable. Clinging to the darkness near the wall of the building, he found a vantage point from which to observe the road. Staying in the shadows, he peered in both directions—and saw nothing. Panic started to rise in his throat. Where was Declan? If he had led his friend to injury or death, he could not bear it!

At that moment, an audible thump issued from a narrow passageway between two huts, not ten yards from where Roland stood. Gripping the bow he moved quickly and silently toward the sound. In the dimness of the passage, he could make out the shape of Declan O'Duinne on the ground, scrambling backwards from a man hovering over him. He stepped forward and swung the longbow, catching the man behind his knees and dropping him to the ground. The man twisted from his back to his stomach as quickly as a cat and started to rise, but Roland clamped a forearm around his neck while bringing his dagger up to prick beneath his chin.

"Move not an inch or you're dead this night!" he hissed. The man momentarily seemed prepared to resist, but the point of the dagger convinced him to remain very still. A flustered Declan O'Duinne managed to collect himself from the dirt of the alley and gain his feet.

"Saw this scoundrel…a creepin' along in your wake," the Irish boy blurted, as he gasped for breath. "I pounced on him. Don't know how he saw me coming. Must have made a sound…lost me footin'…The boy's explanation trailed off into a mumble.

"You flushed him out, Dec. My thanks!" Roland said, cutting off any further apologies. "Now let's see what our friend has to say." He grasped the man by the rough collar of his robe and spun him around, keeping the dagger point close to his neck. In the darkness he could make out no features of the man's hooded face. The boy dragged his captive the short distance to the stables and pulled him inside.

"Declan, go fetch a torch," he ordered. Without a word, the Irish boy bolted back down the village lane toward the inn. Roland kept a tight grip on his captive in the dark, ready to strike if the man made a move, but the dark figure remained motionless.

181

"Who sent you?" he demanded. *"Was it the Earl of Derby?"*

"Heavens no," a calm voice replied.

"Then who—if not the Earl?" Roland countered harshly, easing the tip of his dagger closer to the man's throat.

He could hear Declan approaching at the run.

"It's a puzzlement to me, lad. Perhaps God," returned the voice, as the breathless squire burst into the stable with a blazing torch.

All around them horses shuffled about, disturbed by the sudden light and commotion. Roland was too stunned to notice. Standing before him in the guttering torchlight was Father Augustine—*Tuck!*

"It seems God keeps making our paths cross, my boy," the burly monk said with a grin.

"You know this man?" Declan asked in disbelief.

"Aye, Dec. The friar is a friend," said Roland lowering his dagger.

"Friar?" the Irish boy asked with a snort. "Seems to lack a certain *gentleness* of spirit to be a churchman! Thought he'd broken me back!"

"Forgive me, my son. I've truly a more kindly nature…when not leapt upon in the dark," The priest said, with a hint of amusement.

"Thought ye were a brigand," Declan grumbled.

"Dec, I'll sort this out for you as I've promised," Roland interjected, "but first I must speak with Father Augustine—alone."

Declan shot the monk a suspicious look, but nodded curtly and stepped out of the barn and into the night. Roland turned eagerly to the priest.

"Father…my family."

"They are well, my son, and safe away in Nottinghamshire. They grieve for your father and fear for you, but they are well protected and cared for. Your brother is a restless one, but the girl is a delight. The monks who shelter them are quite smitten."

"Thank God." The boy sank to the floor.

"Aye, He deserves the thanks…and, He appears to have guided your path well. When last I heard you were hard pursued by Ivo Brun, a man who rarely misses his target. By the time this word came to me, there was little I could do but pray."

"Aye, father. When I fled from Derbyshire I thought I had gotten away free. I swear I left hardly any sign as I passed, but it was not enough. I was tracked to York and attacked there," the boy said. "I thought it might be Brun. It was sheer luck I survived."

"De Ferrers must have been desperate to turn to Brun. He is a weapon that can cut both ways," the monk observed with a grim look. Then he brightened.

"And how did you come to be here, Roland? This knight I saw you with at the inn—you are in his service?"

"Aye, father, he is Sir Roger de Laval and he's taken me as squire," Roland answered. "He's a Norman, but seems to care naught for bloodlines. He's married to a Saxon lady of great character and his Master of Arms is a Welshman. He's a good man, Father."

"Then you do well to serve him. And I suppose you are on to London for the coronation?"

"Aye, Father, but what of you? How did you come to be here?"

"Well, I suspect it's as I've said. God directs our feet on occasion. Like you and half of England, I go to London to observe our new king—and to sniff out the politics of things," the little priest said, with a grin and a wink. "The road from Derbyshire joins Watling Street just west of here. Perhaps our meeting was by chance—or perhaps not, but I am glad to see you and to see you have found a place for yourself. I shall look forward to telling your brother and sister!"

"I miss them," Roland said, with a catch in his voice.

"Aye, I know ye must, but ye cannot return to Derbyshire," Tuck said, with a shake of his head. "Young William still rules the land during the Earl's convalescence and I'm not sure he is anxious to hand back the reins of power should his father recover."

"Aye, Father, I had no mind to return—for now, but I must ask after a member of your flock, a strange hermit who aided me. Does he live?"

"Oh, aye, lad. Angus yet abides in the deepest part of the forest. He told me of your brush with Ivo Brun."

"The Earl's son...he still searches for me?"

"I cannot say. William has many scores to settle in his own

183

mind and he has kept Brun busy with them these past months. Oh, I've no doubt he hasn't forgotten you, but he has other concerns at present."

"Concerns, father?"

"The old Earl has always been a hard man and one to maintain firm control over his lands, but not truly cruel by nature. He understood that wanton abuse of his vassals and peasants was bad politics in the long run. Young Lord William has learned nothing of this from his father. His rule is savage. He uses terror to subdue the peasants —and unrest is beginning to grow."

"He will be here for the coronation?" Roland asked, eagerly.

"Aye, he is already in London, seeking favour with Richard, or perhaps John, or—more likely—both." The monk looked sternly at the boy before him.

"I gather you still have an account to settle with de Ferrers. The Bible says that God reserves vengeance unto Himself."

"You said God would understand," Roland countered.

"I said God *did* understand, not that he would *always* understand. Listen to me, boy, you have more at stake here than revenge for the murder of your sire. You are squire to a knight. You injure an Earl, and the full wrath of the nobility will fall, not just on you, but on your knight and his family as well. He would be executed, and his lands confiscated. *Can you live with that?"*

Roland hung his head and clinched his fists in frustration.

"I would not bring this down on Sir Roger, Father, but I have sworn to make de Ferrers pay and the day will come when I will."

The priest shrugged his shoulders. "God moves mysteriously, my son. We shall all receive our due here—or in the next world."

"God may do as he will in the next world, but by my oath, de Ferrers will reach there before I." the boy spoke with finality.

"Very well then!" Tuck replied, slapping his hands together. "I notice ye still have the longbow."

"Aye, Father. And I've had to use it again," the boy said, with a touch of embarrassment. "Welsh raiders."

"Fair game, I'd say!" the monk said, seeing the boy's discomfort. "Will ye enter the archery tournament, then?"

"Tournament, Father?"

"Aye lad, there's been a proclamation issued by Duke Richard that there will be knightly games to celebrate his crowning—jousts, wrestling matches and a great archery tournament. The finest bowmen in the land will be there, but I'd wager that a lad who knows how to use a longbow would have a fair chance. I know of only one other who has the skill, and he's coming from Loxley."

Roland listened sceptically to the friar. He recalled Sir Roger speaking of an archery tournament back on that first day when he had shown him his skill with the bow. His master had seemed confident that he could hold his own in such a contest, but to vie against the best in all of England? He'd hardly stand a chance.

Outside, he heard Declan strike up a conversation. Another squire must be returning to the stables, and his friend was giving him warning and delaying the fellow in the process. Tuck smiled.

"I like your friend. I think he can be trusted, though he needs a bit of work on his handling of brigands. Now, I must be gone, but I'll be about. Watch yourself, for there are hazards beyond Lord William in London."

Without another word, the monk slipped out the back entrance of the stable. Roland went to the front entrance and motioned to Declan, who quickly concluded his conversation with the other squire. They two boys walked into the darkness at the edge of the village.

"Dec…I have a story to tell you," Roland began. The Irish boy stood silently in the dark, waiting. "That day we met…on the road to York…"

"Ye mean the day I almost ran ye through for trying to filch our breakfast?" the other squire corrected him, dryly.

"Aye, that day. That day I was fleeing from the Earl of Derby, Declan. Fleeing for my life."

As he told of the deer he had poached, the attack on his father and the terrible vengeance he had wreaked on the killers, the Irish boy listened silently in the dark. Roland longed to see his friend's face, to gauge his reaction to this tale, but could not. He told of his meeting with Tuck in the forest and how the churchman had protected his family. When he spoke of Ivo Brun and the attack in the stable at York, he heard a short grunt of surprise. Finally, he was finished. He prayed that Declan would understand, but knew that a secret such as this could undo a friendship—whether told or kept. Only Millicent and Tuck were aware of the awful events that had propelled him here, and the girl only knew the barest of details.

For long moments, the boy stood in the darkness and waited for some response from his companion. Perhaps he had misjudged the Irish boy, he thought. A poor lad like Declan, who so yearned to be wealthy, could be tempted to betray him to the Earl of Derby. He would be handsomely rewarded for his trouble. Whatever the outcome, Roland felt a great relief for having unburdened himself. After an agonizing wait, Declan spoke.

"I've always thought the Irish were born to trouble, but you put us all to shame," the boy said, with just a touch of admiration in his voice. "Are ye *sure* you're not Irish, then? Nay, don't answer that, I've heard yer singin' voice and yer *definitely* not of the race."

"Declan, I'm sorry...sorry I didn't tell...sorry I've drawn you into this," Roland stammered, his throat going tight.

"Oh, be quiet." The Irish boy said in exasperation. "Where I'm from men have been known to kill each other for less than nothing. To survive, ye must be loyal to your family, your clan. I'm a long way from Ireland, and I count you, Roland Inness, as my clan." The Irish boy stepped a little into the dim light flickering from the stable door and spit in his hand. He held it out to Roland.

Roland spit in his own palm and grasped that of his friend.

"Clan then," he pronounced, pulling Declan to him and draping his arm around the boy's shoulders. Together, they headed back up the narrow lane of the village. "I think Sir Roger, may be willing to go another pint of ale," Roland said.

"If he doesn't agree, you can threaten to *sing* for him," Declan replied.

Chapter 18

The Crossing of Paths

Roland had never seen so many people in one place. The crowds that had been growing as they approached London were now a throng, and one had to take care not to trample the fellow in front, or to be trampled by those who followed. For as far as he could see along Watling Street, the travellers crept forward. Some of the knights abandoned the road all together and trampled acres of ripening grain under their horses' hooves. The pitiful cries of the peasants tending those fields were simply ignored.

For his part, Sir Roger was undisturbed by their snail's pace and scowled darkly at his peers, cavalierly wasting good grain.

"No wonder the peasants revolt!" he muttered, to no one in particular.

Likewise, Sir Alwyn could only shake his head at the arrogant display. Among those who were in such haste to reach the city, was the Earl of Chester, trailed, as always, by a flock of admirers.

"Looks like a gaggle of goslings chasing the goose," observed Sir Alwyn.

While the crowds made for slow going, the colourful nature of its members relieved the tedium. Jugglers, merchants, magicians and poets, mixed freely with knights, squires and peasants. For Roland, it was like a moving carnival. He found himself twisting, first left, then right, to see what wonders might next appear. Beside him, Declan O'Duinne did the same, though his gaze was a bit more intense. Roland's revelations of the night before had left him anxious for his friend's safety. As he scanned the crowd he studied each face with suspicion. Roland eased his horse up closer and leaned over to his friend.

"*Declan*," he whispered. "It's not likely that assassins are about. Back in York, Bucephalus kicked the only one who knew my face into the next county. So, *please*," he pleaded, "calm yourself. You make me nervous!"

Declan grinned sheepishly. He knew Roland was right and tried to relax. Nevertheless, he kept his hand on the hilt of his short sword, as they moved with the crowd.

The nearer they approached to London proper, the more settled the countryside became. Widely scattered peasant huts had given way to more prosperous and numerous dwellings belonging to wealthier landowners. It was hard to believe that the crowds could grow any larger, but as they approached the suburbs, progress slowed to a near stop. Standing in his stirrups, Roland could just make out the top of some great structure in the distance. Off to his right, across a level field of grain, he could see another large building looming. Sir Roger watched the boy's obvious excitement with amusement.

"That, straight ahead is St. Andrews church, just outside the city walls. That …off yonder," he said, gesturing across the fields, "is the temple and monastery of the Knights Templar."

"Knights Templar, my lord? What sort of knights are these?" Roland asked.

"Fierce ones, lad, and that's a fact. They come from all over Europe and many from noble stock. They've given up all their worldly trappings to dedicate themselves to the liberation and defence of the Holy Land. These knights have taken priestly vows of poverty and, it's said, they be as gentle as sheep when not in battle, but fierce as lions once engaged. Only known a few in my day. Wouldn't want to cross any of 'em!" This last, Sir Roger said with clear conviction.

"Will we see any of these knights in London, my lord?"

"No doubt. They will be few in number, but easy to spot. I'm told, they prepare to join the new king on Crusade and, as token, wear a red cross on their tunics," the knight answered.

"They are few in number, my lord?"

"Aye, tis true enough, though they may have claimed some new members of late. Almost two years ago, lad, terrible news reached us from the Holy Land. You know of Saladin?"

"Aye, my lord. He's the Saracen commander that took Jerusalem. We are taxed in his name." Roland replied, proudly.

"Aye, he took Jerusalem, but he did so after defeating the Christian army in the field. At some God-forsaken place called the 'Horns of Hattin,' he crushed our force, taking the King of Jerusalem and thousands of our knights and soldiers captive, many Templars among them. It is said that he had a particular hatred for the Templars. I don't know the truth of that, but, he gathered all of the Templar Knights he captured on that field and had them beheaded, save the Grand Master."

Sir Roger shook his head sadly. He looked at his squire and could see the shock written on the boy's face.

"It was a foul deed, Roland, but one not uncommon to war. If—as seems likely—we must follow our King to that killing ground, you can expect nothing better—neither from the Saracens nor perhaps from us." The knight paused, looking keenly at his young companion. "Can you face that, Master Inness?"

Roland was still trying to grasp the notion of hundreds of men executed in some far off battlefield, as Sir Roger's question rang in his ears.

"My lord, if face it I must, I cannot say how I may fare." He answered, truthfully. "I can only say that I will go wherever you lead...and do my best."

Sir Roger slapped the boy on the back.

"An honest answer, lad! Any man who says he knows how he will face his first battle is a fool. I practically messed me britches the first time the bugle sounded and a horde of Burgundians came chargin' our lines. Still get nervous when swords are drawn," he continued, lowering his voice to a whisper and leaning over to Roland. *"Hurts like hell to get poked with a spear or slashed with a blade,"* he confided. Rolling up his tunic sleeve he pointed to an ugly raised scar on his left shoulder. *"Cried like a baby over this one, I did."*

Roland was a bit astonished at this admission from a veteran warrior, but comforted as well. He remembered the almost paralyzing fear he had felt in the dark woods of the Clocaenog and, somehow, that no longer seemed so shameful.

"Roger, let's cut across here to Aldersgate," Sir Alwyn interjected. "Newgate is tight as a cork in a bung hole."

Sir Roger stood up in his stirrups and saw the crush of pilgrims seeking to enter the city along Watling Street, which passed through the Newgate.

"Aldersgate it is then," he ordered, and tugged his reins to the left to follow the slightly less-crowded lane that led through the stockyards of Smithfield to the old gate on the northwestern wall of the city. Sir Alwyn spurred up beside him.

"Horde of Burgundians, Roger?" he asked, looking straight ahead.

Sir Roger suppressed a laugh.

"As I recall old friend—and I was there—there were about twenty Burgundians and a like number at our outpost. Even odds I would say and hardly a 'horde'," he said gravely. "Ye did have one thing aright, though. Ye can always tell where the English lines are in battle by yer sense of smell. I just follow the scent of soiled trousers!" With that, Sir Alwyn rode smugly ahead toward the Alders Gate.

***

Lodging was difficult to procure in a city swollen with celebrants preparing for the first coronation in thirty-five years. Nothing was found in the Saddlery area, or near the dairies on Milk Street. Finally, the weary travellers made their way to the bakery district. There, Sir Roger and Sir Alwyn found a small room above an inn to share. The innkeeper agreed to let all four horses and the two boys share space in the cramped stable for an extra pound for the week.

"Told you the extra horses would pauper ye," Sir Alwyn observed, dryly. Sir Roger only grunted.

Once the boys had deposited the large bundles that contained the personal effects of the two knights in the tiny room, Sir Roger called them together.

"Boys, we've arrived later than I thought, given the pace set by our liege lord," he announced. "Still, there are four days 'til the coronation. Enough time to get a feel for this city and…to get into mischief." He said this with a clear warning in his voice. "Heed me well, young squires. I'm no stranger to mischief, meself, but have a care. This is not Shipbrook. I have no power here, and there are many who would do you harm for profit, or just for sport." The man looked closely at the two boys, gauging whether they understood him. They looked back at him earnestly. Satisfied, he continued.

"Now, you'll be released from duty, if your chores are done, *but y*ou'll be abed in the stables afore the crier marks midnight— and I'll be checkin'. Do I make meself clear?"

"Aye, sir!" both boys said in unison, then snickered in embarrassment at their own eagerness.

Sir Roger nodded, and turned to whisper to Sir Alwyn. *"Catherine made me promise to keep 'em reined in."*

Sir Alwyn smiled and nodded his agreement with abiding by instructions from Lady Catherine.

"If the horses be fed and watered and brushed, yer on your own," Sir Roger concluded. The two boys bolted toward the low entrance to the tiny room. "but remember—*midnight!*" the knight shouted, as the boys jockeyed to be first through the door.

"Aye, my lord. Aye, my lord." The boys shouted in turn. *"Midnight! Midnight!"* Then they were gone.

"Ah, to be young again, eh, old friend?" Sir Roger sighed and shook his head. Alwyn arose and gave him a clap on the shoulder.

"You're only as old as ye feel. And I, for one am not too old to forgo the pleasures of London. Don't bother checking me bed at midnight Roger. I won't be in it!"

***

Midnight came sooner than they could have imagined. For hours, the two roamed the torch-lit streets of the capital and marvelled at the activity and commerce that continued far into the night. The crowds had thinned a bit from the afternoon, but were still substantial. They had first followed Bread Street until it met

191

Old Fish Street near the Thames. Turning westward they came to the sprawling compound of the Dominicans friars, built directly into the western wall of the city. A goodly number of these monks, dressed in black robes could be seen entering and leaving the gate of the enclosure. They had passed the large monastery of the Franciscan "Grey Friars" nearby Aldersgate earlier in the day. These Dominicans must be the "Black Friars" they had heard of.

It seemed odd to Roland that a city so heavily populated by churchmen could so openly flaunt some of the behaviour he had seen this night in the shadowy alleyways and even under full torch light, but this was not a time to dwell on such things. Sinful the city might be, but exciting all the same!

Turning eastward again they followed Watling Street further into the city, finally arriving at the banks of the Thames where they beheld a marvel. Here the river was as broad as the Dee as it entered the sea, but London was many miles upriver from the sea. It was a great river indeed, and spanning more than half of its width was a great bridge of stone. A little upstream of this was a ragged wooden bridge that had once spanned the entire river, but now had entire sections missing. Here the dark swirling waters hissed and frothed and sucked at the timbers that supported the mass.

The new bridge was being constructed in a series of great arches. Here too the tidal current sucked and swirled and roared. Even though it was fully dark the span was well illuminated by torches and, since none seemed to object they ventured out onto it to the very end where several hundred yards of dark water separated them from the southern bank. There a few feeble lights could be seen, but all else was darkness.

Looking back across the dark water, they could see the city arrayed before them. To the right, was a large fortress, also illuminated by torches. Declan believed it to be the "Tower Castle," built by King William the Conqueror. Sweeping from that great structure westward, the lanes of the city could be seen as illuminated strands in a darker tapestry. To Roland, it all looked too beautiful for words. As they returned to the northern shore, the crier was just calling midnight. The two boys ran, like their lives depended on it, back to the stable, and were just catching their breath when Sir Roger peered in, carrying a torch. Seeing the boys safe, though winded, he nodded and left without a word.

***

The few days remaining until the coronation flew by as Roland and Declan tended to their chores and roamed the city when placed at freedom. Mischief, they saw aplenty, but managed to avoid any of their own. The city was as wicked as Sir Alwyn had described it. Thieves, pickpockets, and worse abounded in the crowded thoroughfares and narrow lanes of London—but so too did minstrels, magicians, jesters and other artists. Vendors were everywhere. Some were concentrated in districts, such as the bakers near their own inn and the fishmongers down by the river. Others roved where they could find customers.

All the talk was of Richard and his mother Eleanor, the Queen. News travelled fast in the streets of the capital, and, thus far, the news appeared to be good. The Queen, with Richard's blessing, had personally ordered the commutation of sentences for the many men languishing in prison for the crime of poaching the king's deer. King Henry had taken great personal offense at the taking of his game, and the dungeons of England were full of men who had paid a great price for a bit of venison. The Queen, it was said, knew that each released man had a family and that each family had neighbours and that soon, all across England, grateful multitudes would be hailing the mercy of the new King. And so it seemed, at least in the streets of London. For Roland, the news of clemency was bittersweet. His crimes had gone far beyond poaching. Nor would his Rolf Inness be returning to his family in this life.

In the last two days, the boys had grown fairly comfortable with their ability to get about in the crowded city and hardly made note any longer of where they were wandering. When you are free to go where you will, any direction is a good as another, Roland thought to himself, as they turned onto Watling Street and made their way out the Newgate. Declan was eager to see some of the grand mansions that were said to crowd along the Strand, which ran from the Templars' compound directly to the Abbey and Palace at Westminster, where the King kept his residence.

The great Barons of the realm, Earl Ranulf among them, had built their city residences here on the Strand. It was to the Earl's city manor that Sir Roger and Sir Alwyn repaired on most days, though primarily to lounge about the grounds and keep company with other knights who were vassals to the Earl. The Earl spent his days and nights entertaining other members of the high nobility and prelates of the church. His lands in Cheshire were of great strategic importance to the kingdom, which made him a man to be reckoned with.

Once the boys left the crush of newcomers entering the city at Newgate and turned onto the Strand, the going was easier. On their left, they passed the fortress-like Temple and quarters of the Knights Templar. Both boys, impressed by Sir Roger's account of these knightly priests, peered through the dark entrance gate, but saw no one. Disappointed, they pressed on toward Westminster. As they entered the district, Roland wondered if they could pick out Earl Ranulf's dwelling among all the splendour.

"Dec, which is it?" he asked his friend, plaintively, as he looked at one great mansion after another.

"Gad, Roland…they all look fit for an Earl. *Where* do they get the funds to build such palaces?" the Irish boy replied, amazed at the grandeur of it all.

"The peasants!" The two squires turned to see who had spoken to them. There, leaning against the trunk of a spreading shade tree, was Sir Alwyn.

"Ho! What have we here? Two lost babes?"

"Sir Alwyn!" Declan shouted. "Well met! We're looking for the Earl's palace and seem to have stumbled upon it."

"That ye have, lads," the Welshman replied. "Come take a seat and view the pageant." As the two boys complied, he lowered his voice and continued. "From here, you can see more perfumed cocks strutting by than anywhere in London," he whispered and winked. As the boys found places beside him beneath the tree, they saw what the knight meant. The Strand was full of well-bred horses and equally well-bred noblemen and women. All seemed in a bit of a rush to visit with the others. Roland marvelled at the finery of their dress. Even the horses were adorned in brilliant colours and bore saddles of incredible workmanship and beauty. It truly was a sight unlike any he had ever seen.

Presently, they were joined by Sir Roger, who had just

completed attendance at a tedious audience with the Earl.

"Ho, what's this the dogs drug in, Alwyn?" He laughed as he caught sight of the boys.

"Puppies," the seated knight responded.

"Well, they have the best seat on the Strand. Think I'll join ye." The big Norman knight settled on the grass beside Roland.

"Squire Inness, I've been giving some thought to how I might recoup the expense of providing you and your companion with mounts for this trip. Alwyn thinks I should withhold food, but I have another plan."

The mention of withholding food had caught Declan's attention, and the two boys waited, anxiously, to hear how they would have to repay their master for the luxury of riding to London.

"Lad, it's time ye used that bow for something other than shootin' gourds...or Welshmen." Sir Alwyn gave his friend a sour look. "Only a handful of folk in all of England know what ye can do with that thing, and therein lays our profit!"

"Profit, my lord?" Roland asked.

"Aye, lad. I plan to enter ye in the King's archery tournament, and lay a small wager on yer performance."

Roland had known about the contest since his encounter with Friar Tuck on the road to London, but hadn't really considered the possibility that he would compete. He had no notion of how skilful the other bowmen were, but he was sure that many could best him.

"My lord, are you sure that's wise? I've never been in such a competition."

"That's what makes it perfect, lad. No one will know ye. I'm sure to get excellent odds."

"Odds, my lord?"

Sir Roger looked at Roland and Declan, then at Sir Alwyn. "Perhaps, Sir Alwyn will explain the meaning of it, when yer a bit older. For now, concern yerself only with shooting as well as I know ye can. The rest will take care of itself."

"But, my lord, what of the ban on the weapon? Will they not arrest me on the spot?"

Sir Roger smiled, undeterred.

"The weapon is not banned for Normans, son, and if I choose to call it mine and have my squire employ it, none will question it."

The man's confidence made Roland very nervous. He did not want some of his master's already stretched finances frittered away on his performance, but Sir Roger would listen to none of his protests. The decision was made.

For the next hour, they watched the pageant passing by, and the boy was able to forget his new dread of the archery tournament. Though they were never close to boredom, Declan was starting to get restless and proposed to Roland that they complete their expedition down the Strand. He wanted to continue on to Westminster to view the Abbey and Palace. Roland agreed, and the two boys rose and started toward the crowded roadway. Suddenly, Roland froze.

There, not more than twenty yards away, stood Sir William de Ferrers. The man had just dismounted from a magnificent black charger and was straightening his cape and tunic. There was no mistaking the sharp, hawk-like features. This was the man who had ordered the death of his father! Roland felt rage swell in his chest. Instantly, the pledge he'd made to Tuck to forgo his vengeance was forgotten. The image of his father, falling face down in the tilled field of their farm, was etched cleanly in his mind. Here at last was his chance to settle accounts! The boy moved, as if in a trance, toward the nobleman, his hand drifting toward the hilt of the dagger in his belt. Sir William was completely unaware of the approaching danger—but Sir Roger de Laval was not.

He saw the boy freeze, as the nobleman dismounted, and was alarmed at the look on his squire's face. If ever a boy had murder in his eyes, this one did. The big knight was up in flash. Roland had the dagger half drawn and was coiling to leap on the man when he was deftly tripped from behind and went sprawling, face down, at the feet of Sir William de Ferrers. Sir Roger grasped him by the collar from behind and hauled him to his feet. The unexpected flurry of movement startled the future Earl of Derby.

"What's this then?" he said. There was alarm in his voice, as he stumbled backwards and bumped into his horse.

"Forgive the boy, my lord," Sir Roger interjected. "He's from the country and a bit *clumsy*, ye know." The big knight now had Roland firmly in his grasp. "It's me sister's boy, my lord," the knight continued, rolling his eyes for the benefit of the nobleman.

"He loves the horses, and just wanted to have a look at your magnificent beast."

Recovering a little, Sir William stared at the man and the boy before him. He didn't notice Declan O'Duinne and Alwyn Madawc, holding their breath a few yards away.

"And who might *you* be?" he asked pointedly, as he brushed at his tunic. His own squire was frantically calming his master's startled horse.

"My lord, it is an honour to meet you," Sir Roger resumed hastily, fearful that Roland might speak. "I am Sir Roger de Laval of Shipbrook, vassal to Earl Ranulf. I fought with your father, Lord Robert, in Ireland. He is a magnificent soldier."

"Quite..." the future Earl replied, absently. He seemed bored and about to dismiss the incident, when he stopped and looked hard at the boy.

"Where did you come by that dagger," he asked, pointing to the weapon still in Roland's belt. "I've seen one like it—somewhere."

Before Roland could reply, Sir Roger twisted his grip tighter on the boy's collar—a silent warning to hold his tongue.

"It was his father's—God rest his soul—my lord. Died a year ago, and left it to the boy. He's lucky one of these cursed London pickpockets haven't lifted it from him by now. I told him to leave it back in Cheshire, but..."

Sir William raised a hand for silence. He looked at Roland suspiciously, but spoke to Sir Roger.

"See that this imbecile squire of yours stays clear of me and my horse in the future," he said, in a harsh, commanding tone, "or I'll have him flogged—and perhaps you as well." With a final sniff, he turned and was gone.

Roland could hardly breathe, partly because of the sudden fury that had seized him and partly because the grip of the large Norman knight was practically strangling him. For a moment, no one moved. Then Sir Roger whirled him around, released his collar, and dragged him by an arm into a nearby alleyway.

"Hear... me...well, Master Inness." He spoke with barely contained anger, as he gripped Roland's tunic in his scarred hands and pulled the boy's face close. "I owe ye much for saving

197

Millie—more than I can probably ever repay—but ye almost were the ruin of us all there!" The big man struggled to form his words. "That man may be a murderin' pig, but he rules half the midlands and could have us in a dungeon or worse *instantly*, with *none* to gainsay him. Do ye not understand that?"

"My…my lord." Roland stammered, searching for a reply.

"Shut…up!" the big knight snapped, and shook the boy. "I know he killed yer father! There's nothin' to be done about it—at present. Trust to God, and wait yer time, Roland—*wait yer time.*"

The boy stood silent. He knew the man spoke the truth, but could barely accept it. *Wait? For how long? Until de Ferrers expired of old age?*

No, no matter how long he must wait and endure, he swore that William de Ferrers would die no peaceful death in his bed. And for that, he would bide his time.

Chapter 19

Long Live the King

Dawn broke on coronation day to the sound of church bells chiming everywhere in London. Indeed, church bells throughout the land rang out the happy occasion. England would have a new King! Roland was long awake, when the first notes in this chorus sounded from the belfry of St. Paul's. Still shaken from his encounter with William de Ferrers, he had slept little. He felt in no mood for celebration.

In the still-dark shadows of the stable, Declan stirred, rose, and stumbled over to join his friend by the entrance.

"Infernal racket!" the Irish boy complained, groggily. "Should wait 'til they've crowned the man...then have a proper party." He concluded his comments with a great yawn. Roland remained leaning against the doorway and said nothing.

Declan looked at his friend and draped an arm over his shoulders. "I see, while all England rejoices, you remain in a foul mood, my friend. Let's go find some breakfast. That should cheer ye up!"

Roland was forced to smile, just a bit. It was hard to stay troubled for long around Declan O'Duinne. For Declan, life was a straight-forward proposition...eat well, sleep well and—somehow—find your fortune. Roland thought it was an excellent outlook, as he trailed after his friend toward the nearest bakery. After all, he was hungry!

To the boys' surprise, they found Sir Alwyn at the bakers before them. "Try the apple tart," he managed to advise them, through a mouthful of the pastry. "Magnificent!" Catching the sweet smell of baking apples coming from the rear of the shop, this was easy advice for the boys to take. Soon, their mouths were equally stuffed with the delicious, freshly baked confection.

"Glad I ran into ye," Sir Alwyn said, as he licked the remnants of apple from his fingers. "Sir Roger wants ye in his quarters, first thing. I was just comin' to rouse ye."

Together, the knight and two squires made their way back to the inn. Roland noticed that the streets were far more crowded than usual at this hour and that there was a great sense of urgency in the movements of the people. Despite his bad temper, he couldn't help but catch a bit of the excitement that coursed through the streets around him. He still couldn't believe that a peasant boy from Derbyshire was going to be present at a coronation!

Of course, only the highest nobility would be in attendance at Westminster Abbey for the actual ceremony. Like many of the lesser nobility, Sir Roger and Sir Alwyn had been ordered by their Lords to join the cordon of honour near the Abbey to hold back the riff raff of London as the new King proceeded from Westminster Palace to the Abbey. The boys were to join them in this duty. It was an exciting prospect.

As they entered the tiny room shared by Sir Roger and Sir Alwyn, the Norman knight rose and smiled broadly at his two squires. Both boys gasped at his appearance. The plain, rough cloth tunic and leather breeches that seemed to constitute the man's total wardrobe were gone.

He stood before them, dressed all in black. His perfectly tailored black breeches were tucked neatly into the top of soft, black leather boots. From his shoulders hung a black tunic, made of a shiny cloth Roland had never seen before. Emblazoned on his chest was the de Laval coat-of-arms, the rampant white stag. Below this skilfully embroidered crest, a belt of black leather, secured with an ornate buckle of pure silver, girded the knight's waist. From his left hip, hung a black scabbard, inlayed with silver. The grip on the hilt of the broadsword was of black leather with a spiral of silver thread woven in.

"What do you think?" he asked.

Declan let out a low whistle.

"Fit for a coronation, my lord," Roland said, with complete conviction.

"Pretty," Sir Alwyn said, with a smirk.

Sir Roger gave his old friend a sour look. "Are we jealous, Alwyn? Well, don't fret, for Catherine has provided for everyone." He turned and swept his arm toward the small cot by the far wall. There, in neat bundles, were three outfits—all, near replicas of Sir Roger's attire. The Welsh knight and the squires eagerly examined their new clothes. None had ever owned anything remotely so fine.

Sir Alwyn, for once sincerely moved, turned to Sir Roger.

"Roger, as God is me witness, ye got the last good lass in Britain when ye snagged Catherine!"

"Aye to that, Alwyn, aye to that," the big knight said. "Now, let's get 'em on!"

No further urging was needed, as the three discarded their rather tattered old garments and slipped on the new. Roland thrust his prized dagger into his belt to complete his preparations. They all agreed that the men from Shipbrook would cut a rather dashing figure at the coronation.

"Well then," Sir Roger said, signifying the end of further preening, "we are to assemble at Earl Ranulf's quarters by mid-morning. So let's be off!"

***

Less than a league away, in a magnificent manor house that fronted on the Strand, Sir William de Ferrers was finishing his own breakfast. He enjoyed having the man in front of him wait, as he daintily dabbed at his mouth and sipped at a cup of honey mead. Things had changed since his father had fell ill and left him in charge—changed for the better. The old man had grown soft through the years, but *he* ruled in Derbyshire now, and there would be no further softness.

Nothing illustrated his new status more than the man who waited patiently for him to finish his morning meal. Six months ago, he had actually been frightened of this creature, but no longer. His power was so absolute, that even Ivo Brun must bow before it. When the assassin spoke to him now, it was with proper deference.

"Brun, I was wondering what became of that dagger of yours—the fancy one with the jewel in the handle. Haven't seen you wear it since spring." The young nobleman spoke with studied nonchalance.

Ivo Brun hesitated but a moment, before answering. "Sold it, my lord. Didn't like the balance of it."

"Did you sell it to some stupid varlet, with two left feet?

"Pardon, my lord?"

"Oh…yesterday, I happened upon a young squire from Cheshire with a dagger—much like yours. In fact I'd swear it was the very same one. Clumsy fool almost fell on top of me on my visit to Earl Ranulf. He claimed it was his father's blade, but unless *you* are the idiot's sire—and I see no resemblance—or your dagger has an exact twin, then we have a mystery here. Aren't you curious as to how your blade came to be in the possession of this boy from Cheshire?"

"Curious, my lord? Perhaps, the man I sold it to sold it himself—to this young idiot, or the idiot's father. If so, the clumsy boy has got himself a clumsy blade."

"Perhaps…perhaps, but still, I am curious. I may have this boy brought to me, to inquire further. He squires for some vassal of de Blundeville—*de Laval*, I think the man said. I'll let you know if I solve this little mystery."

"As you wish, my lord." Ivo Brun knew he had been dismissed and backed out of the presence of his master. He was sure he had given nothing away by his answers, even though near panic gripped his gut. That dagger had been unique—enough so as to make it unlikely to have a twin. *The boy!* It had to be.

Ivo Brun cursed the luck that would bring this troublesome boy to London and to the attention of his master. There must be no chance of a further meeting. He must finish the job he had started—

and soon.

***

As the delegation from Shipbrook covered the distance between their inn and the Strand, they mixed with thousands of Londoners streaming toward Westminster. The crowd hoped to secure a vantage point from which to catch a glimpse of their new monarch. Most gave way at the approach of the tall Norman knight and his three black-clad companions. When all had assembled at the Earl's residence, the Earl's Marshal, Sir Edmund Rose, organized the vassal knights and their retainers and led the group along the Strand to Westminster. There, they were given stations along the processional route that led from the Palace to the Abbey.

The entire length of the path had been covered with a fine woollen cloth. Knights from throughout the realm were taking their assigned posts to form a barrier against the friendly, but unruly, crowds of commoners, who were out to see their King. Roland noticed that a small group of knights, uniformly dressed in white tunics emblazoned with a red cross, lined the processional route for the final hundred feet leading to the Abbey. With a start, he realized that these must be the warrior monks of the Knights Templar! Sir Roger and Sir Alwyn were posted less than fifty feet from the Templars. Roland and Declan took up station just behind the two knights, who faced inward. The boys turned outwards. They had been instructed to alert the knights to any threats posed by the crowd.

For over an hour, they watched as the crowd swelled. The mood was one of excitement, if not positive joy. Duke Richard's reputation as a warrior and the skilful political moves made by the Queen since her release from imprisonment had completely won over the people of London. They were in a proper temper to celebrate. No threat seemed likely from this happy mass of people.

At last, a trumpet sounded from the direction of the Palace and an excited murmur ran through the crowd. Richard was coming! Moments later, a great cheer could be heard from the people gathered near the Palace. As the procession approached, the cheering grew deafening. Roland alternated between scanning the crowd and looking over his shoulder for the approach of the royal party.

The procession finally came into view, led by a host of clergy. A priest proceeded all, casting Holy Water before him. Another priest came next, carrying a great golden cross. Behind the cross came an assortment of priors, abbots and bishops. The slow progress of the group made it easy for Roland to see all, without neglecting his duty to observe the crowd.

The high nobility of the land followed close on the heels of the churchmen. Roland could not recognize which of these men held which great landholdings in the realm, but there was no mistaking their wealth and power. As fine as the boy's new clothing was, it could not compare to that of the great barons of the land. One nobleman carried a golden sceptre topped with a cross and, another, a rod of gold topped by a dove—symbols of the royal authority. Behind them, a group of six—including Earl Ranulf—carried a litter on their shoulders, upon which rested the royal arms and robes. Other great nobles followed. Roland searched, but could not identify William de Ferrers in the large group, though, doubtless, he was there.

After a short gap in the parade, came four barons, bearing a canopy of silk on lofty spears. Shaded under this canopy was the Queen, Eleanor of Aquitaine, wife to two kings and mother to a third. Roland studied her intently. She was quite old, but there could be no mistaking the regal bearing and commanding presence of the woman. There were no signs of frailty.

In her wake, came her youngest son—the surviving royal brother—Prince John. The Prince, who was also shaded by a canopy, seemed distracted and had a sour look on his face. He was taller than most, but seemed to hunch over as he proceeded toward the Abbey. Roland was vaguely disappointed. Having seen the Queen, he expected all royals to possess a certain majesty. Prince John did not. He merely looked anxious to be done with the ceremony.

Next came an Earl, carrying the massive, golden crown of England, encrusted all around with precious jewels. Directly behind him came four more Barons bearing a second silk canopy. Beneath the canopy strode Richard, the Duke of Anjou, known on the continent as Couer-de-Leon...*Richard the Lionheart*! He looked, to Roland, as one might imagine a warrior king. Tall and well-muscled, he moved with a disciplined grace. His long, reddish hair hung to near his shoulders, from which draped a dazzling cape of ermine and red silk. His tunic and breeches were of purest white, with elaborate inlays of gold embroidery.

The crowds went wild at the sight of their new sovereign and surged forward. Roland and Declan pushed back, while Sir Roger and Sir Alwyn locked arms to hold back the crush. In the bedlam, a man edged his way out of the crowd. He was not comfortable surrounded so closely by all this stinking humanity. Nor did he care who was King of England. He was a hunter, and while he preferred the forest paths, his game was somewhere here.

He turned, one last time, to watch the new king entering the nave of Westminster Abbey, and was turning back, when he froze. Above the milling throng he caught a glimpse of a man, taller than the rest, standing along the processional route with his back to the crowd. Instantly he recognized the silhouette that he had followed for hours on the road to York. It was the big knight! He waited patiently as the crowd dispersed now that the King had passed. Then, through a brief gap, he saw it. The face he had expected and hoped never to see again. *The boy!*

It was an unlucky trick of fate that had brought this accursed youth here, but this was an opportunity to undo his failure, to repay this troublesome peasant for the pain and humiliation he had endured. Each morning, when he arose, he felt the place in his side where the damned horse had kicked him and his nose had never healed properly where this stupid boy had struck him!

"This time, young friend, I shall not miss," he hissed to himself. *"And I shall have my dagger back, as well!"*

***

For over two hours, the cordon of knights held back the people of London, while inside Westminster Abbey, Richard Plantagenet was crowned Richard I, King of England. At the conclusion of the rituals, a mass was said and the new King reemerged from the nave to the cheers of his subjects. Upon his head he now wore the ceremonial crown of the realm and in the crook of his left arm, he carried the golden sceptre.

As he retraced his steps to the palace, the King acknowledged the cheers with an occasional wave and nod. Then he was gone. Within the hour he would host a great coronation banquet for the lords of the realm and by mid afternoon, the royal family and their guests would repair to the tournament grounds to view the jousting and archery competitions. He had declared that the winner of the joust would receive a golden dagger and the winner of the archery competition a golden arrow.

As Sir Roger and the party from Shipbrook made their way back along the Strand toward the inn, Roland found himself growing increasingly nervous. His name had been entered among the contestants in the archery competition, but the excitement of being in the city had kept his anxiety at bay. Now, the time was upon him, and he felt ill-prepared to face the finest bowmen in England. Sir Roger noticed the worried look on the boy's face and drew him aside as they reached the inn.

"Listen to me, Roland. I've seen many a man draw a bow, but *none* better than you. Do ye even know how good ye are?"

"Aye, Sir Roger. I know I have skill. My father taught me well. But…I'm afraid…afraid I will fail you…and myself, in front of the king," he blurted.

"Har!" the big knight snorted. *"Fail me?* I care little for whether ye win or lose this little competition. I won't be wagering the title to Shipbrook on the outcome! What matters to me is if ye can take a man down in the thick of the battle, when all is confusion and fear. *That* matters. I know what ye did in the Clocaenog, so— win or lose this contest—I'll be proud to have ye with me when it counts."

He paused a moment to gauge if his words were having an effect, then continued. "These fellows…these knights, who play at war in the jousts—I wouldn't give a copper coin for the lot of 'em, not until they've stood in the line and held their ground against a real enemy. Roland, just shoot like your sire taught ye and win that gold arrow! A little gold can't hurt."

By this time, Roland was feeling better. Sir Roger had lifted a burden from him and his fear was starting to turn to excitement. What if he did win the golden arrow? It would be a fortune to a poor squire.

Longbow

"Go fetch yer bow and join us in the inn," Sir Roger said. "The innkeeper has promised a banquet of his own an hour hence to celebrate the coronation." Roland had not realized how hungry he was, but the thought of a banquet caused his stomach, which was ever vigilant, to rumble loudly.

"*Quiet,*" he scolded his gut, as he hurried around the inn to the stables in the rear. The horses seemed a bit agitated by his sudden entrance, but he knew they were just anxious to get out of their stalls and get some exercise. Quickly, he went to the one empty stall that he and Declan had claimed for sleeping quarters. He moved his rolled up woollen blanket from its spot and dug through the layer of straw underneath. To his alarm, he reached the dirt of the floor without finding the wrapped bundle that held his longbow. Frantically he clawed through the remaining straw covering the stall. The bundle was gone! He leapt to his feet in a panic, his mind racing. It had been there when they left for the coronation! Somehow a thief...

"*Are you looking for this?*" A guttural voice came from directly behind the boy. He whirled to see its source. Standing before him was a dark, muscular man with a scarred face and horribly crooked nose. In his hand, he held the longbow.

"*Who are you?*" Roland blurted.

"Mayhap ye' don't recognize me," the man said, as his face broke into a wicked grin. "Ye gave me this," he growled, pointing to his mangled nose, "and ye took that from me." He pointed to the dagger in Roland's belt. "*I've come t' settle accounts.*" The man dropped the longbow at his feet and withdrew a long dagger from his boot. He advanced slowly into the stall.

Roland drew his own dagger and went into a fighting crouch as Sir Alwyn had taught him. His mind raced. He had always feared that one day there would be a final reckoning with Ivo Brun—for undoubtedly it was Brun who stood before him. He had escaped the man once through luck and surprise. Now it was he who was surprised. Centring his weight on the balls of his feet he made ready to meet the man's thrust. It was quick in coming. Brun feinted once, then lunged forward. Roland had begun to react to the feint, but stopped himself in time to dodge the main thrust. As he leaped backwards, he came up hard against the wall. He had no more room to manoeuvre.

Brun recovered quickly from his miss and could see that the boy was now cornered. He moved in. The game was over. But to the assassin's surprise the boy went on the attack, feinting a swipe at his head, then thrusting at his chest. He had to leap backwards quickly to avoid the blade. *Someone has been teaching the whelp— but no matter.* Brun gave ground slowly, countering each manoeuvre the boy made, judging his skill with the dagger. *Passable*, he thought, *but not good enough.*

Now he went over to the offensive. His thrust at the boy's gut was so convincing that it forced a counter. Too late, Roland saw that it was a feint. Brun's blade sliced into the muscle of his left shoulder as he twisted to avoid the surprise blow. Despite the searing pain of the blow, the boy was able to recover and keep his guard up. Luckily the wound was not to his sword arm. He could still wield his blade.

Slowly Brun forced him back once more into the stall as he manoeuvred for a clean strike at a vital spot. Roland could see that his skill was no match for the man in front of him, but he fought with the desperation of a cornered man. He gave ground slowly, but knew that, inevitably, he would miss a counter or react to a feint and Brun would finish him.

He resolved to close with his tormentor. If he could get within the arc of the killer's blade it would nullify his skill with the weapon, but even so his chances were poor. The man was heavily muscled in his shoulders and thighs and at close quarters would certainly overmaster him. As Brun moved forward, Roland managed to counter a sweeping blow from the dagger and lunged forward. His left hand frantically sought the wrist of the man's knife hand—and found it, just as an iron grip seized his own. Now it would be a test of strength, rather than skill with a blade.

The boy was big for his age and stronger than most. A lifetime of hard labour had made him thus, but he was not yet a match for Ivo Brun. His disadvantage was made worse by the wound to his left shoulder, which now burned like fire and felt strangely weak. Slowly the assassin brought his knife hand down. When it reached an awkward angle he forced it forward and the boy felt the blade just miss his ribs. He twisted away and scrambled to his feet. The pain in his shoulder was now a fiery agony, but he would not give this man the satisfaction of giving up. He raised the dagger and motioned Brun forward.

"Come… take back your blade—*if you can!*"

The assassin moved in to finish a job long overdue.

"Brun!" a commanding voice froze the boy and his attacker. Ivo Brun whirled around instantly, prepared to strike. Before him, stood a short, stocky man in a white tunic with a bright red cross inscribed upon its front—unmistakably a Templar! To Roland's utter astonishment, he recognized the face. It was that of Father Augustine—*Friar Tuck!*

With a chilling growl, Ivo Brun leapt at the man, his dagger arcing downward with blinding speed. The blade never found its mark. With a movement, too quick to follow, the little monk sidestepped and brought a meaty fist down on the back of Brun's head. The assassin went down in a heap, but leaped instantly back to his feet, his dagger thrust before him.

The Templar knight stood motionless between the killer and the boy. He had not even drawn his broadsword.

"This is not your fight!" Brun spat out at the strange knight before him.

"Oh, but it is, my son," Tuck replied calmly. "You see, I have a small wager placed on young Master Inness here, in the archery contest…and you seem to have taken his bow!"

"Die then!" Brun shrieked, and leapt again at the monk. To the attacker's surprise, his target met him in mid leap. In one swift motion, his wrist was seized and the dagger turned inward. The man could not halt his forward motion, as the blade sank into his chest. He fell to the straw, sputtering and choking, a surprised look on his face. Then he was still.

The Templar Knight leaned down and withdrew the dagger, wiping it on the fallen man's sleeve. "I believe this is yours," he said, bending down to retrieve the longbow and tossing it to the boy. I see you've been nicked, lad. Let's have a look."

At the friar's urging, the boy slipped the tunic over his head. The wound was not crippling, but would be stiff and painful for weeks. Tuck ripped a strip of white cloth from his own tunic to bind the boy's shoulder.

"You're lucky!" he said, tossing the boy his new tunic. "The blade did more damage to you than to this fine looking garment. You can hardly notice the rip."

Roland slipped the long shirt over his head and smiled at this man, who had again been his protector.

"Father, how did you come to be here?

"I told you I'd be about in the city, my son," the monk said. "I saw your party leaving the coronation, but I lost you in the crowd. It was plain luck I spied our mutual friend Master O'Duinne laying about in front of the inn. I figured you might be in the stable, but had no notion you might have...*company*." Tuck nodded toward the inert figure on the ground. "*Ivo Brun.* He's troubled my flock over long. I should have killed him long ago. You seem to make deadly enemies, Master Inness."

"Aye, Father, I certainly do...but how...how did you come to be a Templar?"

"Oh, I've been a Templar for near twenty years, lad. When the uprising in the North failed, your father and I were hunted men. Somehow, he managed to blend in with the rest of the Danish peasants. The Earl never knew that one of the fiercest leaders the rebels had was hiding in plain view. His neighbours never betrayed him. Your sire built a simple life up there on Kinder Scout, but a good one. I envy him that."

The warrior monk paused and seemed to reflect on the choices made so long ago. "As for myself, well, I was a Saxon, and had fewer places to hide. I fled to London, and there was recruited as a 'Soldier of God'. At that moment, the Holy Land seemed a very good place to hide. So I went."

"You have been to the Holy Land, Father?" Roland asked.

"Aye son, I was there for near fifteen years," the friar replied, shaking his head. "It is a magnificent and fearful place, full of the glory of God and the weaknesses of men. Somehow, amid all the hate and fear and bloodshed, I found myself growing to be more the monk and less the knight. I had my fill of the endless skirmishes with the Saracens. The change was noticed and the Grand Master felt I had lost my edge. I took leave of the Order and returned to England. I made my way back to the north, there to minister to the sheep in the farthest pastures. I had changed much in the years since I fought with the rebels as a young knight. None recognized me, which suited my purposes. I go where the parish priests fear to tread. The forest people, who are my flock, know me as Tuck. They also know I can dispense a cracked skull, as easily as a prayer." He paused and smiled.

"This seems to help with my acceptance among them."

"But you have returned to London, and you dress as a Templar."

"Aye, it felt a bit odd to put on the red cross once more, but times have changed. Two years ago most of the men I knew among the Templars died at the Horns of Hattin. You know of this battle, my son?"

"Aye, father. Saladin had the Templars…*beheaded*." The boy stopped, embarrassed by his own bluntness.

"That he did, Roland, all save the Grand Master, Gerard de Ridfort, a man of surpassing courage and monumental stupidity. Saladin spared his life, I'm convinced, to ensure that a madman would continue to lead the Templars. A year later the man led the Order into another disaster. He was again captured and, this time, Saladin had no further patience. He too was beheaded."

"And now?" Roland asked.

"Now, England has a warrior king who has taken the cross. Make no mistake, Richard will spare no effort to liberate Jerusalem from the Mohammedans," Tuck said, with conviction. "He is selling titles and lands to finance his army, and it's said he'd sell London—if he could find a buyer who could afford it! I have been recalled by the Master of the London Temple to aid the King in this Crusade. I know not my role as yet, and I would rather return to Derbyshire, but it shall be…as God wills it."

The priest paused and made the sign of the cross. "I must go now. I have some refuse to dispose of." He lifted the crumpled body of Ivo Brun over his shoulder, as though it were a sack of turnips and turned back to the squire. "Can ye shoot with that arm boy?"

Roland flexed the shoulder. It was still painful and very stiff, but he would be hanged if Ivo Brun's last act would keep him from this tournament.

"Aye, Father."

"Then, win me some money at the archery tourney—and we'll be square," the monk said, and left through the alley entrance to the stable.

Roland's head was swimming. Friar Tuck, the odd priest who had found him in the forest was a warrior of the Knights Templar. Declan and he were lucky to have survived their attack on the man in the alleyway outside St. Albans! For a moment, he saw again the lightning quickness of the monk, as he turned Ivo Brun's blade back on its owner. *Brun was dead!* Suddenly the magnitude of that fact came home to him. Ivo Brun was the only man who could tie him to the killing of the soldiers in Derbyshire! For the first time in half a year, it seemed that he might truly escape punishment for his crime.

"Roland, Sir Roger says you'll miss the feast!" It was Declan O'Duinne. Roland turned to his friend and smiled.

"Wouldn't want to do that," he said. "Hard to shoot straight on an empty stomach!"

Longbow

Chapter 20

The Tournament

The new King finally arrived at the archery pavilion in the late afternoon. He had come directly from the jousts, where he had presented the golden dagger to Sir Oliver Stafford. It was said that Sir Oliver had unseated his final foe with a mace, after his lance had splintered. Sir Roger had scoffed at the account.

"Play actors!" he snorted.

The foursome from Shipbrook had joined a growing multitude of archers from all over England and, judging from a few kilts, Scotland as well. All were gathered in a cordoned area set off from the archery range and shaded by spreading oak trees. The afternoon had grown bright and hot, as they waited for the new ruler of England to open the competition.

Suddenly, there was a ripple in the crowd waiting near the royal pavilion. The King had arrived! Cheers started to rise from the crowd, and the tall figure of Richard could be seen entering the viewing stands. With him was the Queen, who looked as energetic as she had that morning, and Prince John, whose mood seemed not to have improved. Roland watched as the King called the tournament master forward and bade him proceed. The match was on!

For the first time, he withdrew the great longbow from its

wrapping and applied the powerful leverage needed to bend and string, the weapon. The effort produced an alarming pain and a slight tremble in his left arm—his bow arm. Distracted, the boy did not notice that he had drawn the interest of some of his rivals.

"It's a Viking bow!" a tall archer announced, advancing toward Roland. "Let me see that, boy. These cursed things are forbidden." He reached for the bow with complete authority. Roland jerked it away

"Don't touch it!" he snarled, surprising himself with the passion of his reaction. The tall bowman had not expected this response from the boy.

"Why you...*stripling*," he sputtered. "I'll thrash ye for that!" He advanced again toward the boy. Roland did not hesitate. Reaching into his belt, he drew his jewelled dagger and held it before him.

"Touch the bow and you eat this," he said grimly.

The man hesitated. He was much larger than the boy, but the dagger looked lethal and the boy was not cowed by his threat. A crowd had gathered as the two exchanged words, and the situation was growing awkward. Sir Roger de Laval made his way forward from the rear of the crowd. He had been watching this encounter from a short distance away—and with some amusement. The knight had judged correctly that Roland could fend well enough on his own, but the other man was in need of a graceful exit.

"Good sir!" Sir Roger approached the man with a broad smile. He slapped the tall archer on the back, pulling him close and whispered. *"Don't trifle with my squire, good sir. He knows how to use that pig-sticker."* In a normal voice, he continued so all could hear.

"Forgive my squire. He is forever in a foul mood, and is far too touchy when it comes to protecting *my* longbow. As you say, it is forbidden—but not to the gentry. It's been a de Laval family heirloom for two decades. I only wish I knew how to shoot the damn thing myself!" As he spoke, he casually held out his hand to Roland who delivered the bow to his master. "Incredible workmanship, don't you agree?" he asked the man. The tall bowman was unsure what to make of this very large Norman knight who had swung an arm over his shoulder, and held him—a trifle

214

too tightly, but he recognized a face-saving opportunity when it presented itself.

"Indeed, it is a wonderful bow, my lord." The man managed to mumble.

"May I have a look at that?" A new voice was heard from the back of the crowd. The other archers parted to see who had spoken. A handsome young man walked forward smartly. There was an air of complete confidence about him, and over his shoulder there hung....another longbow!

"Sir Robin of Loxley, at your service, my lord." The man said, and quickly executed a sweeping bow, his doffed hat in his hand. Sir Roger was delighted with this new amusement.

"Sir Roger de Laval, at *your* service, my lord." He affected a stiff little bow of his own. "I see we both share the advantage of bow length," he said, eyeing Sir Robin's longbow. "Perhaps it will make up for any lack of skill."

"Ho, ho!" The young man laughed. "Well said, Sir Roger, but speak for yourself. I won the last royal tournament, presided over by good King Henry, and propose to do the same in this little contest for good King Richard. Indeed, I know how to use this infernal weapon and I intend to have the golden arrow!" All around the young knight jeers and groans rang out from the other archers. Sir Roger was enjoying all this immensely.

"Perhaps I spoke out of turn," he countered, "for it is my squire, young Roland Inness here, who shall do the shooting for the house of de Laval this day." The Lord of Shipbrook grasped the great buckle at his waist. "I would wager this silver buckle that *he* takes the gold!"

More taunts and catcalls came from the crowd. Sir Robin looked past the big Norman knight at the young squire standing behind him. He studied the boy for a moment, untied a small money bag from his belt and held it high. "Done!" he said, and clasped hands with Sir Roger, sealing the wager. He signalled to the crowd for silence.

"Gentlemen," he said, pointing toward a small man waving at the edge of the crowd, "if I'm not mistaken, that is the Master of the Tournament yonder, trying to get our attention. It seems His Highness, the King, would like us to begin! *Shall we?"*

***

The archery range had been constructed to handle up to sixty competitors, and the lanes were filled as the competition began. Each lane was marked by a white strip of cloth that ran from the bowman's firing position to a target set fifty yards away. The King, seeking any means to stir up support for his planned Crusade, had decreed that the targets be in the shape of a man with a turban mounted on top, to represent the Saracens who now occupied Jerusalem.

Archers were given marked arrows to ensure the integrity of the contest. Each target had a heart painted on its left front. In each round, competitors would take three shots. Each shot would be scored as a heart, a torso, or a miss. The thirty contestants scoring the highest would advance to the next round. The thirty lowest would be eliminated. Retainers from the numerous Earls and Barons had been volunteered to score the contestants.

Roland stood by the knee-high post which was his firing position and stared at the target. He tried to block out the sounds from the crowd and the thought that the King of England was watching. His stomach churned, but he was determined to remember all his father had taught him, and all he'd taught himself in the endless hours of practice at Shipbrook.

A bugle sounded signalling the beginning of the first round. He had three arrows stuck in the ground before him. His were marked with a black circle, just ahead of the fletching. He took this as a good omen—as it matched the colour of the garments prepared for them by Lady Catherine. A few archers had already released their first shaft, and all appeared to be striking home. Roland nocked his first arrow and drew.

The weakness in his left shoulder was worse than he had feared. He felt the arm gripping his bow tremble slightly and willed it to grow still. He, breathed, held the draw, then froze. Without warning, a vision had come to him of a mountain glade and a roebuck. For an instant, he was once again on Kinder Scout mountain and had not yet released the fateful shot. He lowered his bow and gathered himself. In the long months since that day his life had been a struggle for survival and against despair. Survive he had, but the struggle against despair had been harder. He must not give in to it now—not when so much was at stake.

Again he drew, steadied himself and loosed the shaft. Without waiting to see the result, he reached for the next arrow, and the next. The bugle sounded to cease shooting, and the retainers ran forward to check the results. The contestants had to wait behind the firing line while the Master of the Tournament walked the length of the range, verifying the scores and having the results recorded by a scribe. After the man had passed Roland's station, the young page scoring the target ran back to the firing line and breathlessly reported the results.

"All...hits," he gasped. "All...hearts." Roland nodded. He thought this page could use more regular exercise, if such a short run could wind him so.

After a lengthy wait, the survivors of the first round were announced. Roland, knowing his results, was not surprised to be among them. He did note that Sir Robin of Loxley had advanced as well. Now the targets were moved out to one hundred yards. The shrunken field of thirty was faced with the same challenge. Be in the top fifteen...or be eliminated. The boy stretched his left arm to relief the increasing stiffness there and vowed he would not let some scratch, especially one from Ivo Brun, decide this tournament.

He knew his bow was capable of great accuracy at this distance, something the other contestants, using conventional bows, could not claim. With the longbow, Roland could reach targets at this range with but little adjustment for arc—and less chance for error. He steeled himself against the pain and quickly nocked, drew and shot. He was the first archer finished in the second round. Many of the contestants were taking considerably longer to complete their shots, as they tried to gauge the proper arc. When the bugle sounded and the boy marking Roland's target returned from the considerably longer run, he took a moment to catch his breath. He grinned at the Roland and spoke.

"One in the heart...one very near it...and...one in the head!"

Roland felt a wave of relief and anxiety. He knew he had hurried his shots to avoid the growing pain and weakness in his shoulder. He was relieved that all had hit the target, but troubled as well. At this range, *all* should have been in the chest. The head shot could just have easily been a complete miss!

Again, the Master of the Tournament seemed to take forever to make his announcement. To his relief, his name was among those advancing to the third round. Only six contestants managed to put even two arrows in the second group of targets, and the Master declared that only these would continue. Sir Robin of Loxley was among them.

The targets were now moved to one hundred fifty yards, and the six remaining contestants were assigned new posts, all near the royal pavilion. From here, Roland could see the King clearly. All around him, the great nobles of the land were cheering on their favourites and making wagers on the outcome. He had to hold his anger in check, as he saw William de Ferrers in the stands. The young nobleman was sitting next to Prince John as was his own Earl Ranulf. The Earl of Chester and the heir to the Earldom of Derby were engaging the King's younger brother in an animated conversation. *Manoeuvring for position,* he thought—just as Lady Catherine had predicted.

Roland had expected his father's killer to be there. De Ferrers would be representing his own father, Robert, still abed in Cheshire. The boy thought he had prepared himself for this encounter, but the sight of the man was still disturbing. It would take less than a second to put an arrow in his enemy's chest, but the cost could not be calculated, for him and his companions. He must wait—and endure.

From where Roland stood, he could see money bags being brought forth. It appeared as though Prince John had agreed to hold the stakes for a wager between the two nobles. The boy suddenly realized that both men were looking directly at him. He saw in de Ferrers face a brief shock of recognition, as the nobleman realized that he was the same clumsy country squire who had practically trampled him the day before. Roland could see him heatedly questioning the Earl of Chester, who simply shrugged his shoulders.

The boy turned away, and tried to recover his composure. From the lesser nobility, gathered behind the ropes that cordoned off the field, he heard a familiar voice call out.

Longbow

"Shoot straight, ye dog-eatin' Englishman!" It was Declan, cheering him on as only he could do. He turned and gave a small wave at the three black-clad members of the Shipbrook delegation shouting encouragement his way. De Ferrers could wait. He had a golden arrow to win and a few side wagers for his friend. He blanked everything else from his mind, as the bugle sounded for the third round of shooting.

Roland surveyed his target. It was still a reasonable shot at this distance, but now he could feel a warm wetness spreading from his shoulder. The strain of drawing the powerful longbow was opening the wound wider and blood was beginning to soak through the dressing that Tuck had provided, though it was not much visible against his black tunic. *No matter,* he thought, *I'll not bleed to death.*

He took his first arrow, drew, adjusted just a bit for the new range, and released. The arrow leapt across the distance and the crowd that had gathered near the target, let out a murmur of approval. It was a hit. He was determined not to rush his shots, no matter the ache in his shoulder. With careful precision, he let his next two arrows fly. He knew before they struck that they would find the target. He turned back towards the stands and saw that Earl Ranulf was now smiling broadly and chatting with the Prince. Sir William did not join in. He was staring at Roland, his fists clinched on his knees.

Once more, the scorers sprang forward. An excited buzz went through the crowd, as they waited for the announcement. The Master of the Tournament cleared his throat and began.

"Only two archers put all three arrows in the target. The other contestants all failed to get more than one hit at this range. The contest will be decided between Sir Robin of Loxley and Roland Inness, squire to Sir Roger de Laval of Shipbrook!"

A great cheer rang out as the results were declared. The King called a pause to the contest and summoned the two archers forward.

"Well done! By God, well done I say!" King Richard's voice boomed across the crowd for all to hear. "We shall have a need for such shooting when we take back Jerusalem from the heathens!" To this, the crowd screamed its approval. "Now—bring me those

219

targets." Two pages quickly brought the remaining targets and presented them to the King. The crowd strained to see what the monarch was doing, as he hunched over these cutout figures of men. At last he arose and proudly turned the targets for all to see. He had painted a face on each…a face with heavy brows, a moustache and pointed beard. "My lords and ladies," he cried in triumph, "I give you… *Saladin the Saracen!*" The crowd exploded into cheers as the king turned the image of the great Muslim general first one way, then another. "Let's see who can rid me of this enemy!"

On the King's signal, pages sprang forward and ran to the farthest reaches of the range, two hundred yards away, to place the targets. The Master of the Tournament instructed that on this final round, the contestants would alternate shots, with results announced after each. Sir Robin of Loxley would shoot first. The signal was given and the bugle sounded to begin.

Sir Robin turned to Roland and nodded. "Win or lose, Master Inness, you are the finest archer I've ever faced. Luck to you!"

"And to you," Roland replied.

The young knight raised his bow, taking considerably longer to gauge the distance before loosing his first shaft. At this range, the slightest miscalculation would produce a miss—even with the longbow. He took a deep breath exhaled slowly and released. The arrow arched through blue September sky. A mighty roar from the crowd announced that he had aimed true. He turned to the boy and grinned.

Roland nodded to Sir Robin and turned toward the target. Carefully, he drew his bow, gauged the elevation and took aim. Now the pain in his shoulder had grown from an ache to an agony. He blocked the screams of protest coming from the wound and forced his mind to clear. Any shot of two hundred yards was a challenge, but he had made many such in the forests of Shipbrook and the slopes of Kinder Scout. He thought of his father, and hoped that Rolf Inness could see him—from wherever his soul dwelt.

He loosed the shaft. The arrow arched into the sky following a great curve toward the target. The roar from the crowd gathered far across the field signalled a hit long before the official result was announced. The boy was grateful that he would have a few moments gather himself while Sir Robin took his next shot.

His rival once again aimed with deliberate slowness, then let fly. Again a hit!

Now it was back to him, and Roland wished only that he could lie down somewhere. He knew his wounds were not mortal, but he had lost just enough blood that his head was beginning to feel a bit light. He shook himself and took up a position next to his firing stake. Looking downrange, the target now seemed impossibly far away—yet it had not moved. The boy closed his eyes tightly then opened them. The target had returned to where he expected it to be. He drew breath, held it and released the arrow. He had no notion if his shot would hit home or not. Time seemed to stand still for a long moment—then a cheer echoed back from the far crowd. Somehow he had made the shot!

Now each contestant was down to a final shot. Sir Robin turned and bowed toward the King, then looked at Roland and stopped as he reached for his final arrow.

"You look a trifle pale, Master Inness," he whispered loud enough for only the boy to hear. "Are you ill?"

The boy managed a weak grin. "Nay, my lord. Perhaps just a bit of nerves."

Sir Robin smiled and nodded toward the King. "He would make anyone nervous, but screw up your courage, lad—or I'll have your master's silver buckle. He does not look the sort to appreciate such a loss!"

With that, Sir Robin nocked his final arrow, aimed carefully and released. The great roar announcing a hit seemed very far away to the boy.

Now Roland prepared himself for his final shot. For his master, for himself, he was determined to strike the target. His left arm trembled as he drew the bow, but he steadied it. He released. Though he knew before his arrow struck that it had flown true, it would decide nothing—and the boy desperately needed a decision. Sir Robin had not missed a single target this day and Roland knew he did not have three more shots left in his own arm. He was finished. The match and the golden arrow would go to the young knight from Loxley.

The two competitors waited while the scorers ran to the targets.

In the distance, they could be seen gathering up the two images of Saladin and running back toward the King's pavilion. When they reached it, they knelt and turned the targets for the King to survey. Neither Roland nor Sir Robin could see the results, but they already knew the outcome.

"By St. Thomas—*it's a tie!*" cried the King, over the cheering of the crowd. The kneeling boys turned the targets about for the two contestants to see. Both targets had three shafts in the chest near the heart. None could judge which archer was more accurate.

The King did not hesitate. "We'll have no ties this day!" he declared. "We must make the challenge more difficult, thus making our winner more worthy!"

Roland's heart sunk at the King's words.

"Your Highness," the Master of the Tournament spoke up, "we cannot move the targets further, or they shall be in the trees!"

From the edge of the crowd, another voice shouted. *"Let 'em take a target on the wing!"* Roland was certain it was Sir Roger's voice!

"Excellent!" roared the King, who had now roused himself into a full passion over this match of skills. "Someone bring me a...a...*melon!*" Pages and servants scattered to the winds, and in less time than seemed possible, the King held in his hand a small green melon. Roland felt a glimmer of hope. In endless hours of practice, he had never fully mastered this shot, but he knew he had a chance. He could ask for no more. Somehow, he would coax one last shot out of his arm.

"I shall throw this but once into the field," the King declared. "Each of you shall take your shot. By all the saints, I pray one of you misses, for I am running short of ideas and the day grows hot! Now make ready."

Sir Robin and Roland looked at one another.

"I've never done this," Sir Robin said, with a weak smile. "Have you?"

The boy's slight grin spoke for him as the King flung the melon in a great arc over the two archers. Roland and Sir Robin drew as one. Sir Robin released first, just before the target reached the top of its flight. His arrow flew close, but did not strike the target. The crowd groaned. Roland watched the melon as it reached its highest point and started to curve downward. He led it slightly—and released. His arrow pierced the melon cleanly through the middle.

Pandemonium broke out in the crowd. Even the King could be seen slapping barons on the back and pointing at the boy who had just shot a melon out of the sky. Roland was dazed by the cheers. He turned and saw Sir Robin, watching him with a rueful smile on his face.

"Well shot, lad. Well shot. Someday you can teach me how to bag a wild flying melon!

"With pleasure, my lord," Roland beamed. "With pleasure."

Suddenly, he was surrounded by Sir Roger, Sir Alwyn and Declan. All three danced a little jig, in celebration of the victory.

"Ye did it, Roland!" Declan screamed, at the top of his lungs. *"Ye did it!*

"I'm the boy's weapons instructor!" Sir Alwyn shouted to no one in particular as the crowd milled about.

"Well done, my boy, well done!" Sir Roger said, with obvious pride. "Let's go see the King, and collect your prize!" He took Roland by the arm and led him to the royal pavilion, where His Highness, Richard I of England stood waiting.

"Roland Inness, is it?" the King whispered hastily to the Master of the Tournament as the two approached.

"Aye, my lord—squire to Sir Roger de Laval."

The King seemed to be searching for the familiarity of that name, as he saw Sir Roger approaching with Roland in tow. Then it struck him.

"Roger de Laval! Of course!" the King exclaimed. "We campaigned together in Normandy. What was it…ten years ago?"

"Aye, your highness," Sir Roger replied, bowing low. "We were both a lot younger then!"

"Now that's a fact!" the King bellowed, beckoning the knight closer. "So tell me your station now, you old war-horse. Haven't seen you on the continent since Normandy."

"Your highness, I've been busy aplenty on the Welsh Marches. I am vassal to Earl Ranulf. I secure the route from the high country in the north to Chester—from my castle at Shipbrook. I am well satisfied."

"Roger, I shall have great need for veterans like yourself, when we move on Saladin," the monarch said. "Are you with me?"

"I am at your command, your highness." This was the only reply the knight could be permitted to such a question from the King.

"My lord Earl of Chester." King Richard summoned Earl Ranulf. Seeing his vassal in the presence of the King, the young nobleman was hovering near by and immediately presented himself.

"Earl Ranulf, you will not, I'm told, be joining us on Crusade?" the King inquired.

"No, your grace. I regret that I must continue to secure our western marches against these Welsh devils, but I shall be sending a full contingent of knights and archers, to represent Cheshire. I am sure your grace will make good use of them in the glorious recapture of the Holy Land."

"Yes indeed," observed the King, dryly. "I shall have particular need of this man of yours, Sir Roger de Laval of Shipbrook. Do you release him?"

"As you wish, my liege. He is yours to command." The Earl bowed low. Roland could see relief written on the young man's face. He had clearly feared that the King would command him to go on this campaign.

"Good. Now take care, Ranulf, that his lands and people are perfectly provided for in his absence or I shall be gravely offended."

Earl Ranulf nodded his understanding and backed away from his monarch. As he retreated, he saw Sir William de Ferrers joining the crowd streaming out of the pavilion.

"Sir William!" he shouted. "I believe we have a wager to settle!"

De Ferrers stopped and glared at the Earl. "The Prince has your money, my lord." He jerked his head to the back of the pavilion where the Prince was now surrounded by a new group of favour-seekers. He turned slowly to stare at Roland, who was waiting a respectful distance behind Sir Roger. Without a word he approached the boy. With all attention on the King, none noticed as he stepped behind Roland and whispered in his ear.

224

"Not so clumsy with a bow, are you, boy?" His voice was a low hiss that none, save Roland, could hear. *"Saw a fellow this spring shoot like that—up on Kinder Scout."*

"I wouldn't know of that, my lord." Roland replied with more steadiness than he thought possible, his emotions warring between fear and anger.

"I think you lie, boy. I can tell by your speech you're Danish peasant scum—the kind that live up there like animals. If you are that fellow, Master Inness, in time I will know, and then you will die." Without waiting for a reply, the nobleman backed away, turned and disappeared into the crowd.

During this exchange, the King had beckoned Sir Roger to come near him. "I have a special task that I think you well-suited to," he whispered. "Come to see me on the morrow and we shall discuss it. Now—where is this extraordinary squire of yours?"

Roland was still pondering Sir William's threat and did not realize at first that he had been summoned. Then he saw Sir Roger and the King staring at him oddly. He hurriedly stepped forward and bowed low to Richard.

"Lad, I've been a soldier longer than you've been alive and I've never seen shooting like that." The King spoke with genuine admiration in his voice. "Where'd you learn?"

"From my father, your grace," Roland replied, through his nervousness.

"Aye, I learned a thing or two from my own sire!" the King said. Considering the civil war he had recently fought with his late father, no one laughed at his joke.

"Now, let me see that bow," the King commanded. Roland handed it over.

"This is a Viking bow, is it not?" the King asked, with genuine curiosity.

"Aye, your grace."

Richard hefted the weapon and drew it to test the pull. "If we had five thousand of these we could conquer China." he pronounced. "And if five hundred were in the wrong hands—we might lose our own kingdom! He turned to Sir Roger.

"Where'd you ever get such a thing?"

"My grandsire found it in a cave, your highness."

"A cave, eh?" The King had a touch of scepticism in his voice. "The craftsmanship is superb, but the secret to building these has been lost," he announced to the crowd, as he held the bow up for inspection. "This one, though, looks like it could have been made yesterday!" The King handed the longbow back to Roland.

"You're a damn fine shot, Master Inness, and it's my pleasure to present you with the grand prize for archery." The King nodded to the Master of the Tournament, who passed the prize to Richard. He held out the golden arrow in his two scarred hands. Roland bowed his head and took it in his own.

"I'm honoured, your grace."

"Roger, be sure to bring this one with you on Crusade. We may get a shot at Saladin at two hundred yards—and I'd want this boy to take it!"

"As you command, your grace," Sir Roger replied.

The King turned away, signalling the end of the audience. Roland and Sir Roger made their way down from the pavilion to where Sir Alwyn and Declan were waiting. The Irish boy was in a high state of excitement and was waving him forward—for beside him was Friar Tuck, still in his Templar's tunic.

"Roland, look who I found!" Declan exclaimed, throwing his arm around Tuck. "It's your friend… he's a Templar!" Sir Alwyn and Sir Roger looked quizzically at the two boys. Roland had learned a bit about the courtesies of noble life from Lady Catherine—more in truth than his friend Declan had. He bowed quickly to Tuck then turned to Sir Roger.

"My Lord, may I present Father Augustine. He ministers to the poor in Derbyshire and has other *duties* on occasion."

"I dare say he does," Sir Roger said looking at the red cross emblazoned on the man's tunic. "Do ye favour more the bible or the sword, Father?" This he said with a broad grin.

"Why, my lord, I favour each according to the need!" The monk returned the knight's grin and rested the heel of his hand on the hilt of his broadsword. It had taken but a quick moment for the two veteran soldiers to take the measure of the other.

"Aye, and I'd expect I'd not enjoy a lesson from either," Sir Roger countered, "but a friend of Master Inness is welcome at Shipbrook or wherever we may meet!"

"I am honoured, my lord, and if I may have a moment of your squire's time?"

Sir Roger nodded and Tuck pulled Roland aside. He withdrew a small money bag from his belt and jangled it. "I've you to thank for this, Roland. I feared Sir Robin would prevail, but you won the day! Fine shooting." The boy nodded then looked down at the prize in his own hands.

"You have done much for me, father. I know you shield my family and that you do much good work with the poor in the north. I give you this to use in whatever way you see fit." The boy handed the little monk the golden arrow. The Templar Knight hesitated and seemed determined, for a moment, to give the prize back. Then he nodded curtly to the boy, and tucked the treasure inside his tunic.

"It's a noble act, my son, and one that will bring food and shelter to many this winter. They shall know that the son of Rolf Inness has provided for them—but I cannot leave you penniless. I think it only fair, that you take my meagre winnings for your own purse. Methinks you'll need it fore long!" Without waiting for Roland to protest, he tucked the small money bag into the boy's belt. "I'm back to the north for now, Roland, but I think God is not finished tangling our paths. 'Til then, may He be with you always."

"And with you, Father," the boy replied, solemnly.

Tuck gave Roland a final wink, bowed toward Sir Roger, and disappeared into the crowd. The boy turned back to where his master and the others stood. He hadn't known they'd been watching him.

"Couldn't help but overhear, Roland," Sir Roger said, his voice gone husky. "It was a noble gesture. I'm proud of you."

"Well, I think you've gone daft!" Declan put in, only half jesting. "That arrow was worth a small fortune."

Roland shoved his friend gently and laughed. "I thought only big fortunes interested you, Dec!"

"Boys..." Sir Roger looked at them sternly. "Tomorrow, I speak to the King. I think we will not be long here in England and it will be far longer before we return. It's time we were to home—to Shipbrook.

Chapter 21

What Lies Ahead

Roland stood on the sterncastle of the *Sprite,* his longbow slung over his shoulder and felt the unfamiliar rocking motion of a ship at anchor. He no longer needed to conceal the weapon, but still liked to keep it near. Overhead the rigging of the single square sail groaned in a rare cool July breeze coming off the Channel. The vessel was a converted trading cog of about eighty feet in length, and to his untrained eye, seemed to be well kept. Below, Declan still slept, wrapped warmly in a woollen blanket while Sir Roger did the same in his makeshift quarters under the forecastle.

The King had been in no hurry to hasten their departure. Throughout the winter and spring, he had exhorted and at times extorted funds from the great barons for his cause. Richard was no Henry, raising funds for a Crusade he never intended to undertake. Richard would go, and glory would follow—but not until all was ready. A fleet had to be assembled, siege engines built and food and forage planned for. It would take many more months, perhaps even a year for him to arrive with his host in Palestine.

Without doubt, the King had spies aplenty among the forces contending in the Holy Land, and these would keep him abreast of the constantly changing political landscape of the region, but he had wanted a soldier—a soldier whose judgment he trusted—to precede him there. He was too seasoned a warrior himself to underestimate his foe or sally forth unprepared. When he arrived, he wanted a full and accurate report of the military situation on the ground. Sir Roger de Laval had been given this mission.

Ten months had passed since the coronation, and the time had flown by in preparation for this day. Much had to be done to put the affairs of Shipbrook in order before sailing for the Holy Land. The harvest had to be gotten in and the spring planting done. The thousand and one things required for the upkeep of even as small a castle as Shipbrook had to be attended to.

The tools of war they would need in a hostile land also required attention. Sir Alwyn had redirected the efforts of Shipbrook's blacksmith from peaceful pursuits to war preparation, repairing armour, mail and weapons. A local fletcher had been found to make three hundred fine ash arrows for use with the longbow and, at Sir Roger's request, the Earl of Chester had provided three hundred steel heads for those arrows. While winter gusts still came off of the Irish Sea, Roland, Millicent and Declan rode out in search of proper yew staves. They would not be ready in time for the voyage, but they would be well cured by his return.

The two squires had little time to dwell on the journey to come. Roland's shoulder had healed quickly and each day, Alwyn Madawc drilled them in the arts of close combat with a renewed intensity. There were many bruises but steady progress as Roland became proficient enough with a sword and Declan approached near mastery of the weapon. As often as not, he bested Sir Alwyn in their sparring. On such occasions, the Welsh warrior would beam like a proud father.

The winter that followed the coronation had been blessedly mild, with but a few weeks of shrieking storms coming from the sea to the west, and now the first signs of spring were about. Throughout this long period, Sir Roger displayed a restless energy in all he did—one day passing judgment on a dispute between peasants, the next leading patrols out along the Welsh marches. All had been quiet on that front since the death of Bleddyn the previous summer, but there were always more raiders in the Clocaenog to take his place.

For many weeks, Roland had feared that Sir William de Ferrers would act on his suspicions and arrive with men at arms to seize him at Shipbrook. He wondered what Sir Roger would do, should the son of an Earl arrive at his gate and demand he turn over his squire. He prayed his master would never face such a choice.

As the weeks turned to months, his apprehension lessened. Perhaps Sir William was not truly certain that Roland was the man he sought. Or perhaps he feared to court trouble with his powerful neighbour, the Earl of Cheshire. Earl Ranulf would not care a whit about a squire, but would have a concern for the sensibilities of his loyal retainer, Roger de Laval. By the time spring approached, Roland had banished Sir William to the back of his mind.

Lady Catherine maintained a brave and cheerful front during this long farewell, but Roland could see her heart was fairly breaking in the way she looked at the big knight when he wasn't aware.

"I'm a soldier's wife," she said to the boy, as though this explained all. He had not expected the leave-taking from Shipbrook to be so painful.

As the day of departure approached, Sir Roger filled his days with the final arrangements for his absence. He had grudgingly decided that his long-time companion in war, Sir Alwyn must stay behind. Sir Alwyn's protests had been brief. He knew as well as Sir Roger that, while Lady Catherine could more than manage the affairs of the land holdings, a trusted warrior must remain to secure the border from the Welsh—and to ensure the safety of Shipbrook and all that was precious within it. He was the only man in whom Roger de Laval could place such a trust.

The final leave taking of these men had been without joy, for duty had overruled their hearts' desire. After his final farewells in private to Lady Catherine and Millicent, Sir Roger mounted Bucephalus as dawn crept out of the east and turned to his old friend who stood at the gate of Shipbrook.

"Guard them well, Alwyn", Sir Roger had said, in a husky voice that made both men redden.

"I'll not fail in that, Roger. You just get yerself back in as many pieces as ye left with," the knight replied, fighting to belie the reputation of the Welsh for making emotional displays. Sir Roger only nodded and spurred the great war horse through the gates and onto the road toward Chester. Their master never looked over his shoulder at his home as they rode out of sight.

***

So it was on a blustery dawn in July, 1190, that the lord of Shipbrook and his squires had come to be at Dover. Roland had slept little the night before, and had come out on deck long before the sun was up. The ship's master said they would set sail with the ebb tide, an hour past dawn, and he didn't want to miss anything. As the sky started to lighten across the Channel in France, he watched the few points of light still visible in the dark shape that was the port city of Dover. To his right, he could see the luminous whiteness of the chalk cliffs that girt this shore of the island. Absently, he touched the small, round piece of metal which hung at his breast. It was a parting gift from Lady Millicent—a good luck amulet, she called it. Etched on the front was a skilful rendering of a yew tree.

"It's an English yew, Roland," she'd said, "to honour your skill with the bow and to remind you of England—of your home." Roland had accepted the token graciously. He could see how the girl struggled with the idea that her father and the squires were leaving for the Holy Land—for what would likely be years— without her. She knew she had to stay at Shipbrook, but it was no less a bitter pill.

"You'll have your heads lopped off by some fellow on a camel and we'll never see you again," she said one day half in jest, half in earnest. "I couldn't bear that—never seeing you return."

"I'll not let any man mounting a camel anywhere near your sire Millie. You have my word on that. I have no doubt, that should ten thousand heathens on camels bar his way, Sir Roger would yet return to Shipbrook!"

The girl nodded, but did not smile.

"And what of you, Roland Inness? Will you find your way home as well?

***

231

"First time at sea, lad?"

Roland turned to see the master of the ship approaching.

"Aye, sir," Roland replied. He could think of nothing more profound to say.

"Perhaps you'll like it," the captain continued. "I did, from the first moment. Nothin' else quite like it."

"I can't really picture it, sir," the boy admitted.

"Oh, you will, lad. By the time we've beat down the coast and through the Pillars of Hercules, you'll be a regular salt. Mark me words!"

"Aye, sir."

As the man left him to attend to his duties, Roland noticed, for the first time, a small skiff being rowed vigorously from the port area toward the *Sprite*. In the dim light, he could make out a boatman and one passenger. He wondered who it might be. Finally, the boat drew near and the passenger, carrying a small sack, scrambled up a hastily lowered rope ladder and onto the deck of the ship.

Roland was stunned to see Friar Tuck standing before him. The monk, again dressed in his rough brown robes, stepped forward and embraced the boy. *"All is well in the north, my son,"* he whispered.

"Oh, thank you, father. Thank you," the boy said. News of his family was welcome but bittersweet. He wondered how many years more it would be before he saw them.

"What brings you here, father?"

"The same as you, Roland, and your Sir Roger—the King commands it! Richard is a fearsome and sometimes rash man in combat, lad, but a prudent general for all that. He trusts Sir Roger to judge the battleground accurately, but worries that he may run afoul of the treacherous political landscape in that troubled land. It appears he has spoken to the Master of our Temple in London and asked his aid in this. There are few of my brother knights left who know the land well—after the massacre at Hattin. Thus the Master recalled me from my mission in the north. Said it was my penance for keeping my head on my shoulders."

"Weigh anchor!" the Captain shouted, at the top of his lungs, and crewmen appeared from nowhere to begin reeling in the anchor chain. The captain grinned as a man will when turning to work he

232

loves and slapped the boy on the back. "Say goodbye to England boy! If you ever see her again, I'll wager you'll be a full growed man!"

As the ship got underway, Tuck moved off to secure his meagre gear and Roland saw Declan sit up and yawn on the deck below. He turned to the rail as the offshore breeze filled the sails. Gulls, rising from their perches formed a squawking honour guard as the *Sprite* leapt forward with the tide toward the mouth of Dover harbour. The sun was now up, and golden rays pierced the remnants of early morning clouds to brilliantly illuminate the white chalk cliffs. *England! When would he see her again? Would he ever see her again?*

He left his station at the stern and ran leaping across ropes and baskets of fresh produce to the bow, as the ship began to encounter the deeper swells of the Channel. His ancestors had come across this sea to find a new home in England and now he was setting off on the same sea to serve her. His people had won a place for themselves on this green island as he had at Shipbrook. He thought of his father and felt the familiar pang of loss, but somehow knew that if Rolf Inness could see him now, he would smile.

As the *Sprite* heeled into the freshening breeze, he looked out over the grey water and absently found his hand moving to the grip of his bow. His fingers curled around the wood as hard as iron and its sturdy strength calmed him. His longbow had gotten him this far. He prayed it would bring him home again.

Historical Note

While I have tried to stay true to the history of the 12th century in this novel, it is not intended to be a rigorous work of historical fiction. The presence of Friar Tuck and Sir Robin of Loxley as characters hopefully will alert readers that there is as much myth as history in the story of Roland Inness.

There are a number of actual historical characters that appear in Longbow. King Richard, Queen Eleanor and Saladin are, of course, major players during this period. I have used a number of actual English earls as significant characters in Roland's story; most notably my villain, Sir William de Ferrers. While these characters are real, their motives and actions are entirely fictional. I suspect Sir William was no more or less villainous than any of his fellow earls of that period.

I did make use of some excellent historical works to provide some of the flavour needed to bring this tale to life. In particular, I would recommend *Warriors of God* by James Reston, Jr. and *Dungeon, Fire and Sword* by John J. Robinson as great places to get insight into Richard of England, Saladin, the Knights Templar and the complex politics of the time.

In my research, I discovered that there are differing opinions among historians on the origin and history of the longbow. The most popular theory is that it was developed by the Welsh, but other researchers believe it was brought to the British Isles by the Vikings. Bows similar in style to the longbow have been found in bogs in Denmark with ages dating to over nine thousand years ago. For the purposes of my story, I've used the Viking origin theory. It should also be noted that, though the longbow became the dominant weapon of English armies by the early 14th century, it was not commonly used by Norman armies in the late 12th and early 13th centuries.

Longbow

Longbow is the first in a planned trilogy of novels which will take Roland Inness from England to the Holy Land for the Third Crusade and back to England where he will seek to settle accounts for his father's murder and find a place for himself in a restive land where kings, princes and nobles all manoeuvre for power.

To learn more about The Saga of Roland Inness and the author, please visit www.waynegrantbooks.com and follow the author's blog at http://bestboysbooks.wordpress.com/.

ABOUT THE AUTHOR

Wayne Grant grew up in a tiny cotton town in rural Louisiana where hunting, fishing and farming are a way of life. Between chopping cotton, dove hunting and Little League ball he developed a love of great adventure stories like Call It Courage and Kidnapped.

Like most southern boys he saw the military as an honourable and adventurous career, so it was a natural step for him to attend and graduate from West Point. He just missed Vietnam, but found that life as a 2nd LT in an army broken by that war was not what he wanted. After tours in Germany and Korea, he returned to Louisiana and civilian life.

Through it all he retained his love of great adventure writing and when he had two sons he began telling them stories before bedtime. Those stories became his first novel, Longbow.

Warbow, the second book in the Saga of Roland Inness is now available on Amazon.

42746613R00135

Made in the USA
Lexington, KY
03 July 2015